THE SECRET OF
EVELINE HOUSE

THE SECRET OF EVELINE HOUSE

SHEILA FORSEY

POOLBEG

Published 2020
by Poolbeg Press Ltd.
123 Grange Hill, Baldoyle,
Dublin 13, Ireland
Email: poolbeg@poolbeg.com

A catalogue record for this book is available from the British Library.

ISBN 978178199-755-0

Printed and bound by ScandBook, Lithuania

www.poolbeg.com

ABOUT THE AUTHOR

Sheila Forsey's childhood was steeped in listening to stories. They were told not from a book but from memory. Stories that gave her a love of words and were the stepping-stones into her writing. Ireland's windswept coastline, rugged mountains, valleys and ever-changing sky inspire her writing and a deep interest in Ireland's intricate past has led her to write historical fiction.

She is an honour's graduate from Maynooth in creative writing. She is the recipient of a literature bursary award from Wexford County Council and Artlinks. She facilitates creative writing workshops throughout the country.

She lives with her husband and three children (very soon all to be teenagers), close to the tapestry of the Wexford Coast.

ACKNOWLEDGEMENTS

I am indebted to the wonderful Paula Campbell and all her team at Poolbeg Press. I am so very grateful for your belief in my writing. To my incredibly talented editor Gaye Shortland for being so insightful and patient and for her astounding knowledge of Ireland's history.

Sincere thanks to Wexford County Council and Artlinks for awarding me a bursary in literature recently. To my agent Tracy Brennan for your constant support across the ocean. To the many writers across Ireland who are there to help, guide and have a giggle with, especially when the going gets tough.

To my family and friends who constantly support me.

Finally, to my husband Shane and my three children Ben, Faye and Matthew. For all that they do every single day. Also thank you all for never batting an eyelid when I get quite distracted, especially when I am deep into my writing. Yes, the washing powder has ended up in the fridge! Thank you for being the best.

For those who are still searching for the truth

PART 1

CHAPTER 1

New Year's Eve 1949

Draheen, Ireland

Violet Ward's elegant frame, sheathed in a jade-green silk dress, shimmered with tiny glass beads as she walked swiftly from room to room in her home, Eveline House. Her dark hair was pinned up in a tight chignon, her high cheekbones enhanced with just a touch of colour, her lips a ruby-red set against alabaster skin, a string of pearls around her delicate neck.

She looked behind the red-velvet chaise longue in the drawing room for her daughter Sylvia, checking to see if the little girl had crouched there as she often did. Sometimes Sylvia would take her dolls and create a perfect little world there or behind the shelter of the heavy gold-velvet drapes.

She hoped that Sylvia's sensitive little ears had not overheard Betsy Kerrigan, their housekeeper, whispering to her earlier, relaying the latest vicious gossip that she had overheard at Miss Doheny's grocery store that day.

Betsy had been putting the bag of sugar she had just purchased into her bicycle basket when Nelly Cooke rushed into the shop, leaving the door ajar. Nelly had just come from a parochial meeting of the 'church ladies' of Draheen and was almost shouting across the counter in excitement as she delivered her latest gossip. Betsy had overheard every vindictive word against her employer.

'Nelly Cooke said that you were evil and that the Devil was surely in you, to go and write what you have written. She said that the bishop himself would not be able to absolve you of your sins. Miss Doheny said that you were possibly cursed. Nelly Cooke then said that she had warned the women at the meeting to keep their young people away from you for fear of the Devil getting into them.' Betsy shook her head in disgust. 'Such a group of auld hypocrites! There they are at the church every morning, scrubbing the altar until it shines, making sure the flowers are not allowed to even *think* of wilting, and not a Christian bone in their bodies! I am so sorry, Mrs Ward, but I felt I had better let you know so you can be on your guard. That Nelly Cooke is nothing but an auld sleeveen! Oh, an awful sleeveen of a woman!' Betsy put her hands on her hips as if she was ready to thrash the lot of them for saying a word against her employer. 'My mother always said that there was more religion in a stick of wood than in the whole body of Nelly Cooke. Of course, Agnes the Cat is the ringleader of the lot of them and her tongue is pure evil.'

Agnes the Cat lived alone in a small house at the bottom of the town and was known to have at least thirty cats in the house with her.

Violet had felt sickened as she listened to Betsy. Her first play, *Unholy Love*, certainly flew in the face of Irish Catholic morality. She had expected hostility from the people of Draheen but she had never expected such vitriolic attacks.

Violet had known how the townspeople felt about her from her earliest days in Draheen. A few days after their arrival she had met Miss Doheny on the road outside Eveline House. A tall rake of a woman with skin so thin it was almost transparent, skinny purple lips and hair secured in a tight grey bun, Miss Doheny had not held back. She had told her in vivid detail how Father Cummins had announced from the pulpit that a notorious playwright and her family were taking up residence in Eveline House. He had informed them in no uncertain terms that her first play, which had been put on in London, was unchristian in every way. He said that Draheen was a good Catholic town and it needed no scandal. Miss Doheny had not given Violet time to respond to this but had jumped on her bicycle and cycled off.

Later, of course, Violet had heard in further detail about the priest's rant from Betsy, after the housekeeper had come to work at Eveline House.

Betsy would never forget it till her dying day.

'*You will be cursed to damnation if you even talk about this play or to this woman who has penned such filth!*' he had roared. '*I believe an illegal copy of this ungodly script has found its way to our town. I forbid any of my parishioners to have anything to do with it – or the writer of it, I might add. If you do, you should never enter this church again. In fact, I forbid you to!*'

Violet knew that it was very unlikely anyone in Draheen would ever see a performance of the play and, even if there was an illegal copy of the script in the town, most of the townspeople would be too afraid to look at it. The play was, of course, banned in Ireland by the severe censorship laws. Obviously, Father Cummins himself had got his hands on a copy as he seemed to be such an expert on it.

It turned out that indeed an illegal copy of the script had somehow found its way to the town. A love story between a priest and a young woman, the dogeared script was literally pulled apart as a group of girls tried to read separate pieces at the same time and then swap them over. Father Cummins was alerted by one of their mothers. The pages of the play were gathered together and delivered into the safe hands of the priest who promised to pray for the souls of those who had dared to read it. Betsy was a horrified witness when he threw the torn sheets down in the street and stamped on them like a child in a temper tantrum.

Things appeared to quieten down a little as time passed and, when a neighbour who had lived down the road from Eveline died, Henry persuaded Violet to attend the Requiem Mass.

They took Sylvia with them. They set out, Violet wearing her fur stole of steel grey over a stylish burgundy suit, with her hair pinned up under a black half-hat and her chin held high, Henry dressed impeccably in a pinstripe suit, tie and navy Crombie coat, and Sylvia all in blue.

Violet had gone to Mass on rare occasions in London but stepping into a church in Ireland was almost overpowering. The aroma of the lingering incense and the stillness that permeated the air triggered deep emotion in her. Whatever her belief, Catholicism was in her bones. There was no removing herself from it. In the same way, Ireland was part of her consciousness. In London, when she slept, she had dreamt of Ireland, a dark brooding landscape that had captured her soul.

But her emotional response to being in the church was soon swept away.

That morning, the priest was not concerned about praying for the deceased – it was the presence of Violet Ward that ignited his sermon.

'We have a darkness in our midst! Mrs Ward forgot her

religion when she was writing such filth. She is a shame to Ireland, a shame to the Church and its teachings. The Devil found her on the streets of London!' Then he shouted from the pulpit as all the parishioners stared at Violet with their mouths open. '*Well, not here! Not here! Not in my parish!*'

Violet wrapped her fur stole tightly around her. Protectively she put her arm around Sylvia to shield her from the priest's abuse. Sylvia had started to tremble. Violet wanted to get up and run as far away as possible, but she was frozen to the spot.

Henry was sitting beside her and she could feel the anger building in him at the priest's outburst. He stood up to his six feet and walked purposefully towards the pulpit.

The congregation held their breath. They had never seen the like of it before. Nobody ever confronted Father Cummins like that. He expected a huge level of respect and if one of the parishioners happened to be on the road when he drove his shiny Morris Minor at speed down the town, well, they simply jumped out of the way. He was the priest after all. Now, here was Henry Ward walking threateningly up to him as if he was just anyone and not the parish priest of Draheen!

When Henry reached the pulpit, he stood and stared up at the priest.

'You should be ashamed of yourself, shouting at my wife as you just did!' he spat at him. '*How dare you? I demand an apology!*'

The priest's face became purple and his eyes bulged.

The congregation were wide-eyed and were afraid to blink, expecting him to explode into tiny bits.

'*Get out! Get out!*' he shouted, spit spraying from his mouth. '*You have no place in this House of God! Let the fires of Hell judge you and your kind! Get out!*'

7

Henry Ward looked in disgust at him, then he turned to the congregation.

'You are as bad as him, if you allow this. Have you no shame?'

Then he walked back down and put his hand out to Violet and the other to Sylvia. They rose and took his hands and, as they walked silently down the aisle, every eye was on them.

A few weeks after the church episode Father Cummins had a heart attack and died. Betsy told Violet that he was resting after an enormous dinner of roast lamb with all the trimmings when his eyes bulged, and it was as if his heart exploded and drove him six feet under.

There were many who blamed Violet for his death – not Henry, even though he was the one who confronted the priest, but her – and the gossips eagerly went on the attack. There were even whispers that she had cursed him.

The young curate Father Quill took Father Cummins' place. Father Quill was a tall handsome man with a gentle air about him. Much to the outrage of his flock, he befriended the Wards and began to visit Eveline House quite often. He told Violet over the odd glass of sherry that he was sorry Ireland had closed the door to her theatrical achievements and apologised for the treatment she and her family had received from Father Cummins.

But the Wards never ventured into the church again.

Ireland had indeed shut Violet out. She had expected it though. So many books and plays were banned. The census was severe and anything that was not about horses or the 1916 Rising seemed to be scrutinised and banned from penetrating Ireland's pure shores. If it gave as much as a hint of promiscuity, adultery, homosexuality or contraception it was banned. She was aware that her second play *The Lightship* fell foul of these laws, so her future in Draheen promised to be even rockier than the present.

Seeing Violet become more and more disturbed by the situation, Betsy tried to reassure her. She told her not to worry as most of the townspeople were just curious about her, and that possibly the women were hostile because the men had never seen anyone as elegant as her and were fascinated by her.

'I heard Timmy Moore describe you as having the looks and allure of Vivien Leigh,' she said with a giggle. 'His wife almost gave him a wallop right there in Miss Doheny's shop. Miss Doheny had to beg her to calm herself and told Timmy Moore to go to Confession for having such thoughts!'

Violet had laughed but she increasingly had huge misgivings about their return to Ireland.

CHAPTER 2

Violet Ward was born Violet Clarke in County Westmeath, in the midlands of Ireland, and had run away from home when she was seventeen. Her parents were small farmers and were exhausted from trying to understand their wayward daughter. She was unlike her siblings. She rebelled against everything. Instead of going to school she would vanish to Lough Deeravaragh with her bottle of milk and bread-and-butter and spend the day talking with the birds and watching the clouds form over the brooding landscape. She knew that her mother prayed extra hard that she would become normal, but no number of rosaries seemed to cure her. Her father had to drag her to Mass and when she refused to go to Holy Communion the priest called on them. He prayed over her and told her parents to be wary – that something had got hold of her. The rosaries continued but, as the bells rang across the land from Whitewater church, Violet would have disappeared back to the lakes and the woods. She barely ate, and her thin frame and frail features began to look so fragile that the priest was called again. This time he performed more prayers and rituals and said he would have to call on the bishop for help if it continued.

Just before she was seventeen her father arranged a place for her in McBride's Drapery Store. He would pay Colm McBride two hundred pounds for the year, for his wayward daughter to learn how to work in the shop and eventually become a paid clerk. Violet went the first day and on the second she was back at the lough, the place where the legend of the Children of Lir began. She sat with her pencils and paper, trying to capture the mood of the lough as the mist shifted from blue to white and eventually to silver.

Her father went spare and threatened to call the priest and the doctor. Violet would be locked up if she didn't behave. Her mother begged her to settle down and try to give McBride's a chance.

Her mother was a slightly severe woman whose body was bent from prayer and toil. Her prayers as she knelt beside her daughter's bed that night were the last words Violet ever heard her say. Violet listened as she called on all the saints to make her daughter settle and obey the rules set out for her. She prayed to the Virgin Mary to give her strength.

Then she blew out the candle and kissed her daughter on the forehead.

'Sleep now and when you awake any badness in you will be gone and you will go to McBride's and all this will be forgotten. Tomorrow you will dress in your good Sunday clothes and your father and Father Burke will see for themselves that you are a good Catholic girl. No more running off to the lough and writing and drawing all that nonsense. It's filling your head with bad things.'

While her family slept, Violet put the few clothes she had into a bag, with some bread and milk. Then she put in a photo of her parents. There were very few photos – this one was of their wedding day. She took some money from the savings her mother had for the Christmas dues which were to be paid to the parish. She promised herself that she would send it back as soon as she could.

The road was still except for the dawn chorus of the birds. She walked fast – she needed to escape before anyone in Whitewater was up. The break of day would come soon. She picked a few sprigs of wild violets, the flower her mother had called her after. She walked and walked and eventually got a lift on the back of a milk lorry bound for Dublin.

In Dublin, her eyes were glued to the sights and smells. Shop windows with hams crusted with mustard, cakes and buns making her mouth water. People of all shapes and sizes walking up and down, bicycles whizzing past. She made her way to the docks and, after sleeping on a bench, the next morning she stowed away on a ship for England. She wept as she saw Ireland disappearing. A land that she so loved but also could not live in – the constraints of society and the fear of the Church were too much. Her mind needed to be free. But she would miss the lough, the hills, the woods – and the music most of all. For Ireland had the most beautiful melancholy in its music.

Violet had a friend who lived in London. Luckily, from her letters she had her address. But London was like another planet. So many people, so many strangers, smells and sounds she had never witnessed before. Somehow she navigated her way to the boarding house on the Kilburn Road. She sat on a wall near it, hoping to see her friend. Three hours passed and then she heard some girls giggling as they walked up the street.

Elsie Morton, who worked in a factory in Kilburn, had arrived home.

Elsie wrapped her in a hug when she saw her.

'Mother of God – well, I cannot believe my eyes!' Elsie's warm brown eyes crinkled up in delight at the sight of her friend and her dark ponytail bobbed up and down as she jumped in pure excitement.

Elsie knew of Violet's love for fancy writing and drawing. There had been very few books in Whitewater, but those Violet could get her hands on she had devoured. Elsie knew a boy who worked in a bookshop, an English boy called Ralph she'd met at one of the dances, thin as a whippet with dark-rimmed glasses. He got Violet a job in the bookshop. It was heaven for her. She worked hard but the big bonus was being able to borrow books to read.

She read everything, from the Brontes to Dickens to Joyce. Eventually she found a shelf which contained scripts of plays and she knew she had found something that spoke to her. She fell in love with the works of Tennessee Williams, Lady Gregory and Yeats. She couldn't afford theatre tickets so she began to queue and stand outside the theatres, trying to sneak in when no one was looking. If she was lucky enough to get inside, she would watch, transfixed, as the words she had read were given life.

When she was off work, she would disappear off up to the heath and write and draw. The bookshop owner, Mr Watson, a tall thin man with glasses and a serious face, was kind to her and loved introducing her to new books, authors and plays.

Two years in London, doing little else but working and reading and watching every play that she could get in to see, amongst all her scribblings and little sketches she eventually wrote a play. She showed it to Mr Watson. He read it and showed it to a friend who was director of a small but reputable theatre and Violet's play *Unholy Love* was performed.

It was a love story about a priest who had fallen in love with a young woman, but in it she had also expressed her love for Ireland – a land that had almost strangled her but had also filled her heart with its music and a landscape that haunted her dreams with its heather-filled mountains and crystal lakes.

She sent back the money that she had taken that last night in Ireland. She wrote several letters home, trying to explain why she had left. But her letters were never answered.

Her writing and the theatre were her salvation.

Then she met Henry Ward. Elsie was getting very serious with Joe Barry, an Irish emigrant from Wexford, and one night he introduced her to Henry.

Henry was tall and fair with eyes as blue as sapphires. He was funny too and, despite living in London, had lost none of his Wexford accent. She loved the way that he seemed to rarely take his eyes off her. She could almost feel him fall in love with her. He seemed to make it his business to try to bring joy to her life. He had arrived as a labourer but had somehow turned his life around and was now a goldsmith.

These were the war years, with days and nights of bomb shelters, fear and rationing. Henry didn't waste time – he soon presented her with a beautiful engagement ring he had made and proposed. She accepted and they were married quickly and quietly.

Violet knew she was pregnant the day Henry was called

up. He was in the trenches in France when Sylvia was born.

When Henry, and his brother Anthony, returned home safely from France Violet's happiness was complete.

Silvia was like a tiny version of her mother, except her hair was blonde like her father's. Her skin was white as milk. She was almost ethereal, too angelic for this world. Violet worried about her as she seemed to live in her own world, shying away from people. As she grew older it was clear that the little girl found life outside of her family very challenging. Social encounters were very daunting for her sensitive nature.

Then Henry began to talk about returning to Ireland. He felt an Irish upbringing would be better for Sylvia. He had often told Violet that he felt London was cold and indifferent, and that he had sworn one day he would return. He begged Violet to move back, to somewhere near Dublin. She could go back to London when she needed to, he said. She said no. But she knew that Henry adored his Irish heritage and had never fully recovered from leaving it behind.

Eventually he wore her down and she agreed to look at a house in Wicklow. In a small town called Draheen.

They were intrigued by Eveline House. It was perched on its own piece of land just at the edge of the town and there were views over the Wicklow Mountains that would take your breath away. They put a bid in and secured it.

Henry was happy and sure that life in Draheen would help Sylvia to make sense of the world. Violet had doubts about how positive it would be for her.

They sent her to school, but Sylvia could not handle being in the school environment. Her London accent ensured that she received constant mockery and her timidity encouraged bullies. After a few weeks, Violet persuaded Henry to take her out of school. There was a retired schoolteacher, Mrs Kennedy, who was kind and gave Sylvia private lessons every afternoon at Eveline. Also, Sylvia loved to paint, and Violet turned one of the bedrooms into a little sanctuary for her to paint in. It was there she spent most of her time now.

The woods at the end of the town was the only other place that Sylvia really loved.

Blythe Wood was a cornucopia of colour no matter the season. Violet loved to take her daughter down after the rain, when the oaky smell blended with the fragrant wildflowers and made the air pungent with a heady aroma. Even with its winter coat Blythe Wood was beautiful, covered in a silver frost that crackled beneath their feet.

But as much as Violet loved the woods and the house, that stifling feeling that had almost choked her when she was seventeen seemed to be seeping back into her life. She had found that her mind and heart were free to think and breathe in the anonymous streets of London. But here in Ireland the air of judgement and religion hung like a veil over the land.

She could feel the stares as she walked up the town. But at least she felt secure in the fact that she had changed immeasurably since she had first left Ireland. Nobody would recognise the elegant lady of Eveline House as that girl from Whitewater who had stowed away on the back of a milk lorry.

CHAPTER 3

New Year's Eve 1949

That night, to bring in the New Year, Henry had invited some friends over for drinks. Victor Gettings, the local doctor, and his wife Heather were coming. Trevor Banville and his wife Chrissy were also coming. Trevor was the local bank manager. Father Quill had promised to drop in.

Betsy joined Violet in the search for Sylvia. They found her huddled in the cupboard beneath the stairs, clutching her Petite Suzanne doll. Amy Smith, an American friend of Violet's, had given Sylvia a collection of books by Marguerite de Angeli one Christmas. Sylvia fell in love with Petite Suzanne, the little French-Canadian girl in the stories. Amy then gave Sylvia a Petite Suzanne doll for her birthday and since then she had rarely left it out of her hands.

Sylvia was shivering when they found her, her white skin almost grey.

'Sylvia, whatever are you doing in there?' Violet said softly. 'I was worried about you. Come on out, darling.'

Sylvia shook her head and held the doll closely.

Betsy climbed in and coaxed her out.

'What has upset you so, pet?' she asked gently.

Then she noticed that the little girl was holding something

behind her back. An envelope. She gently prised it from her hand and handed it to Violet.

Violet was taken aback at the look on her daughter's face.

'What is it?' she asked. 'Where did you get this letter?'

Sylvia's blue eyes filled with tears. She dropped her doll and began to sob.

Violet pulled her towards her, hugging her and soothing her.

Later, when Betsy had led Sylvia off to the kitchen for some supper, Violet looked at the envelope. It had Sylvia's name on the front and was already opened. Violet pulled out a letter and paled as she read.

The words were written with a heavy hand in blue ink. Splotches of ink were scattered on the page. One of the words had an ink-stain almost covering it. But the word was still legible. The letter looked as if it had been written by either an uneducated hand or a childish one. But the message was clear despite the amateur appearance.

To the daughter of the Devil
Leave Draheen now with your witch of a mother.
You have been warned!

CHAPTER 4

Who could do such a thing to a child? If ever Violet needed proof that she was not wanted here, she had it now. She could feel her legs give way. Whoever had written this vicious letter had achieved what they set out to do. To terrorise them. She had left Ireland before – she should never have returned. She should have listened to her gut and not allowed Henry to persuade her that things would be any different now.

Her family had turned their backs on her – surely that had been good enough reason never to return? She had written to her mother, asking to meet with her. She had written so many letters over the years. She wrote to tell her that her play was a success and that she had met Henry. She wrote to tell her that she was getting married and then, when Sylvia was born, she wrote hoping that finally her mother could forgive her for leaving. But there was never any response. She wrote to tell her that she was coming back to live in Ireland, in Draheen. But there was only silence. Her friend Elsie Morton was also from Whitewater and had kept her up to date on what was happening with her family. At times she would ask Elsie to try to find out if all was well with them. Elsie would write home and ask her mother discreetly if there was any news about the Clarke family. But, other than hearing about the emigration of her siblings, there was no other significant news for Violet. In the end she stopped asking Elsie to check. She should have seen it as a sign long ago. She was not welcome. She had no place in Ireland.

She had to tell Henry about this wicked letter and somehow convince him that they had to move back to London. It would not be easy. She knew he loved Draheen and had really settled in, despite their terrible encounter in the church. He had a temporary workshop in the town, and he had commissions from as far away as New York. He had made friends with several businessmen and, despite the talk about Violet, the men of the town had really taken to him. He was constantly out to card games and meetings about improving Draheen.

She could feel the tears sting her eyes. She was so worried about Sylvia. She was eight years old but she could read quite well and so had been able to read the letter. Henry had been convinced that Ireland would open its arms and welcome them. But the reality was a different story. She was ostracised because of her plays and Sylvia was bullied and frightened partly because of her mother and partly because of her accent.

Sylvia had made no friends in Draheen and spent most of her free time in a make-believe world where her doll Suzanne played a large part. In London, they had a small circle of friends and Sylvia seemed to feel fairly secure with them. But here in Draheen she was fearful of everyone.

A few weeks previously Violet had to go to London for the opening of her new play. Sylvia withdrew even more while she was away. When she came back after two weeks, she was shocked to see her daughter thinner and paler and more withdrawn than ever. She vowed not to leave her again. Betsy had told her that she had cried and cried while she was away. Henry and Betsy did everything they could to soothe her, but she was inconsolable.

Violet knew she was an intelligent little girl and extremely artistic, but social interactions were becoming impossible for her. They had hoped as she grew older that she would grow out of it, but as each birthday approached Violet knew that her little daughter's desire to live a reclusive life was stronger than ever. Other than their daily walk in the woods, she rarely went out except for tea on a Saturday afternoon at O'Hara's Hotel. Sylvia loved the iced buns and lemonade, but Violet knew that she would refuse to go into the town after this.

They both adored Eveline House and it was certainly Sylvia's haven. The garden at the back was surrounded by a stone wall. When they first caught sight of it the wall was covered in a white rambling rose. The garden was abundant with yellow and red roses. Now in the depths of winter there were the Christmas roses and berried holly. Betsy had filled the house with clusters of holly and ivy behind every picture. She had put vases of Christmas roses throughout the house. When the weather was not too cold, Sylvia would play out in the garden with her dolls. But loving the house and garden was not enough and Violet could see her daughter clinging to home out of fear of being tormented on the streets of Draheen.

Now this letter, this dreadful letter. If Violet had received it, nobody would ever have known, as she would have burned it. But whoever sent it was cleverer than that – they knew the effect it would have on Sylvia. There was a postbox outside the door but normally the postman would knock on the door and chat with Betsy about any news in Draheen and would often come into the kitchen for a cup of tea. But this letter had no postmark and as it was a Saturday no post had arrived. Sylvia would not tell her where she had found it. Or, God forbid, if the writer had arrived up to the house. Sylvia had been playing in the rear garden earlier. Although it was cold, dressed in her coat, hat and mittens she loved to run around with Milky the cat for a few minutes before it was too dark. Could someone have crept up the avenue and given it to her over the wall? This worried Violet even more. It could be anyone.

'Don't let them bully you out of Draheen,' Betsy implored. 'They're just a bunch of bullies! There are always a few bad apples, but there are good people here too, don't forget that. They would be ashamed of their town if they knew that you had received this. They have their own way of dealing with these kinds of bullies.'

'I know there are good people here, Betsy. I have made some friends like the doctor and his wife and Father Quill and you of course. But most of the townspeople will never accept me. Father Cummins put a stop to that. I had a gut feeling about it before we came. We should never have come.'

'If I could get my hands on whoever wrote that, I would fry them! Some little good-for-nothing!' Betsy grimaced, her green eyes bright, her face flushed.

'It was an adult who wrote this,' Violet whispered. 'A child couldn't express themselves like that – I know it looks a bit childish but from the words it strikes me as written by an adult.'

'But who could do such a terrible thing to a young girl?' Betsy asked.

'Somebody with an agenda – to run me out of this town – and I believe they will not stop until they have their way.'

'But, if you go, then you are allowing them to win,' Betsy said, aghast.

Violet knew that Betsy would hate to see them leave. But it was the only answer. Betsy was so good to them. She was about seven years older than Violet and felt like an older sister at times, always looking out for her.

'They have won already, I want to go,' she said, 'but convincing Henry of this will be difficult. I have never seen him so content. He always longed to return to Ireland.'

Henry's father had left Ireland with his two sons and just the clothes on his back after his wife died. He had to leave the small world he knew and loved and live in what seemed the dark dungeons of London. She knew it would break Henry's heart to leave again, especially as it seemed they were being run out of the town. But she was sure it was the only way to protect Sylvia. She could not risk something even worse than today's letter happening to her.

Violet looked into her daughter's eyes and smiled reassuringly. Sylvia looked ghostly in her white nightdress she was so pale, her frightened blue eyes shimmering with tears.

'I will check on you every ten minutes tonight and you are not to worry about that letter. It's just some very silly person. Try to put it out of your mind.'

'I don't want them to hurt us, Mummy. I'm afraid. What if they come in here, somehow break into our house? They said such horrible things in that letter.'

Violet felt sick, thinking of its contents. So, they considered her evil. A witch of some sort. Well, she'd had enough. She would talk to Henry later and tell him that they would have to leave. As much as she loved Eveline, living here was impossible. They could sell the house. They could rent an apartment for the moment in London. It would be more upheaval, but it was for the best.

'Nobody will hurt us, pet. Try to put this out of your mind. Pop into bed now.'

Sylvia climbed into bed and Violet tucked her and Petite Suzanne in.

She kissed both child and doll on their foreheads.

'I must go down now to get everything ready for our guests, but I will get Betsy to bring some hot cocoa and cake up to you, alright?'

'Thank you, Mummy,' said Sylvia and at last she smiled.

Henry looked dapper in a tailored suit, his fair hair curling at the back of his white shirt. Violet tried to relax, but all she wanted to do was run up to check on Sylvia and make sure she was not lying awake.

Betsy had managed to get some lovely canapés from O'Hara's Hotel, and they sat with their drinks in the large drawing room, listening to the songs of John McCormack.

Victor Getting, the doctor, and his wife were in high spirits. Heather was the height of glamour in a red-silk dress with her dark hair in a fashionable cut that framed her face. Trevor Banville, the bank manager, and his wife Chrissie were a more staid couple but good company nevertheless. Trevor was quite a serious man who spent most of his time birdwatching when not working, while Chrissie was a keen member of the local Flower Club.

Father Quill was looking very relaxed and having some sherry. Violet was very fond of him. He was such a sensitive man. He had very dark expressive eyes, and his soft Connemara accent was soft and soothing. He looked over at her, his dark eyes gazing intently at her and she knew he sensed something was wrong. She longed to tell him. She loved how calm he always appeared but the opportunity to talk alone with him was not going to happen. She had noticed that when he smiled his brown eyes seemed to almost light up. She loved the way he listened to her. As if there was nothing in the world more important than what she was saying.

Two more guests arrived – Stephen O'Donoghue, who ran a woollen factory near the town, and his wife Sarah. Stephen had obviously taken a detour to the pub first. His face was bright red and there was a strong smell of brandy emanating from him. He was dressed in a pinstripe suit, white shirt and multi-coloured tie. Sarah was a quiet lady, dressed modestly in a simple skirt, blouse and cardigan. She looked very uncomfortable. Violet sensed that Sarah did not approve of her and suspected that her husband had persuaded her to come.

Once everyone was seated and had a drink, Henry stood up, a drink in one hand and a folded paper in the other.

'I'd like to say a few words,' he said, beaming.

Violet smiled. It was the New Year. For Henry's sake she would try to make the best of tonight and put the matter of the poison-pen letter out of her mind until the morning.

'I would like to say how happy we are to have you here tonight and I have a small announcement to make.'

Betsy had just come in with another tray of canapés but stood respectfully in the background on hearing Henry make his announcement.

Violet looked expectantly at him. Excitement was bubbling out of him. He looked at her and she smiled encouragingly. He must have received a big commission. His work was receiving wonderful recognition, especially from Irish emigrants in New York who had done well. He was getting the Ward name very well known in all the right circles.

'Ladies and gentlemen . . . I have just bought the old bank on High Street and refurbishments begin on Monday for what will be Ward's Goldsmith and Jewellery Shop. I have clients from London and New York and of course Dublin – and I will bring them all to Draheen!' He was absolutely beaming.

It was as if someone had kicked Violet in the stomach. She sat motionless, staring at Henry as there were cheers and congratulations and glasses clinked.

'Well done!' Victor Gettings said heartily. 'Draheen needs something like this.'

'Good man, Henry!' Stephen O'Donoghue said. 'With everyone taking the boat for London and New York, it's great to hear some good news! A toast is in order.' He reached for the bottle of brandy and filled up his glass, to the obvious disapproval of his wife who was fidgeting and had refused any alcohol whatsoever.

'You are a dark horse, Henry,' Heather Gettings said. 'What a beautiful building it is! And how wonderful that something exciting is happening in Draheen for a change.'

Victor Gettings raised a toast, and everyone clinked glasses with more congratulations.

Heather got up from the fireside chair and walked over to where Violet was sitting. She took a drag from a cigarette in a gold cigarette-holder, inhaled deeply then allowed the smoke to escape from her mouth in small circles.

'So, you're staying in the sticks then,' she said as she smiled at Violet. 'I have to say I thought the bright lights of

London would be calling you back or even New York and Broadway. Well, good for Draheen!'

But Violet was staring open-mouthed at Henry and made no reply.

Henry walked over and pulled her up. He grabbed her waist and swung her around, then took both her hands and held them tightly.

'Yes, we are staying in the sticks, Heather,' he said. 'It's a surprise for Violet too.' He looked sheepishly at his wife.

She didn't trust her voice to speak – how could he do this? Without a word he had gone ahead and bought this building. Without ever discussing it. She knew he had plans to open a jewellery shop and workspace. They had discussed it at length. Opening it in Draheen did make sense but they had talked about having it in Dublin or even London before they moved. Henry knew how unsettled she was living here. He knew how unwelcoming most of the townspeople were to her. There was so much to discuss about it. All the money they had saved, and more, would be needed to open it. Now he had gone ahead without even consulting her, as if her opinion was of no importance.

In that moment, she felt she hardly knew her husband.

'Henry . . .' She tried to speak but her voice was strangled.

Betsy had put her tray down and now she came over to Violet.

'Excuse me, Mrs Ward, but Sylvia would like to see you.'

Violet's eyes met Betsy's, secretly thanking her for helping her make her escape.

'Thanks, Betsy, I will go up to her now.' She pulled her hands from her husband's grip.

'Congratulations, Henry,' she said. But it was barely a whisper.

She went out and up the stairs, her heart pounding. The congratulations and cheers below were getting louder.

She tiptoed into her daughter's room. Sylvia was, in fact, asleep. She looked like a little fairy with creamy wisps of hair over her face, her doll Suzanne snuggled close beside her. A tug of love almost overpowered Violet. She made a vow to herself. Whatever she had to do, she would protect Sylvia. She loved her husband but if he refused to leave Draheen their marriage would be tested to its very core.

CHAPTER 5

Violet had hidden the letter that Sylvia had received in a drawer in her bedroom. She took it out now. She had not gone back down to the party. Instead she had sat beside Sylvia's bed for a while and then quietly left her and came to sit in her own bedroom.

Now she read the letter again, staring at the vicious words. Her party mood had certainly left her.

Almost an hour had passed when the door opened and Henry walked in.

'Violet, you must come down now – I have a bottle of champagne ready to open.'

Violet turned her head away.

'I won't be coming down.'

'Why ever not? Sylvia is asleep.'

Violet got up and walked towards her husband, staring straight at him.

'You have absolutely no idea why I am upset. Do you, Henry?'

'No. What do you mean "upset"? What is wrong? Is it Sylvia?'

'Henry, why on earth did you not consult with me

before you poured all that money into a building here? Did you not think I had a right to know?'

Henry looked completely taken aback. 'I thought it would be a New Year surprise for you. It's such a beautiful building. You will love it. Wait until you see the interior! The light through the windows, the craftsmanship of the architrave! And the wooden floors really give it class. I know it swallowed most of what we have. I did put away a bit for a rainy day, but I have had to mortgage the house. I promise you it will be worth it. I have wonderful plans. Draheen will become known as the home of the finest goldsmiths in Ireland. I thought you would be thrilled!'

He smiled and reached for her.

She stepped away.

'Thrilled about what exactly? That you have tied us to Draheen for good by buying that building? You know that I have had huge reservations about staying here.' She was barely able to disguise the frustration and anger she felt.

He shook his head and tried to grab her hand, but she pushed him away.

'In time things will change,' he said. 'I know it has not been easy for you or Sylvia. But in time things will come right. You have already made some friends here.'

'What about Sylvia? Will *she* make new friends? Is it all going to work out for her, too?' she said, her voice rising.

'Stop worrying so much, Sylvia will be fine. I know the school did not work out for her. But the town will accept all of us in time. It's just their way.'

'Really?'

'You are overreacting here. Maybe I should have told you. But it's done now – can we discuss this in the morning? We have people downstairs and it's starting to look more than a bit odd that you are not down there.'

'I'm not going down.'

'*What?* You are not serious?'

'You heard me, go down yourself. I am not going.'

Henry threw his eyes to heaven. 'You are completely overreacting, Violet.'

'I am not going down there and that's final!' she said vehemently.

'Christ, woman, I don't know why you are acting like this. I have had enough!'

He turned around, stormed out and banged the door shut. Violet could hear him pounding down the stairs.

Shortly after that Betsy came up, bringing her some tea and a little food, for which she was grateful. Betsy told her not to worry and that things would look better in the morning. Violet knew this was far from the truth, but she smiled and wished Betsy a Happy New Year.

As Violet drank the tea, white flakes of snow began to fall outside. She watched them as they covered the windowsill. Snow could make everything look so pure, so untouched, so innocent.

She sat there for a long time, lost in her thoughts.

Eventually she could hear the church bells in the distance, ringing in the New Year, and much jubilation downstairs. 1950 had arrived. She shuddered and pulled her wrap more closely around her. She thought of other New Year's Eves when she was a young girl, sharing a room with her sisters. Now she was shunned by all her family. She thought of her mother, busy cooking, cleaning, sewing and praying. Did she still pray for her youngest daughter?

Elsie Morton had told her that her brother Mattie was in Guildford on the buildings. She knew that if she really

31

wanted to find him she possibly could. The Irish community was tight enough in Guildford. But the thought of him shutting the door on her stopped her.

Elsie had told her that Owen Keane from Whitewater had seen her first play while he was in London and reported that it was a sin against the Catholic Church. The news had spread like wildfire in the village. Violet's father had said he wished she were dead, that she had brought shame to her family. Her sister Kathleen was to be married to Eamon Boyle but when his father heard about Violet he had made his son call off the wedding. Kathleen was heartbroken and had left for America. Violet could not imagine what it would be like for Kathleen who had only been as far as Dublin on a day trip in her life. Elsie said that she went to look after children in Brooklyn. She was to come back after a couple of years. At the time Violet had written yet again to tell her mother that she was so sorry for any distress she had caused. But again, there was no response.

She undressed and put on her nightdress, then went back to Sylvia's bedroom and got into bed beside her, cuddling into her warm little body.

Eventually the guests left, and she heard Henry come up the stairs and go into their bedroom. He did not come to find her.

Tears silently flowed down her face. She would have to talk to him in the morning. But she feared that even if she showed him the letter he would shush it away as some silly kids with nothing better to do.

She was sure it was not from any child. There was pure hatred in that letter. She had not felt hatred before in Ireland. Disappointment, yes. Her family were disappointed and felt betrayed by her. But hatred was new.

She felt suffocated. She had left here over twelve years ago for the same reason. She could breathe in London, even if the air was filled with smog and toil. In Ireland the air was filled with rules that were so rigid she felt she would smother. Her curious mind had been silenced from an early age. She was not allowed to question her mother, her father, her schoolmaster and certainly not the Catholic Church. She had wished for an easier mind that would have accepted the life set out to her. Work in the local drapery shop, attend a few dances and marry a suitable boy. Then rear her children if she was blessed enough and make sure that they knew the rules set out to them. For rules were there to be abided by if you wished to live peacefully in Whitewater and those rules applied in Draheen too. She knew that in the minds of many she had broken the rules and she would have to face the consequences.

CHAPTER 6

Violet had a restless night. While it was still dark, she slid out of Sylvia's bed and went to the window. The light snow had vanished and the garden gleamed under a cover of silver frost. She crept out of the room and into her own bedroom. Henry was in a deep sleep, snoring lightly. She could smell the alcohol emanating from him. She quietly washed in the adjoining washroom and then changed into a flared crimson skirt reaching to below her knees. During the war material had been scarce and clothes had reflected that. Material was never wasted. She knew her skirt would possibly receive some glares from the women of Draheen, if only for the colour, but she was past caring today. She pulled on a warm cream jumper that clung to her figure, some socks over her nylons and her walking shoes.

Downstairs, the waft of freshly baked bread met her senses. Betsy was normally off on Sundays but had insisted the previous evening that she would come in for a little while before she headed off to eleven o'clock Mass.

When Violet arrived down all remnants of the night before had vanished. Betsy had the place spotless. There was a pot of tea on the hob and she poured herself a cup and began to drink it, sitting in the comfort of the warm kitchen.

'Happy New Year, Betsy. My goodness, you should have rested after last night. You are so very kind to come in this morning – and so early.'

'It's no bother at all. To be honest, I was worried about you and the little one after the letter and your husband's announcement. I know you are unsettled here.'

'Betsy, I am not sure what I would do without you.'

'Sure, I am only too delighted to be here. Would you like some eggs – you ate very little yesterday. I can have them ready in a jiffy?' She was mixing an onion-and-butter stuffing for the goose they would have for dinner.

'No, I'm not hungry, but thank you, Betsy.'

'I can see you didn't sleep much.'

'I'm afraid sleep deserted me.'

'I know how you must be upset about that letter, but like I said there's only a few bad eggs, remember that. Draheen might have a few nasty people who feel they run the town, but there are kind people here too.'

'I know that. Betsy, I'm going to go out for a walk up to the woods, to clear my head. If Sylvia gets up, tell her I won't be long. I'm cancelling my trip to London next week. I could not leave her. I'm so worried about her. I feel sick to my stomach about everything.'

'I'll mind her until you get back from your walk, don't worry. It's not my place to say but I don't think Mr Ward meant to upset you so much. He was so pure excited last night. I think he just thought you would feel the same. Men can be strange creatures at times. He didn't stop to think properly but I really believe he thought you would be just as thrilled as him.'

'Thanks, Betsy – unfortunately, though, he was wrong.'

Violet put on her green woollen coat with its rich brown fur collar and tied a pink silk headscarf over her hair.

'You might well meet the early risers coming from first Mass this morning – the 'church ladies' as people call them. Nelly Cooke will be there and Agnes the Cat of course. There is something about that woman that worries me. It's as if she is the opposite to holy even though she is so involved in the care of the church. You'll see them as you pass the church – they usually congregate at the gate to gossip.'

'Thanks for the warning, Betsy.'

Henry Ward lit a Woodbine cigarette. He inhaled deeply, allowing his senses to be enveloped by the tobacco. There was no sign of Violet. He stretched himself and looked out of the window. It had a view of the rear garden. Even now it had a calming effect on him with its winter coat. This is what he had dreamed about those nights when he secretly cried to go back to Ireland. He could never have imagined that he would be so lucky. His work as a goldsmith had gained him exceptionally well-off clients who were not afraid to spend their money for something unique. He was getting commissions that he could hardly keep up with. Some of the high society of New York were noticing the name Ward Jewellery. London society had already noticed him, and the brand was beginning to flourish in all the right circles. A bespoke piece of jewellery from Henry Ward would soon be the gift of the rich of London and New York for their society wives. He could hardly believe his luck.

He had longed to live under an Irish sky again. London's streets were far from being paved with gold, but they had allowed his father, his brother and himself to begin again.

The small farmhouse where they had lived with his father's parents seemed to become more and more unreal in his memory as the years passed. The famine may have driven their people out in the last century, but people were still leaving in droves. The chance of a better life. The chance of an education. But the streets of London stole the souls of many who had Ireland tattooed on their heart.

The fields, beaches and roads of Wexford had been his playground. He knew every fairy fort and fairy myth, thanks to his grandmother. He knew where every battle had taken place and how grateful he should be to the men who fought for a free republic. She had told him the stories of the 1798 rebellion and how Father Murphy, a young curate, had led his people to fight the English army on Vinegar Hill. How the children with their parents went to fight, picking up shovels and pikes and anything that they could find, how valiantly they fought but were beaten and how Father Murphy was brutally executed. She had told him of the Banshee who would comb her hair and keen as a warning of death. He had often thought he could hear that dark angel as he slept in the black smog of London.

His father Jim may have left with barely the price of the boat to England. But they had conquered London. Luck had found them there. They had started on the building sites but Jim being hired by Mr Bayley the jeweller to do some carpentry work after hours had changed everything. Henry had assisted his father and Mr Bayley had taken to the hardworking young Irishman. He hired Henry first as messenger boy and general help but, when Henry displayed a keen interest in the goldsmith's craft, Mr Bayley began to take him aside in the evenings to train him. It wasn't long before he was working full time side by side with the jeweller. He fine-tuned his craft under Mr Bayley and then, after the war, established his own goldsmith business.

His father had wanted him to stay working for Mr Bayley, but Henry had bigger plans. They had worked. He never would have had the money to buy Eveline or acquire the loan needed to help buy the new premises if he had remained working for Mr Bayley.

The time had come when he knew he could no longer only dream of returning to Ireland – he had to make it a reality. He had finally convinced Violet. Finding Eveline House had sealed the deal. He knew she loved it as much he did.

When they first arrived, and Father Cummins had insulted them from the pulpit, he thought he had made a serious mistake dragging his family back to Ireland. Religion and tradition still ruled the state. But he could live with that. It was harder on Violet. She was such a free spirit. It was why he had fallen in love with her but being back in Ireland Violet was less content. Maybe announcing his big purchase in front of everyone was not the best idea. He hated fighting with her, but he was gutted at her reaction. This was what he had dreamed about. He wanted it to be her dream too. Somewhere in the depths of his heart, he was afraid that it was far away from Violet's dream. He knew she was worried about Sylvia. He had really hoped that coming to Ireland would help. But he could see how their little girl was withdrawing.

But running away was not the answer. He needed to persuade Violet to give it a proper chance. He had enough commissions for two years. He would train a young prodigy and have a proper jewellery and goldsmith shop. He would have a clerk on the front and a workshop at the back. He would put Draheen on the map.

He just had to convince Violet. But that was not going to be easy. Her career was beginning to flourish in London. The theatres were very interested in her work. Here in Draheen she was so different to anyone else. But he was sure it would be good for Sylvia. They both worried about her. But maybe when the shop was up and established in years to come, Sylvia could come in with him. He could train her as a goldsmith. Father and daughter working alongside each other in one of the most prestigious jewellery shops in Ireland.

It didn't help that Violet's own family in the midlands had refused to have anything to do with her. He wanted to drive there and face them. How could any parents turn their backs on their daughter?

He would just have to make it his business to try to convince her that it was best for her and for Sylvia to remain in Draheen. He had to convince them because, no matter what she said, nothing was dragging him out of Ireland again.

The frost was beginning to thaw, a light winter sun peeping through the sky sending rainbow colours out to dance. Violet would have loved if Sylvia was with her this morning but getting Sylvia to leave the house would now be a huge undertaking. She would barricade herself in Eveline House after that letter.

Walking down the street and over the bridge, the woodsmoke filled her nostrils. As she walked up High Street, she could see Miss Doheny eyeing her from an upstairs window. The shop owner was apparently unaware that it was quite easy to see her peering out through the lace curtain of what was probably a bedroom. There was

39

certainly not much that Miss Doheny missed. Her mind drifted back to her first visit to Doheny's shop.

That first week, she had visited the grocery shop with plans on buying something to make for tea. But, although there was no one else but her and Miss Doheny in the shop, Violet was left to stand at the big thick counter while Miss Doheny rearranged some tomatoes.

Then another woman bustled in with two children in tow, her face as red as a beetroot. Miss Doheny ignored Violet and went to serve her.

'Good afternoon, what can I get for you today, Mrs Hogan? I have some lovely tomatoes.'

Mrs Hogan took a long look at Violet, openly examining her clothes.

'Good afternoon to you,' she offered to Violet.

'Good afternoon. What lovely children!'

'They are pure devils. I am going home to scrub them for Mass tomorrow.'

'How are your new Rhode Island hens?' Miss Doheny butted in.

Mrs Hogan threw her eyes to heaven. 'If they don't lay soon, they will find themselves in the pot with an onion for the supper. Give me some of those tomatoes and a bag of flour, please, and a bit of that nice ham.'

Miss Doheny carefully wrapped the ham and the tomatoes. Then she got a bag of flour. They chatted for another few minutes about the hens and what she could do to make them lay. Eventually Mrs Hogan bid good day to Miss Doheny and took a long last look at Violet before bidding her goodbye.

Violet had decided not to make a fuss while they chatted

but when Miss Doheny eventually turned to serve her, she felt the full force of her thin scowl.

Violet smiled back at her. 'I would like some tomatoes and a head of that lovely lettuce, please.'

'Well, are you settling into Draheen?' Miss Doheny asked through her scowl.

'Yes, thank you.' Violet smiled, not acknowledging Miss Doheny's rudeness.

But Miss Doheny ignored her pleasantness and began to sort the tomatoes again, then stopped to stare at her. 'I saw your husband yesterday. A jeweller, I believe.' She took some tomatoes and put them in a brown bag and then got the head of lettuce.

'Yes, he is a jeweller and a goldsmith too,' Violet replied.

'Sure, there will be no need for you to write plays anymore now. I hear you have a daughter too. You will be busy keeping Eveline in the state it should be kept in. Your husband will be busy with his work and you will need to tend to him. Eveline is a fine house to call home.'

There was something about the way Miss Doheny said *home* and eyed her with one eye half-shut that made Violet realise that she knew that neither Henry nor herself had come from as fine a house as Eveline.

It was not that it was such a grand house, but it was full of charm. No, she had not come from a house as charming as Eveline. It had been a small old farmhouse handed down from generation to generation, beside the back of a hill – her father's people's homeplace, people who had kept it much the same for the past two hundred years. Thick walls and small windows with a little porch to enter and take off your mucky boots and old coat. There was a range in the kitchen and a round table with a faded oilcloth with little

41

red roses painted on it. A sink overlooking a window with the wall as thick as two feet. There was an armchair for her father, an old bench for the children and a hardbacked chair for her mother, not that she sat very often there. A tea chest in the corner. There was the parlour that was papered in big blue flowers and dark furniture that Violet often thought a rat or mouse could jump out of. On the dresser was an old picture of her parents when they were courting, both looking tentative. Him a large man with deep eyes, her mother fair and graceful, unaware of the hardship that lay ahead. There was a pantry of sorts that held the slop bucket for the pig, potatoes and milk. In the kitchen was a stairs that led up to three small bedrooms. One for the boys, one for the girls and one for her parents. When she thought of her house, she could see her mother, knuckles sore from work, hair pinned up with a horseshoe nail. Steel-blue eyes looking at her, worried, disappointed. Blonde hair gone to grey.

'So I suppose you can put all that stage-writing business behind you now that you are in Ireland?' Miss Doheny said, bringing her out of her reverie.

Violet looked at her. This was a question and one that was demanding an answer. Miss Doheny had her hands on each side of her waist, looking at her accusingly.

'My husband is well capable of minding himself and we are recruiting someone to help look after the house and keep an eye on Sylvia while I write,' said Violet. 'I am writing a new play, not that it will be performed here – I am sure the good people of Ireland will ban it. Good day to you, Miss Doheny. I think we will go to the hotel for our tea. Our little conversation has reminded me that I am much too busy writing to worry about preparing food.'

With that she walked out, leaving Miss Doheny for once speechless.

She walked past the shop now and had to resist waving at Miss Doheny to let her know that she could see her clearly peeping through her lace curtain.

It was unusual to have a town built so close to a big wood. When they had first visited the town, it was Blythe Wood that had held the magic. Sylvia was fascinated by the little holy well with rosary beads and holy pictures hanging from a hawthorn tree over it, and loved running along the winding paths. It being the height of summer then, thistles, ragwort and cowslips were tangled amidst the hawthorns, birch and large oaks. There were ancient yew trees that seemed to haunt the wood, ancient trees holding secrets for decades.

Today the woods would have a winter coat.

Two other women she recognised from her walks were walking down the street and were eyeing her suspiciously. She could feel them staring at her clothes. The tapestry of clothes that morning was brown and grey except for hers. She held her head up high and walked on, never acknowledging the two women, who were openly standing and staring at her. Well, they didn't own the street, as far as she remembered – at least you could still walk the street without permission. Unless the Catholic Church had made some rule that she was unaware of.

She remembered her own mother following the rules set out for her religiously. Obeying the rules of the Church was a way of life.

One morning her mother told her that she had to go to Father McBride to be 'churched'. She had recently had her younger brother Mattie. But in the eyes of the Church her mother would be impure until she was churched by the priest, a blessing that took away the sin of childbirth. Virginity and celibacy were akin to holiness. She also remembered her having to be churched when her baby sister died. The night that baby died her mother had screamed and roared as the village midwife took the dead baby from her and her father buried the little corpse at Blackthorn Hill under an acorn tree. It was said there were other babies buried there too that had died at birth, never having the chance to be christened. Violet used to think she might see them dancing there on days like All Souls' Day, or on a Christmas Eve. She was sure she saw a glimpse of what looked like a fairy there one day, a misty day, when the fog was shifting blue and white.

As she drew level with the church, a couple emerged through the gates. Mr and Mrs O'Brien who ran the bakery. She was small and stout, and he was tall and thin, his neck bulging with large veins protruding as red as Miss Doheny's tomatoes. Mr O'Brien tipped his hat to Violet and was about to pass a pleasantry, when Mrs O'Brien pushed him on – but not before giving Violet a look that left her in no doubt that she thought she should live on the sole of her big flat shoe.

As she walked past the church more people began to emerge, eyeing her with wonder and suspicion. A couple of men tipped their hats and Liam Barrow, who delivered the milk every morning, wished her a pleasant day. Mrs Kennedy, who taught Sylvia in the afternoons, smiled encouragingly at her and waved good morning. Her son was with her, a thin, gangly-looking man, and he tipped his hat but not before he looked around as if making sure no one was watching.

There was no sign of the 'church ladies'. Presumably they were still inside, talking to the priest, tidying the church, engaging in vicious gossip.

She walked on, a light breeze blowing.

It was unfortunate that the church was so close to the entrance to the woods. But seeing the judgemental faces on the local parishioners was not going to stop her on her walk this morning. The woods were what made Draheen magical and this morning they did not fail her.

The silvery light of the morning now faded and the dark trees allowed a half light through. She stepped on gnarled twigs and decomposing leaves that gathered around the thick trees, their roots sleeping. The frost crackled beneath her steps. Then she came to a clearing and a brook. She walked on. Shadows circled the yew trees, throwing shades of light and dark in her path. But the air was clear, the frost penetrated her nostrils and she breathed deeply.

She knew what she had to do.

Ireland had not changed. It was like the woods, full of dark and light, full of magic and myth, full of kindness and maliciousness. The holy and the unholy. Like the gnarled branches around the sleeping roots, she felt it smothering her. She would not allow Sylvia to be a victim of hatred. She would leave soon and hopefully she would leave with Henry. But one thing was certain: she would not leave without her daughter.

CHAPTER 7

When Violet arrived back, Betsy was taking a fresh loaf of soda bread out of the oven. The goose was stuffed and all prepared to be cooked for dinner later. Potatoes and vegetables were peeled and chopped and a trifle was setting in the pantry. Betsy amazed her, she was so capable.

'My goodness, you have been so busy. What a feast you have prepared! I know you said you are off to see your cousin after Mass but are you sure you won't come back for some dinner later with us?'

'Thank you but no. I will leave you to eat in peace. I will go to eleven Mass and then head to see Patricia. I will eat with her before I leave. Get some good dinner into you all and hopefully all will come right. That goose needs about two hours in the oven.'

'Thanks, Betsy. It all looks wonderful. You are so kind. I hope your cousin is better today.'

Patricia suffered badly from arthritis.

'Ah, she's a great character despite all and normally has me in the fits of laughter.'

'Wait – I have something for her.'

Violet gave her a bottle of rum and a box of chocolates

that she had bought in London on her last trip there to see her play being performed.

'Oh, this is very grand,' Betsy said, delighted.

'You get yourself off – and thank you,' Violet said.

Betsy put her coat and hat on. She would cycle up and back.

Violet wished her a great day and went upstairs in search of Sylvia.

Sylvia was playing in her room. All her dolls were sitting in a circle and Sylvia was talking to them. Petite Suzanne was sitting right beside her.

'So, what's the story?' Violet asked. 'May I listen?'

'Well, it's not a story but of course you may listen. Sit beside Suzanne. I am just telling the girls not to go outside, because there are bad people who can hurt us. That it's safe here, but never to venture outside of Eveline. There are people who do not want us to be here. Suzanne will be watching out for everyone and will report if there are any nasty letters.'

Violet was alarmed at the seriousness on her daughter's face.

'Let's go into the garden for a little while, it's quite safe out there,' she suggested. 'I think Suzanne needs a little fresh air.'

'Are you sure?' Sylvia asked worriedly. 'I don't want to go into the garden.'

'You love the garden. It's very safe,' Violet reassured her.

Reluctantly she agreed.

Violet helped Sylvia into a warm coat, hat and mittens.

Grabbing Petite Suzanne, Sylvia followed Violet downstairs and out to the garden.

'It's just a letter, a very unkind letter, Sylvia,' said Violet. 'You are really not in any danger.'

'Yes, we are, I know it. Sometimes I know things, Mummy, and I know this. I can feel things that are dangerous, and I know that danger is near us. Please do not go outside or into the street. You should not have gone out today.'

'But we cannot live like that, Sylvia. Then we are prisoners in our own house.'

'But we must, they are after us. They think you are some sort of witch and they want to hurt us. *I know it, I know it, I know it!*' Her eyes were now filling with tears and her little body was beginning to tremble.

Violet tried to calm her down.

'It's alright, Sylvia, there is no one going to hurt us, I promise. Whoever wrote that letter may be just a little unwell in the head but, whoever it is, they cannot hurt us by what they say.'

There were tears streaming down her daughter's face.

'They are going to hurt us. I don't know how I know, but I do,' Sylvia whispered through her tears.

Violet hugged her daughter who was now crying inconsolably. Then she wrapped an arm around her and led her back inside and up to the safety of her bedroom.

Sylvia looked as weak as a kitten.

Violet took off her coat and hat and led her to the bed where she took off her shoes.

'Lie down for a little while,' she said, pulling back the blankets.

Sylvia climbed in and Violet tucked her in.

She lay down beside her, speaking soothingly to her until she calmed. Eventually she lay peacefully, and Violet left her with Suzanne to keep her company.

Violet went to look for Henry. This was not going to wait. He had to know.

She found him in his study, going over the finances of the new building. He had papers everywhere.

He pulled out his plans to show her, his enthusiasm overwhelming her, as if their difference of the night before had never occurred. He got up and began to talk about the plans as if he was talking to himself.

'I am going to hire only people from Draheen, make it a really local business. There are some great craftsmen around. George Kelly is a fine carpenter. I will ask him to kit out the shop and he can get his brother Willy to help. I met them at one of the meetings in the town hall. It is shocking seeing the likes of such men getting their cardboard boxes and boarding the trains for London and anywhere else that they might get work. Gifted men with so much craftsmanship. I thought the forties were bad but everyone I meet now has most of their family in England. The women are going too. What is to become of the country if they can't keep the young here? It will be on its knees. We need to do things to help this town. No one here needs jewellery, but buyers will come to the town. If they travel to Ward's Jewellery, they will have to eat and stay here, so everyone will get something out of it. That is why I want to stay here – why give London even more reason to keep us all there? I will employ people. I will need to source the finest shop windows with the name inscribed. Ireland will not have a shop like it. I am telling you it will put Draheen on the map. People will come from as far as New York, to purchase a once-off piece of jewellery from Ireland's finest Jeweller and Goldsmith. I will make you a piece to celebrate the opening. A bracelet of rose-gold set with the finest diamonds.'

Henry was almost dancing with excitement.

Violet tried to remain calm.

'Henry, I want to show you something.' She took the letter in its envelope out of the pocket of her skirt. 'Can you read this, please? I found it with Sylvia yesterday. I only discovered it just before anyone arrived last night.' She handed him the letter.

He read it, then took off his glasses and pointed at it as if it was contaminated.

'Where did she get this piece of filth?

'I don't know how it got here and that is even more worrying. I have tried to find out. Sylvia refuses to tell me if someone dropped it off or if it was in the postbox or if somehow it was shoved through the door. Betsy has tried to ask her too. She has never been outside of the house on her own so perhaps someone came to the door or saw her in the garden and gave it to her. It scares me to think that someone was here that we don't know about. You can see Sylvia's name is on it.'

Henry sat down and read it again. He looked up. Raw anger was evident in his blue eyes.

'This is disgraceful. Who on earth sent it?'

'I know it's not a child – it's definitely an adult. The wording on it is not from a child. It is too cruel. I know you have all sorts of plans, but that letter has just finished me. I can't expose Sylvia to any more cruelty from these small-minded people.'

Henry stood up and came closer to Violet. 'What are you saying?' he said, his voice rising.

'I am saying we need to leave, for our daughter's sake – we need to get back to London,' Violet replied, her calm disappearing.

Henry threw his eyes to heaven. 'Are you quite mad? Yes, it is a vicious letter, a dirty piece of pure filth, but you are hardly going to let them get away with frightening us out of our home? That is plain lunacy!'

'It's not just the letter! Our daughter could not stay in school in case you have forgotten, because she was called an English bitch and daughter of a witch. I cannot walk down the street without the women of this town looking at me as if I were a harlot let loose in Draheen.' Violet had begun to tremble.

Henry went to put his arm around her, but she shrugged it off.

She stared at her husband. 'I am taking Sylvia back to London, Henry. She's not safe here.'

A look flashed across his face that frightened Violet.

He banged his fist on the table. '*This is getting beyond ridiculous!* We have poured everything we have into this house and now this business. We are going nowhere. I know you are upset, but don't get any ideas about moving. We will get used to it and they will get used to us. Maybe we should try to fit in a bit more?'

'What do you mean by that?' Violet replied, alarmed.

'Well, you are busy enough now – you could take a break from writing and the theatre and just concentrate on Sylvia and maybe get involved in something in the town.'

Violet felt like she had been struck. A vision of Miss Doheny came to her mind. Did she not advise her to do the same? She tried to remain calm, aware that their voices could possibly be heard by Sylvia. She looked into her husband's eyes.

'Well, unfortunately for you, you married me, and I am not the type of person that you have just described. The sad part is that I thought you knew that.'

She grabbed the letter to leave, but Henry caught her by the arm.

'Violet, I'm sorry, I shouldn't have said that. I'm worried too but running is never the answer to bullies. I will find out who is doing this, and I will stop it. Look, forgive me for what I said. I was wrong.'

But it was too late. He had said it and the awful thing was Violet knew he did mean it.

She left the study, slamming the door behind her.

Back in the bedroom she felt that same stifling feeling she'd had when she lived in that small farmhouse when her mother and father did everything to make her fit into a community she felt alien to. She would be married off by now if she had stayed, to a suitable lad from the village, and her hands and knees would be sore from scrubbing and cleaning and kneeling for Mass. There were few options for her if they could not get her married. She would possibly be still working in the drapery store – the position that her father had secured for her. She could have trained to be a typist or a seamstress. Most from school were gone to England to work in factories. Her mother had hoped to make a priest out of at least one of her brothers. There had been a spinster aunt who had left money to help get one of them into a seminary. But, from what she remembered of her brothers, they were far too wild to be priests. Her mother had prayed and prayed that one of them would have a vocation, a call from God that he was destined to be a priest. She had said enough novenas and prayed at enough missions. But the call had not come – instead, as far as Violet knew, except for her younger brother Paul they were scattered between London and New York, all working as labourers.

She took a deep breath. She was no longer that young girl, trapped by her mother's prayers and her father's despair at his wayward daughter. She had felt trapped then and she felt trapped now. Her daughter was her priority and she would do all in her power to help her.

But she had to admit, even if it was only to herself, that she missed London. She missed the smell of the streets, the beauty of the galleries, the restaurants and, most of all, the friends she had there. They never questioned her for who she was, they embraced it. She missed the theatre. Although she never directed her plays, she was always there to be consulted with, and loved watching how it all came together. She missed the green room when she would meet the actors. She loved rehearsals where she saw how they interpreted her words. She was writing a new play and, if it was to be staged, there was no way she could leave Sylvia for that length of time. She would simply have to take her with her. She had moved here because she loved Henry, she wanted him to have his dream, but in doing so she had no idea how much it would hurt to leave hers in London. A doubt started to creep into her mind. Was it all to do with Sylvia, or was part of it that she knew she had made a mistake for herself and her career in coming here?

Dinner later was a stifled affair but, for Sylvia's sake, she tried to make the best of it. Herself and Henry being overly polite to each other.

Henry retired to his study for the evening.

That night she slept in the guest room. But sleep would not come. She wanted to go down and make herself a hot drink, but she could hear Henry walking around. Sleep had obviously evaded him too. Eventually she fell into a dream. She was back in her old family home, with her mother. Her mother was crying, telling her how disappointed she was.

Miss Doheny was in the dream and there was a copy of *Unholy Love* in her hand. Miss Doherty began to shred it, tearing it into strips with her hands, and then Henry gathered up the shredded pieces, her words scattered on the flagstone floor. He opened the range and threw the strips of paper into it, making a golden glow, as Violet could hear herself silently and violently scream.

CHAPTER 8

Henry drank the second cup of tea that Betsy poured for him. He had barely slept. It was good to come into the warm kitchen. Betsy cut him a thick slice of the warm soda bread. He spread it with butter and greengage jam.

'You will have to roll me out to do some work, Betsy. You do spoil us. Maybe you can get Sylvia to eat some of this. She's getting very thin.'

Betsy looked at him intently.

Henry heard that Betsy had been devoted to her parents. She was a fine-looking woman and would make some man a great wife. She was still young enough. They were lucky to have her. She had become great friends with Violet and was very close to Sylvia too.

'If only she would eat,' Betsy replied, concerned. 'She has me heartbroken trying to get her to eat something. Her face is as white as snow this morning. I would love to get a bit of colour into them little cheeks of hers.'

Henry decided to ask her about the letter. Betsy was solid – she would never go talk about it down the town.

'Betsy, this letter Sylvia got, Violet has told me about it. She also told me that you saw it.'

'Yes, Mr Ward, I was there when we found it with Sylvia.'

'Have you any idea who might have sent it? I need to get to the bottom of it.'

Betsy eyed him as if weighing up in her mind if she would tell him what she knew. She sat at the bottom of the table and sighed.

'I was at morning Mass this morning and then I went into Doheny's for some flour. Miss Doheny could hardly wait to tell me what she knew. That woman is a danger to herself.'

'Go on, is it to do with Violet?' Henry helped himself to another slice of bread from the plate.

Betsy got up and shut the kitchen door, then sat in a chair closer to Henry.

'It is. I am sick with the worry.' She shook her head.

'Go on.'

Then in a whisper she told him her news.

'Well, there is a certain group of women that go to Mass together most mornings. They are very involved in the upkeep of the church. All Holy Joes, of course. They have not hidden their disapproval of Mrs Ward and her plays and that is putting it mildly. They meet in the town hall a couple of times a week – for a parochial meeting. They are doing some knitting for Africa. Although Miss Doheny has a point in saying it's far from woolly jumpers they need in the heat over there. Anyway, Miss Doheny said that at the last meeting – she is not normally at them because of the shop – but anyway she was at this one. Although it doesn't suit her that Agnes the Cat is the ringleader of them. Even Miss Doheny is fearful of Agnes and it's rare for Miss Doheny to be fearful of anyone. Well, she said that they got no knitting done because they could not concentrate on their work as they are too concerned about the effect Mrs Ward is having on the youth of the town. Already some of the girls are beginning to wear their hair like her and, well, she is a very handsome woman, sure she has a bit of a fan club with the young boys. Then there are the plays – Miss Doheny says that one of them is about a priest who has his way with a woman.' Betsy's eyes looked away in embarrassment at this.

'Well, they have a relationship, that is true – I wouldn't say he has his way if you get my drift,' said Henry.

'There are a few right auld sliveens in that group, let me tell you. I am sure one of them wrote the letter. It's not Miss Doheny because, to be fair to her, she would say it straight to her face. But she knows. I just know it. Then she spoke to me as I was going out the door. "I'm sure her ladyship will tire of Draheen and the bright lights of London will be pulling her back. Wouldn't be surprised if she ups and leaves. You will be out of a job then, Betsy," she says to me, all prim and proper and looking at me as if I had crawled from beneath the rug. Oh, she is something else! As my mother used to say, a wipe of an auld rag is what she would need.'

Henry shook his head. He knew the type. Busybodies with nothing better to do.

'Thank you, Betsy. I am going to try and put a stop to this business before my wife is on the next boat to England. But not a word of this to Violet. She is upset enough as it is.'

'Very well, Mr Ward, I will leave it to you, but you have a fight on your hands, let me tell you. Them women are pure poison.'

She got up and went to the door.

'I'll see how Sylvia is,' she said. 'Good luck.'

Henry put on a Crombie coat and a grey hat and walked out the door. It was a mild morning for the time of year and there was a stillness in the garden as he closed the gate behind him.

He walked up into the town. He bid good morning to a few neighbours and walked up the hill. At the top of the hill there was another street. This was the main street. On the main street was Miss Doheny's shop. He walked in and the bell rang, signalling his arrival.

Miss Doheny did a double take when she saw him and the conversation between two other women stopped in its tracks. All eyes were on him.

'Good morning, Mr Ward.'

'Good morning, Miss Doheny. I want a word with you, if you don't mind.'

The other two women looked crestfallen at having to leave, but there was no excuse for them to stay to hear what Mr Ward wanted to say.

'Close the door tightly, please,' Miss Doheny said to them with an air of importance. 'Now, how can I be of help, Mr Ward?' She smiled sweetly, fixing her shop apron around her.

'I was hoping an intelligent woman like yourself could help me. I have asked around and everyone has said that if I need any advice on a . . . delicate matter, Miss Doheny is as discreet as the day is long.'

Miss Doheny beamed and beckoned for him to come closer to the counter.

'Well, my daughter received a letter. A very nasty letter.

I am not sure if it was put in the postbox or if someone came into the garden and gave it to her. I am afraid there is someone in the town with a very poisonous mind who for some reason would prefer to see my wife and my child on the first boat to London.' Henry examined Miss Doheny's reaction, but her face was unreadable.

'First let me tell you,' she responded sharply, 'I am not exactly surprised. Your wife has caused quite a stir here in Draheen and it's not a good stir by any manner or means.'

Henry came closer to her and lowered his voice.

'I am trying to be patient here, Miss Doheny, but someone sent or delivered a very vicious letter to my daughter, a threat, and I will not take it lightly.'

'Well, perhaps it is your wife you should be talking to, Mr Ward. She is the culprit here, who is upsetting everyone. With her filthy plays. Before Father Cummins died, he did everything in his power to make sure they did not make their way here. We are a Catholic country and there are certain rules of the Church that your wife seems to be ignoring. The people of Draheen must protect the minds of their young from evil. Stop your wife from writing this filth and she might stop upsetting everyone. Father Quill is not doing his job properly, if you ask me. He should be putting a stop to it – instead I believe he is up drinking sherry in Eveline. It's simply not acceptable in a town like this.'

'Miss Doheny, you are a straight-talking woman and I appreciate that. But my wife is her own person. I cannot and will not tell her what to do.'

Miss Doheny looked at him as if he had lost his reason. 'Are you not a married man, Mr Ward? Did your wife not promise in the name of God and Our Lord to obey her husband? Handle your wife properly, Mr Ward. Take

59

control of your household if you want a peaceful life in Draheen. Ireland is a good clean Catholic country with good clean-living people who try to teach the young of the country the right way. Having your wife make a mockery of this in her filthy plays might be accepted in London, but you are not there now. You asked me for some advice and there it is. Is there anything else that I can get you, Mr Ward?'

'There is something actually.' He leaned in closer to her. 'If you happen to hear who has sent that letter, or called on my daughter without my knowledge, warn them for their own sake to stop – because I will find them out if it's the last thing I do and they will regret the day they were ever born when I do. That is a promise. I do not make empty threats, Miss Doheny, and believe me this threat is a very real one. *I am not a man to be messed with*. I will bid you good day.'

Henry turned on his heel and walked out, leaving Miss Doheny staring after him with her mouth open.

CHAPTER 9

Sylvia was becoming more reclusive as the days passed. She barely ate, her face became gaunt and her skin almost transparent. Her blue eyes were haunting, watching every movement, her hands clutching Suzanne the doll close to her frail body.

'This cannot continue,' Violet whispered to Henry as Sylvia pushed the piece of bread and butter away yet again. She had barely touched her glass of milk.

Henry put the paper that he was reading down and looked intently at his daughter. He caught her hand. 'Sylvia, you must eat, or you will become ill. I know you are upset, but you are perfectly safe, and nobody is going to harm you or anyone else.'

Two fat tears rolled down Sylvia's face. 'You don't know that. You can't say that for sure. I know things, I can see things. It is safe in the house. *Only in the house. Only in the house. Only in the house.*' She pushed her chair back and stood up, putting her hands on her ears.

Violet knelt beside her and put her arms around her, trying to calm her down.

'Can you tell us how you got that letter, dearest?' she

said. 'Then Daddy can make sure it never happens again.'

But Sylvia was silent and the tears continued to flow down her pale face.

'I am calling the doctor – he might be able to give her something,' Henry said.

'What can the doctor give her?' Violet whispered.

'I don't know, but he can advise us at least.'

Violet looked at Sylvia. 'Sylvia, why don't you go upstairs and get some paints ready and I will bring some hot cocoa and a biscuit up to you – you might prefer that.'

'Alright, Mummy.' Sylvia hugged Violet before leaving the room.

Violet sat down opposite Henry, her eyes showing new lines that had recently appeared.

'We need to leave here, Henry – why will you not listen to me?' she pleaded.

Henry shook his head. 'For Christ's sake, Violet, I am not being run out of my own country by some stupid old biddy with a stupid poisoned-pen letter. I am going to report it. Let that garda sort it out. I promise this will not end well for whoever wrote that poison. Be reasonable. There are biddies in every town. I am sure in time Sylvia will improve. Let's get the doctor to look at her. Give her a bottle of something to build her up. It will all blow over.'

'Blow over? How can all this just blow over?'

'Why don't we go out this evening to the hotel, just the two of us. It will do us good and Betsy will stay and mind Sylvia. You know she won't let anything happen to her.'

Violet was weary. It was true – Betsy would watch her like a hawk. Maybe she should go. It might give her a chance to talk to Henry and convince him that leaving was the only answer. In truth, she had already decided.

'Please, Violet, you have barely left the house yourself these past few days except to go to Blythe Wood. It will do you good, it will do us both good.'

Violet had continued to sleep in the guest room. Although she was barely sleeping. The fact that she had moved out of the main bedroom was not helping matters. It was driving a wedge between them.

'Very well, let's. I'm just going to lie down for a while, I feel so tired.'

She walked upstairs, back to the bedroom that she normally shared with him.

It was papered in an embossed gold, with plum-velvet drapes and a large four-poster bed. There were ornate bottles of French perfume and a gold jewellery box on the dressing table. A lady's vanity unit lay open on a small table. A rose-gold hairbrush that Henry had bought for her sat beside some creams and potions she had bought in Harrods.

She pulled open the drawer and took out the photo of her parents. They looked so young in the photo, without the creases that life had inflicted on their faces.

She tried to imagine what her mother was doing. After all her chores of feeding the hens and the pig, she would have made some breakfast for the men who were busy with their own chores. Then after that perhaps made a wheaten loaf. Then she would set about getting the washing ready for the day. Her hands were hard and swollen from the work, her back aching from the scrubbing. Her mother perhaps no longer talked about her estranged daughter. Violet wondered if her name was ever even mentioned in her home.

An image of apple-picking came into her mind. They had a large orchard at the back, and it was brimming with the sweetest apples. Her mother would make apple jam, tarts and then wrap the apples not used in bits of old newspaper and store them in the pantry. She could remember how the sun felt on her face as she bit into one of those apples, her mother picking them and smiling at her. How she wished she could talk to her, ask for her help with Sylvia. Introduce her to her beautiful granddaughter. Sylvia would love the freedom on the farm and the kittens who nested in the shed. The birds who built their nests high up in the rafters, ignoring wars and woes, intent on building their homes for their babies. How Sylvia would fall in love with the colours of the heathers on the hillside and the brook where she could fish for minions! She could roam the countryside, picking blackberries just like she herself had done. How she would marvel at the lough as she imagined the three swans in the story of the Children of Lir!

But the morning she had sneaked out that door for England was the day she made her bed – she would have to lie in it now. The first year she had sent her mother a beautiful silk scarf. She could hear her say, 'Sure, where would I wear such a grand scarf?'

But Violet knew that secretly she would love a fine thing like a silk scarf.

She lay back on the bed and thought about the evening ahead. She would have to convince Henry tonight. She slept for an hour and then got up and worked on her new play. But her mind would not settle.

She played cards with Sylvia for a little while and then caught up on some correspondence from the theatres. She wrote to some of her writer friends in London and then walked out to post the letters.

Towards evening she had a bath and washed her hair,

spending time coiffuring it into a style behind her ears that she had seen in a magazine. She picked out a pale-blue silk dress with a full skirt and a wasp waist embellished with flowers. She was possibly a bit too dressed-up for Draheen, but she didn't care. In her head she had already left. She took some time applying some gentle make-up and then her scarlet lipstick. Finally she put on her cream cashmere coat, red half-hat and cream gloves.

Henry whistled from the hall as she came down the stairs.

'Well, you are a picture! Every eye in Draheen will be envious of me,' he said, but Violet caught the look of tension that crossed his face when he saw her so dressed-up.

Clearly he would prefer her to dress in a lower key. The thought upset her. They had always dressed up when they went out in London.

But she was in Ireland now.

It was not too far to walk up to the hotel and, although cold, it was good to be out in the air. Henry bid hello to a couple of people. Violet could feel the stares. She held her head up high and walked on in step with Henry.

The hotel was busy as they walked into the foyer. There was a record-player and Bing Crosby was crooning. They sat and ordered a drink from the waitress, then said hello to the nearby table. John and Catherine Hunt from Blake House a few miles outside of the town were having a drink. The Hunts were Protestants who normally only mixed with their own. At another table were two brothers who lived in another big house called Blackburn Hall. They tended to eat in the hotel two to three times a week. Their father and mother were dead, and they were the last descendants of a long line of gentry. They wore tweeds and were known to smoke cigars and drink only sherry. They said hello to Henry and Violet.

After finishing their drinks, Henry and Violet walked into the main dining area of the hotel. This was known as the parlour. It had a small bar and a fire blazed in the hearth. There were two other tables busy and they nodded good evening to their occupants.

The owner of the hotel, Mrs O'Hara, was wearing a black dress with a starched white collar, her grey hair pinned high up on her head. She was cleaning some glasses behind a small bar.

'Good evening, Mr Ward. Nice to see you out, Mrs Ward. Is it taking a break from your writing you are?' Her tone sounded unpleasant and she surveyed Violet through narrowed red-rimmed eyes.

'Only for the evening, Mrs O'Hara. I will be back to my writing first thing in the morning.'

Mrs O'Hara pursed her lips. She came out, took their coats and hung them on a coat stand. Then she showed them to a table.

'Shall we have another drink first and then have a bite to eat?' Henry suggested to Violet.

She nodded and they ordered a whiskey for Henry and a dry sherry for her.

She took off her gloves and put them into her bag, wondering when would be the best time to tackle Henry. Should she wait until he'd had a few more drinks? She sipped her sherry.

Henry threw back the whiskey and ordered another. He sat back, folding his arms.

'I met with that carpenter today,' he said. 'A brilliant

craftsman. He will do a fine job on the interior. We are just trying to source the wood. But it will look so polished when it's complete.'

Violet could feel herself tense. 'Henry, you are going ahead with the plans?'

'Yes, of course I'm going ahead with the plans. Why wouldn't I?'

'After everything I have said? About the letter. How unsettled we are here. I thought we would discuss the matter further.'

'The building is bought. The deal is signed. I cannot go back on my plans and commitments and quite frankly it's the last thing I want to do. For Christ's sake, give it a rest.'

'I know you have invested heavily in this new building,' she said. 'But we can sell it, you can buy one in London.'

'Violet, stop, I can't listen to this talk from you anymore. We are not moving.'

Violet had a terrible sense of foreboding as he caught both her hands across the small table and lowered his voice. His grip was so tight it caught her off guard. He was staring intently into her eyes.

'Violet, you are my world, you and Sylvia. I know it's hard here, but it will get better, I know it will, I will make it my business to make things better. I hate all this distance. I know you are unhappy, but this is getting out of hand. We have each other and Sylvia, that is all that matters.'

Violet took her hands away. 'How are you going to make things better? This place – this place will never change. I am constantly looking over my shoulder wondering who wrote that poison. Sylvia has not left the house. How is all that going to change? Tell me that!'

Henry spoke very quietly as if to a child. 'I think you

need to stop writing, just for a while, and perhaps let the people of the town know that you are taking a break from your career. It's not unusual. Just until everything settles down. I know you love writing, but until Sylvia has settled?'

Violet could feel a panic inside her belly that almost made her throw up.

'How can you even suggest it? I had put that kind of suggestion down to the likes of Miss Doheny. I didn't expect you to join the army. This is what that evil letter was intended to do. To stop my writing.'

'I am just suggesting that you take a break from writing. This new play can wait for a little while. Just a break. That's all. Then, when things settle, we can see.'

Violet shook her head. 'I can't believe you're saying this. You are blaming me for what is happening to Sylvia.'

'Well, it is the writing that is upsetting everyone. They are just not ready for someone like you. I love you and want what's best for you and everyone. I am just asking you to take a break from it. Just until we all settle here. You can redecorate the house if you like. Put your own stamp on it.'

Violet could feel her body stiffen. She tried to control her voice. 'I don't want to decorate the house.'

'Well, maybe there is something else you could do. Maybe get involved in the community or something?'

Her stomach had turned into a gut-wrenching ache. It was getting very difficult to keep her voice low – she wanted to scream.

'So, you want me to stop writing. Am I making a mistake on this? I need to be clear on what you want.' Her voice was rising now.

'Look, all I am saying is that perhaps if you took a break

from your writing, the theatre, all those theatrical people, it might be easier to settle in.'

'I cannot believe you are saying this.'

'Violet, we need to be sensible – it can take time to fit in somewhere.'

'*But I don't want to fit in! I want to leave!*' she hissed. 'I want to go back to London. Henry, I *am* going back.'

Henry reached for his drink, throwing back the stiff whiskey.

'My God, woman, I am trying to provide for my family, and I think I am doing a bloody good job of it. You are not giving Draheen or me a chance.'

'Well, maybe it's because most of the people living here think I am some sort of harlot.'

'That's some old biddy. I am trying to sort this out. Just give it a chance.'

'No, Henry, that is not what you are asking me, and you know it. You are asking me to stop writing, stop my plays. Leave the theatrical world, the world that I adore. You knew who I was before you married me.' She knew her voice was too loud, but it was impossible to whisper. She could feel people looking at her.

Henry had reached for a cigarette, lit it and breathed it in deeply. His face looked pale and strained.

'You knew who I was too, and you knew I always planned to return to Ireland. It is my home and I am not being run out of it by anyone.'

His voice was colder than she had ever noticed it before.

Violet flinched. 'Are you including me in that?'

'I'm telling you, Violet – we are not moving. '

'What are you saying? That I have no say in this? I must do as you tell me to?' Violet stood up.

Everyone in the room was staring at them.

'*Violet, sit down!*' Henry hissed.

But Violet was picking up her gloves and bag.

'No, Henry, I will not sit down.'

'*Violet, I order you to sit!*'

'I do not answer to orders.'

'I need to make you understand, Violet.'

'Maybe it's you who needs to understand, Henry. I am going back to London and Sylvia is coming with me. I have left Ireland before, and I will leave Ireland again. With or without your blessing.' Violet tried to keep her voice even, although inside she was trembling.

She turned to walk away.

Henry stood up and tried to catch her arm, but he missed her.

He called after her. '*Don't threaten me, Violet! I warn you!*'

Violet's heart was beating so hard she thought it would explode. Her legs were turning to jelly. She walked out of the room, leaving Henry standing alone, every eye in the room on him.

CHAPTER 10

It was as if her legs were carrying her of their own volition – Violet seemed to have no connection to them. She was numb, yet she was moving quickly. Away from the hotel up towards Church Road. The air smelled of woodsmoke, wood from the dead trees of Blythe Wood. She caught her breath with gasps from the biting cold. The night was still as if the frost hung in it. She wished she had worn flatter shoes. A strong urge to see the river that flowed through the town and was home to a family of swans overcame her. She began to walk towards it.

She needed the solace of the water to calm her mind. The river in Draheen was still pure and clear and in the late evening ducks would nestle in the reeds. She reached the river. The moon had risen and there was a glimmer of brightness that glinted over the water, casting shadows of light and dark.

Normally the water looked clear but this evening she imagined it looked muddy with secrets thrown in and hidden – a river full of conspiracies, prayers and memories of things not mentioned, things long forgotten or buried in the minds of some poor townspeople.

She almost tripped as she walked along, listening to the gurgle of the water against the reeds and the stones, her feet crunching on broken twigs and rotten leaves. When she had left the house earlier, she had never thought she would be walking alone this cold frosty night.

Well, they had certainly given the people of the town something to talk about. A mixture of anger and sadness washed over her. She looked around to see if Henry had followed her. But the road was silent except for the odd dog barking. A man on a bicycle bid her a good evening.

There was a pub in the distance, with an amber glow from the small window. How she wished she could go in and order a large drink and sit quietly to gather her thoughts. But she would certainly be the talk of the town if she did. It was not the thing for a woman to go alone into a pub in a town in Ireland. Suddenly the cold became almost unbearable, her coat no protection from the chill. She turned away from the river and walked back up the street, took the corner and went up Magpie Lane which would lead her to the road that Eveline House was on.

When she reached the house Betsy was at the door, leaving some milk out for Milky the big fat black cat who had decided Eveline had become her home. Milky liked to sit in the back garden during the day but at night roamed the streets of Draheen. Betsy looked up and seemed to be about to say something but obviously knew from Violet's face all was not well. She rushed to Violet and put her arm around her.

'Mrs Ward, you are shaking like a leaf and frozen with the cold. Where is Mr Ward? What's happened? Is Mr Ward alright?

'Yes, Betsy – let's get inside. Mr Ward is fine. I just need to get some warm clothes on.'

Once inside she rushed upstairs, took off her clothes and got into a comfortable nightdress, slippers and a dressing gown. She washed away the earlier make-up and the tears. She could feel the heat of the dressing gown seep into her. There was a knock on the door.

'It's only me, Mrs Ward. I brought you some tea.'

'Thank you, Betsy, you are kind.'

Betsy brought a tray in and poured some tea into a china cup, adding milk and sugar.

'Can I help with whatever is ailing you, Mrs Ward?'

'If only you could, Betsy, but I'm afraid you can't.' She sipped the tea and could feel the hot liquid almost in her veins. 'Is Sylvia settled?'

'Yes, not a bother on her. She was drawing for a long time, and when she grew tired I put her to bed. She just had a few bites of dinner, but at least it was something. She is fast asleep.'

'Thank you, Betsy.'

'Did you have something to eat? You didn't have time, did you? I can rustle something up for you.'

'No, Betsy – but you get home for yourself. I can make some eggs later, but now I couldn't eat anything.'

'Very well, but there is some soup on the hob in case you're hungry. I can stay, Mrs Ward, if I can help at all.'

'No, Betsy. All is fine. I will talk to you tomorrow. But it is late for you to go home alone. Henry would have driven you home.' If he was sober enough, she thought.

'The evening air will do me good. I will be home in a few minutes.'

After Betsy left, Violet walked over to her daughter's bedroom. Sylvia was indeed fast asleep. A feeling of pure love and determination came over Violet. She knew that there were going to be turbulent times ahead, but she was determined to leave for London with Sylvia beside her.

She loved Henry but tonight had driven a wedge through that. He knew how much her writing meant to her. He knew how difficult it was for her here. He also knew of her past and how she felt she could not live within such a society. It was as if her life was repeating. She had to leave her own family because they wanted her to conform and she knew, as much as she loved Henry and it broke her heart to leave, that it seemed to be happening again. What hurt her the most was the way he now looked at her, as if he was wishing she was different from what she was. Her father had looked at her like that up until the day she ran away. But it was harder when her mother looked at her wishing she was different. Now Henry. Now he had that same look. She knew that he would not change now. He had seemed more open in London. But being back in his beloved Ireland had made him less understanding of who she was.

She thought back to a different time when they would walk up to the parks in London and have a picnic. She would read some of her writing to him and he would tell her of his plans of being a goldsmith who was known from London to New York. They were on their way to their dreams. Her first play was performed to critical acclaim in London and there was talk of Broadway, and he now had commissions from New York as well as London. But somehow their dreams had damaged their love. She had thought nothing could. Her mind drifted to a long hot summer's day in London.

'You are not like anyone, Violet, that I have ever met. You make me feel so alive, like I have only begun to live. I was living some half-life up to now. My heart is filled with need for you and fear too, fear of ever losing you.'

She had seen the fear in his eyes, and she had kissed him. They had vowed to never let anyone or anything pull them apart. But it seemed that something already had. Suddenly living with Henry in Draheen felt like someone had arrived to put her in a straitjacket. She had to break free.

CHAPTER 11

Henry took some money out of his wallet, threw it on the table, gathered up his coat and hat and walked out. John Hunt came over to him as he was leaving. He was an elderly man who Henry had met out at a card game. John was a retired solicitor and very distinguished in appearance.

'Buy you a drink?'

'No, I think I need some air after that but thanks.'

'It will all come right. The bright lights of London are far from Draheen but it will all settle in a while.'

'Thanks. Hope you are right. Goodnight.'

He went outside, lit a cigarette and took a long drag. Looking down the street, he debated what to do. Whelan's bar was close to the hotel. There was no sign of Violet. He knew she would be home by now. Eveline was only a short walk out of the town. It was best to give her time to cool off. He would just pop in for a drink before he headed home.

He opened the door of the bar. It was one long counter. Half a bar and half a shop. It was hard to say what the shop sold most of. You could get bacon, eggs, fresh vegetables, butter and tea. In the pub, there was whiskey, porter, ale from the brewery in Kilkenny and sherry and port wine for the ladies, although it was rare that any women frequented Whelan's bar.

They bought their supplies in the shop but rarely ventured beyond that. Niall Whelan was wrapping a lump of bacon up in brown paper and tying it with a piece of twine at the shop end of the counter.

'A large one, please, Niall!' Henry called down to him.

Niall came up, poured a large glass of Irish whiskey and handed it to Henry.

'Cold night out?'

Henry nodded as he threw the whiskey down his neck as if his throat was on fire and the whiskey was water and he needed to cool it. Then he ordered another. He could feel the hit of alcohol. Together with the low light and the haze of Woodbine, his mind calmed.

When Violet had walked out of the hotel, he had felt a sense of dread descend on him. This was a battle he had not anticipated. So much for taking control of his household as Miss Doheny had advised him. It had met with disaster.

He should have known better than to order Violet to do anything.

The barman was handing a pint of porter to an old man in a corner, sitting beside a wood fire. The man looked as if he had a wisdom that was only bestowed to few and somehow he had found the key to contentment. A fine pint of porter beside a wood fire with no one to bother him. There was no one wanting to drag him back to London or anywhere else.

It was a different scene to the pubs in London. Henry had frequented plenty of them. Pubs where the Irish sang of home, buying drinks for the man who might give them a week's work the following week. The Irish were not afraid of hard work, their vested bodies covered in sweat a common sight on the streets of Kilburn and Camden Town.

His mind was suddenly cast back to a different pub in Camden Town, a small pub with dark velvet chairs and the ceiling so low you had to bend your head. Scholars and poets tended to collect there and Violet loved it. It was there that he had first told Violet that he loved her. It possibly wasn't the most romantic of settings. But to him it could not have been more perfect.

He was drinking a pint of bitter and Violet had a half. There was a man singing a beautiful English love song, the melody hauntingly poignant.

'Are you alright, Henry? There is a faraway look on you there,' Violet said.

'I was thinking of home. It's never too far from my thoughts.'

'Could London ever be your home, your real home, I mean?' she asked tentatively.

'Ireland will always be my home, Violet. I thank London for making a man of me. I was a boy as green as the grass when I arrived here. I thought I knew what hardship was too, but no one really knows what it's like until you get here. I owe it to London for showing me that there is another life, but I don't thank it for stealing me from the place I dream about.'

'So what is it about Ireland that you dream about?'

'I dream of my mother, God rest her, and sometimes just of the rivers and the mist on the mountains.' He caught hold of Violet's hands and looked intensely into her eyes. 'I never thought I would fall in love with the most beautiful Irish girl in the world, right here in Camden Town. A girl who makes my heart leap every time I see her and when she speaks it's like the lilt of an Irish goddess.'

'It's the bitter, it's gone to your head – you should stick to the porter. Where is this girl who sounds like Queen Maeve? She sounds enchanting surely.' Violet grinned.

'Ah, you're teasing me now!' Henry smiled, letting go of her hands.

'Ah, yes, 'tis the bitter gone to your poor heart, making you all sentimental,' Violet said with a laugh.

Henry had tried to embrace London as much as he could and Fortune had smiled on him. It had miraculously opened the way for him to learn the craft of a goldsmith. No such opportunity would ever have come his way in Ireland. And it came through Mrs Thompkins, their landlady. She was a large woman with a heart of gold who had quietly hitched up with Henry's father. To outsiders his father was still only a lodger, but Henry knew when he saw them together that it was much more than that. He was happy for his father, but he could not help thinking of his mother. His memory of her had haunted him when they first left. It was as if they were abandoning her, even if she was buried deep in the clay of Wexford.

Maura O'Riordan met his father at a dance in Ferns and stole his heart. She was the prettiest girl in Wexford, but the years of hardship had thrown lines on her face like a ploughed field. Henry could still see her in his mind's eye – eyes like cornflowers, dark hair with ribbons of grey running through. He could see her praying when she knew she was dying, praying that the world would be kind to her family and begging Mary Immaculate to watch over her sons and protect them from harm.

They first arrived in Camden Town in 1931. The Irish

were not hard to miss. Although he was barely sixteen his father Jim had secured work for him and his brother alongside himself on a building site. That train station in Wexford that they had started their journey from still had the power to haunt him. Each man with a cardboard box and no sense of anywhere except Vinegar Hill and the dances in Ferns and Enniscorthy, with not a clue of what the roads outside Leinster looked like. They each got a tag pinned on to them, quite like you would a parcel. The tag carried the name of the builder that they would work for.

His mother had died the year before – the tuberculosis had finally killed her, that and the hardship of a small farm on the edge of the world. They had tried to conquer the land, as their forefathers had, but eventually there was nothing left – the sea had begun to eat away at it, the last crop had failed and the future in Ireland looked as bleak as Mount Leinster on a November evening.

London had looked like another planet. They got digs with Mrs Thompkins, a widow, and Jim had bonded with her from the very start. Henry knew that she sensed his father's heart was broken, from losing his wife and leaving his humble home and everything he knew. It was normally only the sons who went looking for work, but Jim would have died if they left him alone on that farm. He was strong and fit for his age and they hoped that the work would not be too difficult for him.

Mrs Thompkins had not taken her eyes off Jim that first evening. She had five grown-up children who were all married with their own lives. Her house was warm and cosy, and the sons watched, grinning to each other, as she piled their father's plate high with thick rashers and eggs and fresh bread.

But none of that security and comfort did anything to change Henry's mind about Ireland. He had enjoyed himself after a fashion, gone to dance hall after dance hall, drinking till the early hours and somehow carrying buckets of cement up twenty floors the next morning without falling and breaking his neck. But at night in his dreams he could smell the air in Boolavogue, though it was the smog of Camden Town that he awoke to.

His father, although a farmer by trade, had always had a flair for making things. He had often spent hours making something out of a small piece of wood with his penknife. It was not too long until he was drafted in to do some carpentry on the building site. Although not trained at it, he seemed to be able to turn his hand to it easily. Mrs Thompkins could see how talented Jim was and it was she who recommended him to Mr Bayley, a jeweller she cleaned for, when he was looking for a carpenter to do some after-hours work in his shop. And that had led to Henry being hired by Mr Bayley and eventually being trained by him as a goldsmith. His brother Anthony had stayed on the buildings. He married a Londoner, Tracy, and within the first year of marriage had twins, a boy and girl. Seamus and Siobhán, with big brown eyes like their father.

Every Irishman who left his Irish shore dreamed of making it in London and Henry had. He had done it. He had found the love of his life and married her, and they had their beautiful Sylvia. Then he had arrived back in Ireland with a list of connections and enough money to buy the house he had dreamt he would. His world was perfect.

But now Violet wanted to literally tear it all apart. Sometimes he dreamt he was a young man leaving his home and arriving at that train station in Enniscorthy bound for the cold streets of London. He would awaken in a sweat in his bed in Eveline. It would take some time for his heart to calm down. Then he would thank God he was back in Ireland and thank God for his good fortune.

There was no way anyone, not even Violet, was taking him back. His chat about her curtailing her writing had made her furious. He knew he had made a big mistake saying that and he cursed himself for it. He knew now it was careless of him not to realise how upset the mere suggestion of it would make her. Upset was one thing but threatening to leave with Sylvia, well, that was another matter entirely.

The door opened and Peter Binchy, the local tailor, arrived in. Peter's back was curved at birth and it had handicapped his life with chronic pain. Violet had asked him to make Henry a suit of the best Donegal tweed. When Henry had tried on the finished garment, he knew it was the finest suit that he had ever worn. It was beautifully crafted and Peter Binchy in a different world could have stood tall with any designer of his time.

'A drink for my good friend here,' Henry said. 'Throw another large whiskey in mine and, feck it, a pint of porter to wash it down.'

'Thanks, Henry,' Peter said.

Dan Holland arrived in and, with a pint of porter before him, took out a tin whistle and began to play an Irish ballad. Soon Henry was singing 'Boolavogue' and telling stories of the battle of Oulart Hill and how the boys of Wexford had fought with every ounce of their strength to free Ireland. The rounds were flying, the hours passed and all too soon Niall Whelan was telling them all to go home.

Henry staggered out alongside Peter at ten past one.

'What am I going to do with this wife of mine? She

wants to take us off to live in London. I never want to go back to London, this is my ho ... me. I lo ... ve Ireland. I love every ... one in Ireland. I love you. I love everyone.' He gave a large hiccup as Peter helped him up the street.

'Women and their fancy ideas! She's a good woman, is your lovely lady, but all that fancy writing will have to stop. If she is to be a married respectable woman, she will have to act like one. I have an idea. I can have my missus have a word with your missus. Put her on the straight and narrow, know what I'm saying?'

Henry in his drunken stupor thought this was a mind-blowing idea.

'Brilliant! You get your wife to come visit my wife and explain that she can't be acting like that. Bloody brilliant! Peter, you're a genius!'

'It will be all sorted out in a jiffy and, before you know it, she will be waiting at the door with your slippers and a large whiskey.'

Henry stumbled over a stone and fell to the ground, cutting his face. He stood up with the help of Peter, neither of them noticing the cut. They were outside Peter's house when the door opened, and a very cross Mrs Binchy was standing there with a look of pure vexation on her face. She was a small woman with her hair tied up in a bun and a blue wraparound bib over a brown skirt, green cardigan and cream blouse.

'Just look at the state of you! You are a right pair of eejits! I thought that you, Mr Ward, had more sense. You'd better come in and I will try to make you look halfway respectable before you have the town talking about you. Get in, the pair of you!'

Henry stumbled in, almost knocking over a chair.

'God save all here! You are a good little woman – sure we only had a few friendly little drinks. Your good husband and I got led astray a bit up in Whelan's.'

'Two schoolboys you are, is it? Mr Ward, you don't look like you needed anyone to lead you astray tonight. Oh, two schoolboys with not a whit of sense once the porter enters your veins and I have the misfortune to be married to one of you.'

She filled a bowl with hot water from the kettle on the fire and put some salt in it. She steeped a cloth in the liquid and let it cool for a few minutes before taking it out and wringing some of the water from it. She then bathed Henry's face.

He flinched. '*Jesus!*'

'Sit still, for goodness' sake!'

She took some more water from the kettle and made some strong tea.

Then she took a loaf of soda bread from the press and cut it into thick slices. She buttered them and put a slice of boiled ham on each.

Henry was trying to sit on the chair at the table, but the chair seemed to be moving.

'Eat that up and it might sober you up before you go home.'

'You are an angel and a gift to a man in distress, little woman. Oh, a good little woman!' Henry said, hiccupping.

'A man in distress, my eye – a man with too much whiskey and porter in him!' Mrs Binchy looked like she could give him a slap she was so vexed.

Henry barely touched the bread and ham. He stood up but was so unsteady he collapsed on the nearby settle bed. Mrs Binchy tried to get him to stand up again. But he didn't respond.

Peter Binchy had fallen asleep in a fireside chair.

'Mr Ward, shake yourself up and get home to your good wife who I hope will give you a piece of her mind when she sees the state of you.'

But Henry did not hear a word. He had passed out.

CHAPTER 12

Betsy knew all was not well in Eveline. Mrs Ward had looked a fright when she had arrived home the night before, alone and frozen from the cold. Betsy felt very protective of Mrs Ward and of Sylvia. She had tossed and turned all night thinking about it. All this upset was not good for Sylvia. She was such a frail little thing. She sensed things so strongly. Betsy never said it to anyone, but it was as if the child was here before, almost angelic in ways. She was the nearest thing to a little angel that she had ever met.

Sometimes she saw her sitting and staring into space and it reminded her of what poor Saint Bernadette must have looked like when she saw Mary appear to her all those years ago in Lourdes. There was something about Sylvia. She could act very strangely and she was barely able for the outside world. Betsy feared for her, for the outside world could be cruel to anyone who was different. Some might say she was a bit of a simpleton, but it wasn't that. She was very clever, could read above her age and her paintings were like nothing Betsy had ever seen before. It was as if they were photographs, the likeness was so good. Sylvia had told Betsy that she was convinced that the family was in danger. Betsy saw the fear in her little eyes. It made her so angry to think that anyone in Draheen could hurt such a gentle little soul. Well, she would try to get to the bottom of it if it was the last thing she did. She knew well that Mrs Ward wanted to flee back to London. She hated to think of them leaving. Her life was so changed since the Wards had arrived in Draheen.

She had been worried about working in such a grand house but Mrs Ward was so kind she had nothing to worry about. Mrs Ward was not of the gentry herself and neither was Mr Ward, but she was certainly a lady and he a gentleman.

Miss Doheny had been quick to tell her how the Abbey Theatre in Dublin would not hear of putting on that play, *Unholy Love*. How Miss Doheny had got wind of this she had no idea.

'It was unchristian, the language in it,' were Miss Doheny's words as she counted out eggs for Betsy shortly after she had begun working for the Wards.

'Let God be the judge of that, Miss Doheny. I assume you must have read the script or sailed over to London to see the play, to be able to comment so expertly on it,' Betsy had replied, daring to cross Miss Doheny who lifted her eyebrow into a high arch and fixed a thin scowl on her thin purple lips.

'Indeed, I certainly have not, or have I any inclination to do so. I have it on very good authority, so be careful working up there and mind your job as I have already warned you – it might be hard to get work anywhere else if they were ever to leave.'

Betsy had almost thrown the money at Miss Doheny, who looked immensely pleased with herself at upsetting Betsy.

There was no point in trying to sleep, it had left her. She

got up and went into the small kitchen of her cottage. It was still warm, and she stoked up the fire and put on a kettle to boil some water for tea. From the small deep-set window, she watched the dawn arrive in all its colours, slicing the sky with golden liquid and flashes of pinks, blues and violets. She had so many memories in this kitchen. It was all she ever knew, all of life that had meant anything to her had happened in this kitchen. The leaving of Michael her brother, the past Christmases and the happy times of her younger years, the rosaries and all the prayers that were said on bended knee. At Easter after the weeks of deprivation and prayer, they would eventually come home on the Good Friday after kissing the Cross and waiting for the darkness to pass. Then at last Easter Sunday would come. In jubilation they wore their best to Easter Mass and came home to hot tea and porter cake, made on the fire.

There were memories of her brother on that last night when the neighbours came to sing a tune and have a bottle of porter. Then the sickness and all the looking after her parents. Eventually when they got so sick, they slept on the settle bed. The last time people were in the house was the wake of her mother. Lying still and frail in her casket. She had prayed for a happy death and Betsy was glad she had not suffered too much, her weak body eventually giving in as Betsy held her hand and knew then she was alone.

She got up and took a box from a drawer. In it was everything that was precious to her. Her brother's letters from Australia. Her mother's brooch and her father's pipe. She picked up the pipe, the faint smell of tobacco filling the air. If she closed her eyes, she could see her father as he sat and talked of myths and legends handed down from generation to generation. All the letters that Michael had sent. They would save them and when the chores were done and they were sitting at the fire, her father would take out his spectacles and read the letter aloud as they savoured every word. She remembered all the talk of Michael coming home. The money that was sent over from Australia and very gratefully received. The letters written and sent back with the news of what was going on in Draheen. The money that Michael sent had allowed them to buy good coats, pay the Easter dues without worry. Her father was a labourer for a landowner. Her mother worked in one of the big houses, but the house was closed now, and the family had moved to Dublin. Michael's money had bought a pony and cart and had allowed some little luxuries for Christmas. At one stage there was even a mention of Betsy going out to Australia. Michael had said there was great opportunities for her. But Mother would not hear of it. Betsy was all that they had with Michael gone. Then Michael got married and had two sons. There was less talk about him coming home. He still asked for Betsy to go over, but it was never really discussed, especially when her mother got sick and Betsy looked after her morning, noon and night, Oh, how she would have loved to see those young boys, but alas it had not happened!

When her father died, Michael was good as his word and had sent money home for her, to give him a good send-off. He still talked about coming home, but he was always so busy with the construction business that he had set up. Of course, his life was there now with his wife Jane and the boys. Betsy felt no animosity towards him. She was glad he had a good life, she just wished it was not so far away. She was eight when he left. His picture took pride of place on the mantelpiece. There was one other of her First Holy

Communion. Michael had a big smile on his face with long tall thin legs and a shock of fair curly hair. He was ten years older than her and had always been her protector.

But when her mother died, standing alone at that graveside had almost killed her. Michael had written and told her that he would book a place for her on a ship to Australia. But Betsy was reluctant – she had never been further than Grafton Street in Dublin and that was only three times in her life. She had marvelled at the style and the fancy food. Towards evening as she got the bus the night sky was illuminated with the streetlamps but she was glad to get back to Draheen. Truth was she was nervous of travelling so far alone.

Dublin had seemed like a different world. If she had any desire to go to Australia, it had left her. She now only had a fear of the unknown. What if Jane, Michael's wife, did not take to her? She would hate to be a burden. So, she wrote back to say that she would look for work and if she got some she would stay.

One minute she was a young sixteen-year-old and it seemed the next minute she was thirty-seven. Her years had filled a pattern. The dark winter nights and the howl of the unknown outside her bed, glad of the safety of her home. Then the spring would come, and the briars would start to bloom, the hens would lay much better and after Easter the summer arrived. Autumn was there again, and the pattern continued. She had spent all her years in a continual sense of ritual, prayer, fasting, Stations of the Cross, picking berries, making bread, peeling potatoes, the Missions with maybe a priest home from Africa with tales of black babies and a land unimaginable. The seasons were broken by the different religious ceremonies.

Her mother had taught her how to pray. They prayed together to all the saints and angels in heaven. She had thought of joining a convent, thought she had a calling for it, but her mother had never encouraged it. They needed her at home more than any convent needed her.

Betsy picked a rosary beads from the box and said a decade of the rosary, offering it up for peace for the Wards. Her kitchen was eerily silent except for the prayers. A kitchen haunted with memories and ghosts. She was a spinster now living alone. She thanked God for the Ward family coming into her life.

Yet, she had a terrible fear in her for them. If only she could figure out who sent that dreadful letter. Those women who cleaned the church knew who had, Betsy was sure of it. Hiding behind a poison-pen letter. What an unchristian act!

Morning had finally arrived. She swept up the kitchen and left for morning Mass. She wanted to say some prayers to the Holy Mother for poor little Sylvia.

She loved this time of the morning when there was a white frost and a mist coming up from the river. Draheen was mostly still asleep. She walked briskly to keep warm.

At first she thought it was someone else, but as she walked up the Master's Hill she recognised Mr Ward coming up the road, looking much the worse for wear. He spotted Betsy and called out to her. She rushed over as he looked like he could fall, and he had a cut on the side of his face. But, as she drew closer, the smell of stale whiskey and Woodbines hit her nostrils.

'Mr Ward, what in God's name are you doing out here in this state?'

'I'm afraid I have only myself to blame, too much porter

and whiskey. I had to sleep it off on the settle bed in Binchys'. My head is dizzy, Betsy. I am afraid I am still drunk – we had an awful feed of drink. Peter Binchy was nearly as bad. He's still sleeping it off. I just slipped out without waking him or his wife.'

'What, you never went home? Mrs Ward will be out of her mind.'

'Oh, she went off in a right strop last night. I tried to talk her out of London.'

'I gathered that – she was upset when she came in.'

Henry stopped and put his hand on a nearby wall to steady himself. His face was white and he looked like he would throw up.

'I can't go back to London, Betsy, I can't. She wants to drag me back there. I am telling you I can't do it. I am done with London. You don't know what it was like, Betsy.'

'Hush now and keep your voice down a bit. If anyone sees us, it will be the talk of the town.'

But Henry was oblivious to anyone. He looked haunted by what he was thinking. He looked intently at Betsy who was desperately trying to get him to move.

'I still dream of those men waiting for the boat. It was a human tragedy. I was barely sixteen. I had not seen further than the nearest town. Unless you were there, Betsy, you could not understand. Young men and old men. Knowing nothing but a will to work. Leaving everything they ever knew. It may only have been across the water, but it may as well have been another planet. The stench of sick on the boat – some of them had never been on a boat. Leaving the mothers, wives and loved ones staring after them. There were women on it too. Some who had got into trouble and some who had no choice but to leave. Leave everything they knew for the cold unforgiving streets of London, where we toiled and sweated enough to keep us alive and send a bit home. Oh, we drank to stop feeling so lonely, but we had our dignity even when we had the porter. I can't go back. I dreamt of making it and I have. I made it, Betsy, can't you see? I cannot go back. Ireland is my home.'

Betsy was shocked at his outburst. There were tears rolling down his face. What on earth would anyone say if they saw them on the street and he with his arm around her in case he fell. She had to get him home. He must have had some amount of drink. He could barely walk. She walked slowly alongside him, his arm over her shoulder, trying to balance himself. They were walking so slowly she reckoned they would never get to Eveline.

'Mr Ward, you have to pull yourself together and try to get home, or I will get cross with you.'

Henry smiled at this last comment. 'I can't imagine you getting cross, Betsy. You are far too good-natured.'

They were nearly at Eveline when the keen eye of Mrs Roche spotted them – she was coming up the road on her High Nelly and she almost cycled into a wall watching the goings-on.

Well, that was that – that would feed the gossipers for the next few days, Betsy thought.

And she had missed Mass. She would call in later and light some candles. She said a prayer to Saint Joseph for strength and she eventually got Mr Ward into the house and put him on the sofa in the drawing room. She put a blanket over him as he fell into a deep sleep. She could almost hear what Mrs Roche was saying to her cronies and she could feel her face blush with anger. More gossip to fuel those women.

In the kitchen she stoked up the range. After a cup of tea and a slice of soda bread and butter she felt a bit better. She had some scraps for Milky the cat and a bowl of milk. The cat loved the garden and was constantly found sitting guarding it – she knew she would find her out there.

Sylvia was normally up and about early. She loved to sit in the kitchen and help Betsy making bread. But there was no sign of her this morning. Milky the cat was delighted to see Betsy and rubbed herself against her legs.

Betsy was about to leave when she spotted it. A letter torn into pieces and lying beside it was Petite Suzanne, face down with her head askew. She walked over in dread and picked up the doll whose head was cracked with pieces broken from her face. Her arm was also hanging loose. In dread she picked up the pieces of the letter. She managed to put it together. It was short and to the point, scrawled in large writing.

The Ward Witches of Eveline

Witches die and the daughter of a witch is burned alive. Leave now.

Betsy gasped and dropped the doll. She ran all the way to Sylvia's room. It was bolted. Sylvia never locked her room.

As she pounded on it, Violet came rushing out of her room in her nightdress.

'Whatever is the matter, Betsy?'

Betsy showed her the bits of the letter.

'It was in the garden, I just found it with Suzanne. The doll is broken in bits. I haven't seen Sylvia. The door is locked from the inside.'

She rapped on the door. '*Sylvia! Sylvia, pet, open the door!*'

94

Violet read the vicious words, gasped and then began pounding on the door.

'*Sylvia, open up! Sylvia, open the door at once!*'

But there was no sound. They kept pounding with Violet screaming at Sylvia to open the door.

Henry came up the stairs with his hand on his head.

'What on earth is going on? Are you planning on breaking up the house?'

'It's Sylvia – we think there is something wrong!' Betsy cried. 'She has locked herself in. I found another letter and her smashed-up doll! *Mr Ward, we need to get in there – do something!*'

'Move away from the door, Violet! Betsy, step away now! *Sylvia, if you are at the door move away now!*'

He charged the door like a madman. On his third attempt the latch broke and the door flew open.

Betsy saw nothing but the blood first – heard nothing but the screams of Violet. Small hand-marks of blood were on every wall. Written on the mirror in blood was the word *SATAN*. A vison of being on a relative's farm and the killing of a goat came back to her. She never quite forgot the screams of that goat.

Then she saw Sylvia. She was lying on the bed in a blood-stained pale-blue nightdress, her eyes open with a look that made Betsy's blood run cold. The child's head was lying askew. Her children's prayer book was torn and scattered around the bed. Her white rosary beads broken and scattered around the floor. Blood was oozing from her arms, her torso and her legs from what looked like stab wounds. Her face was covered in bright red marks and her forehead was swollen as if she had fallen and hit it. But it was a large gash at her wrist pulsing with blood that almost took the breath from Betsy. Then she spotted a nail scissors on the floor beside the bed. She recognised it from Mrs Ward's vanity unit. The scissors was covered in blood.

Violet was still screaming.

Somehow Betsy sprang into action.

She checked the child's pulse at the side of her neck. She said a silent prayer of thanks – there was a pulse.

She grabbed Henry who was on his knees as if in pain, animal sounds coming from him.

'*Go get the doctor quick!*' she shouted.

Henry was white. As white as the sheet of the bed. He didn't respond.

Betsy shook him.

'*Go!*' she screamed.

Henry stared at her, his eyes full of horror.

'*There's little time!*' Betsy screamed. '*She's alive but she's dying!*'

He rose to his feet and ran from the room.

Violet was cupping Sylvia's face, tears flowing down her cheeks, screaming at her to come back to her.

Betsy prayed that the doctor was still at his house and had not left for house calls. The house was only down the street. She ran and grabbed a sheet from the cupboard in the corridor. Back in the bedroom, she tore at it with all her strength. She tied one strip tightly around the bleeding wrist, then began to wrap strips around the other wounds. She began to talk to Sylvia. The child's eyes were now closed, but her mouth was moving. Betsy leaned in to hear what she was saying. She could hardly believe the words.

'*I am the daughter of the devil, I am the daughter of the devil, I am the daughter of the devil, I do not believe in deum immortalem . . .*'

96

Then she seemed to faint.

Betsy had prayed at enough Masses to know that *deum immortalem* meant 'immortal god' in Latin.

Violet screamed and fell to her knees in fright while Betsy forced herself to check the child's pulse again.

'She's alive, Mrs Ward, she's still alive.'

Within about seven minutes Victor Gettings arrived with his medical bag. He did a double take when he saw the room as if wary of entering it but then he saw Sylvia and he set to work. He checked her pulse then swiftly opened his bag. He took out a small vial and punched it with a needle and then injected the liquid into Sylvia's arm. She never flinched. She had slipped into an unconscious state.

'We need to get her to the hospital immediately. Quickly, Henry, you carry her – we need to go now,' the doctor instructed.

Betsy and Henry wrapped her in a blanket then Henry picked her up in his arms.

'Is she going to die?' Violet sobbed as she followed them and the doctor down the stairs.

'Her pulse is weak. We need to get blood into her as quickly as possible.'

They put her in the doctor's car, lying in the back seat. Violet jumped in at the other side and Henry placed his daughter's head on Violet's lap. The doctor drove away shouting at Henry to follow him.

Betsy locked the front door. Henry jumped into his own car with Betsy beside him.

The hospital was only a few miles outside of Draheen. It seemed forever but eventually they got there. It was run by an order of nuns who lived in a convent on the grounds of the hospital. A nun in a white habit met them. Sylvia was put on a stretcher by two porters and Doctor Gettings was at the front of the stretcher. The grave look on his face frightened Betsy even more than before. Mrs Ward was crying and Mr Ward looked as white as the starched veil of the nun. An older nun met them and directed Mr Ward, Mrs Ward and Betsy to take a seat in the corridor. Mrs Ward was intent on following Sylvia and Mr Ward tried to tell her to wait. The nun stopped her and told her that she could not go into the room where they were taking the child. Mr Ward tried to hold his wife in his arms while she shouted and tried to pull herself away.

'Hush, Violet, we have to let them do their job,' he whispered.

'Let them do what they can now,' the nun instructed gently.

Violet sat down with Betsy beside her holding her hand. Henry pulled out a packet of cigarettes and dropped the matches his hands were shaking so much.

Betsy put her arms around Violet who was crying uncontrollably. Then Betsy began to pray, the corridor echoing her voice. She prayed to Mary the Holy Mother. She prayed to Saint Martin and she prayed to her mother. The small corridor was silent except for the sobs of Violet and the prayers of Betsy.

CHAPTER 13

Betsy thought the hours would never end. All she could do was pray.

'Please, Mary, in your holy mercy let the child live. I beseech you, Most Holy Mother,' she prayed silently.

They were told little of how the child was.

The strong smell of Jeyes Fluid and carbolic soap permeated the air. Nurses chatted to each other as they went about their business, dressed in starched aprons and veils. Nuns young and old walked up and down doing their various chores in a silent reverie, in white habits with large wooden rosary beads. The Matron, who was a small stern woman, seemed to be walking as if on patrol, making sure the hospital was spick and span. Hours passed and other than a nun giving them tea and telling them that the child was still alive they waited in what felt like a purgatory.

Eventually the first nun they had met came out of a room and told them to go home. The child was still alive, and they would do all they could. She had lost a huge amount of blood and was deeply traumatised.

'I must see my daughter!' Mrs Ward grabbed the arm of the nun.

The nun gently took her hand away and whispered softly. 'The child is alive, and the priest has been called. Go home and thank God for his divine mercy.'

'Why have you called the priest?' Henry said, alarmed.

The nun slowly turned her head to look at Henry and then bowed her head as if in repose.

'Just to pray for her recovery,' she said with no sign of emotion.

Betsy asked no questions, but a burning need to know what had happened to the child almost suffocated her. But, as the nun said, she was alive and for now that would have to suffice. Betsy knew she should go but the nuns would have to throw Mr and Mrs Ward out. Mrs Ward looked like she had been beaten – her eyes had taken on a haunted look and when she spoke it was like something in her throat stifled any words. Henry kept going in and out, barely sitting, smoking heavily and shaking his head in disbelief. Betsy put on her coat and said goodbye to them. She would go back and make some soup for them for their return.

Violet barely noticed that she left – she was lost in some sort of tormented world.

Betsy walked back to the town. It was still light. One of those rare beautiful January evenings with a hint of frost making the air pure like silk. She was glad of the fresh air. It allowed her some time to think. When she turned onto the main street, she met Miss Doheny who was directing an awkward young girl on how to sweep the pavement properly. The poor girl looked almost in tears as Miss Doheny instructed her to put more enthusiasm into her work.

'You are not here to slouch, Peggy McCormick. I want that pavement as clean as a whistle.'

The girl looked at Betsy. Her dark-brown hair was cut in an unflattering style to her jawbone. Betsy knew she was fighting the tears back.

'This is my recruit sent up from Tipperary. Say good morning, Peggy, to Betsy.'

'Good morning,' Peggy said meekly.

'Peggy, when you have finished that go out and make sure all the eggs are clean before you display them tomorrow and then wash out the back yard like I showed you to.'

'I will,' Peggy said.

Miss Doheny shook her head and bent her head towards Betsy.

'She's a bit slow, I think. A cousin of mine asked me to take her on. She has no one – her mother was bad with nerves and had to be put into the madhouse and the father died of drink. He was found dead in a ditch. Poor girl was discovered half-starved in a henhouse. To be honest, I don't know if it will work out here for her. She has no great manner about her. It will be a long time before I can even let her near the customers.'

Betsy felt so sorry for the girl. Of all places to be sent to! Miss Doheny was not going to be the easiest and she knew what it was like to have nobody. She cursed herself for not going the long way around and avoiding Miss Doheny. She hoped she had not heard anything about Sylvia but the minute Peggy was out of earshot she saw that Miss Doheny knew. The excitement in the woman's eyes was too hard to mask, as clever as she was.

'Betsy, have you come from the hospital? How is she? Tell me how the young girl is.'

Betsy knew there was no point telling her to mind her own business. At least she could find out how much she

101

knew and how she could have heard it so quickly. There were a few lay people working in the hospital – it must have been one of them.

'Is it true?' Miss Doheny demanded.

'Is what true?'

'No need to act like that, Betsy, it's all over the town – how the child was almost dead and when she was found it was an awful sight. The room was covered in blood and her body was full of cuts and she was almost dead. Yet there was no explanation for it. It was like she had done it to herself or something even worse than that. Lord bless us and save us, what has come to Draheen? Never have we seen the like of this. Is it true? I heard the bedroom was bolted from the inside. What does it mean?'

Betsy was not expecting this. What blather-mouth had given out this information so quickly? What could she tell her?

She was terrified, thinking about what was happening to Sylvia. She could not care about her more if she was her own. It was hard enough to deal with it without the whole parish of Draheen getting wind of it and making it the talk of the town. What good would it do for anyone outside the family to know? Sylvia would become a spectacle, a circus act. She had to stop this getting out any more than it already had.

'Miss Doheny, it is true that the Wards' child is unwell, but who is making up these other inventions is beyond me. I would advise that you don't add fuel to their mischief by spreading such gossip. I am off now to get the house ready for the Wards when they get home and I'll say a prayer that Mr Ward does not hear such evil gossip about his only daughter. Good day to you, Miss Doheny.'

With that Betsy walked off without a backward glance. But Miss Doheny followed her.

'Say what you like, Betsy, but I heard it on very good authority. The day that family arrived in Draheen a darkness followed them and now it seems to have grabbed hold of that poor child. *I* would advise *you* to step as far away as possible from them.'

The anger was bubbling up inside Betsy. How dare they! Those gossipers had somehow got hold of it. This would spread like wildfire and make everything even worse for the Wards. She felt so ashamed of her town for treating them as they had done. She turned to Miss Doheny, her heart pounding in her chest.

'Well, that is where you and I differ, Miss Doheny. Thank God I have some humanity in me, and I can remember the Christian way that my mother brought me up. I have no intention of leaving the Wards' side in their time of need. *I was sick and you visited me.' Matthew 36.* You have obviously forgotten your religion. Good day to you and I'll pray for you today, Miss Doheny, for holding such dark thoughts in your heart.'

'Well, really, Betsy. It is yourself you should be praying for, to be mixed up with that family. Your poor mother would turn in the grave.'

'Leave my mother out of this, Miss Doheny. She would be ashamed of our town,' Betsy retorted.

It had taken her over an hour to reach Eveline House since she left the hospital. The tears of frustration and anger were flowing down her face as she put her key in the door. She wept for the child when she was safe in the house and bent on her knees praying to God and his Holy Mother for them to help the child. There was an eerie feeling in the house that she had never felt before. What had happened in this house? There was no denying that what had happened to Sylvia looked evil. Betsy had a strong faith. It was why so many years ago she had thought of entering a convent. Her mother had of course instilled a strong faith in her as a child but it was more than that. She loved her faith and it meant a great deal to her. In fact, in some ways it was everything to her. But here in this house this morning she had felt something dark at work in that dreadful scene they had witnessed. Sylvia was an innocent child with a vulnerable mind. If it was a dark force at work, it had picked its victim well. A defenceless sensitive child. Betsy grabbed her rosary beads and, with her voice shaking with vigour, she called out the Lord's Prayer in the Gaeilge of her childhood. A determination so fierce came over her. If it was something dark that had somehow latched on to the child, she would do everything in her power to stop it.

At the end of her prayer she stared up the stairs and blessed herself. She wasn't ready to face the child's bedroom. She went into the downstairs bathroom and washed her face with the ice-cold water. Somehow she felt a little stronger then. The evening was closing in. She went into the garden to where she had found the doll and the letter. She carefully picked up the doll and the broken pieces of her face. Had somebody arrived into the front garden, jumped over the wall to the rear garden and approached Sylvia with the letter? Could they have followed her to her room? But her bedroom was bolted from inside, so no one was in there other than Sylvia. It made no sense. But how did she get the letter? Mr Ward had put a lock on the postbox to make sure that only he or Mrs Ward could open it. It was not really possible to put the letter through the door. There was no gap and no letterbox. So, someone gave it to her. But who? She went into the kitchen and brewed a pot of tea to help calm herself.

She washed and diced some vegetables and put on a soup, then tidied up the kitchen.

Then she walked up to the bedroom and with a deep breath walked in. Somehow, she had hoped that it was not as bad as she had initially thought. But the blood seemed to be everywhere. It amazed her that the child was alive at all. She picked up the small scissors. The cuts had to be from the scissors. She checked the window, but it was bolted tight. The bedroom was so high up that Mr Ward had bolted it in case Sylvia sleepwalked as she had from time to time.

Betsy had heard of strange occurrences happening to people. Perhaps it was some sort of terrible disease that had suddenly come over her. But the thought that it was maybe something else frightened her.

She ran down to the kitchen and found a bottle of holy water that had come from the holy well in Blythe Wood. She went back up to the bedroom and threw the water around the room. Then she brought up a picture of the Holy Family and a crucifix that was in a drawer and put them on Sylvia's dresser. There was talk of people being possessed with an evil spirit that could show itself in bruising and cuts. She tried to block the words that Sylvia had whispered. She knelt beside the bed and prayed to God that whatever had happened in this room could be somehow explained.

She took off all the bedclothes and put them in a bag to be boiled and washed. Then she got a large bucket of hot water and some sugar soap and began to clean the bloodstained room. She washed the mirror with the scrawl of *SATAN*. Then she began the slow process of trying to clean the wallpaper. The small hand-marks of blood almost broke her heart. With a mixture of sugar soap and warm water and a slow process of soaking and gently rubbing, she began to make progress and erase the blood from the walls. Where the blood was heavy she scraped at the wallpaper and removed it. It was better she felt to have faded scraped wallpaper than bloodstained walls. She picked up the blood-soaked rugs and brought them outside to burn at a later date, then she went back up and scrubbed the floor. She scrubbed and scrubbed until all traces of the nightmare had been erased.

She was almost finished when she heard the latch on the door. It was Mr Ward. Please God, she prayed, that he would have good news about Sylvia. But what if it was bad news? A terrible fear gripped her. She couldn't bear to hear it if the child had died. Did she have the right to feel this maternal love so strongly? She didn't think she could be more heartbroken if the child was her own. Slowly she went down to the kitchen. She would need to bathe her hands as they were bleeding from the scrubbing.

Henry was sitting with his head in his hands, sobbing uncontrollably.

Betsy fell to her knees, thinking the worst.

'*No, no!*' she sobbed.

Henry looked up, shocked to see her there. He bent down to where she was kneeling on the floor and grabbed her hands.

'Betsy, sorry for frightening you – she is alive, she is alive, Betsy – they have saved her and they believe she will make it now.'

At that, the anguish of decades was set loose as they both cried for all they had ever lost and thanked God for the life of the child.

When she eventually got hold of herself, she washed and dressed her hands and then made some tea.

'Where is Mrs Ward?' she asked.

'I am going down to collect her shortly. She begged the Matron to let her stay. But I had to promise to collect her in an hour.'

Betsy went into overdrive. 'Here, have some soup and some soda bread. You have not eaten at all. Poor Mrs Ward, she will be beside herself with worry.'

Henry put down his cup of tea and looked intently at Betsy.

'You saw it, Betsy, you saw the cuts, the blood and the state of the room. What does it mean?' Betsy looked away. 'I don't know, Mr Ward – I have never seen anything like it.'

'Violet is saying that perhaps something has taken over our child. Something evil.' He shook his head. 'I will not hear of it, Betsy. Is my wife mad to be saying such things?'

Betsy wasn't sure if he was in denial or if he really had never heard of such things. He was raised a Catholic boy – surely he had heard of evil spirits and being possessed by a devil? But perhaps it was too much to bear – how could he begin to comprehend it?

'Look, Mr Ward, it is quite frightening whatever it is. Don't be too harsh on Mrs Ward – the shock is enough kill a horse. Just bring her home and after she gets some rest you can talk to her.'

'Very well, Betsy, but I won't have my child made out to be something that she is not. She is alive, and I will watch

107

over her night and day until she is well.' Then he got up and paced the kitchen floor.

He reminded Betsy of a wild horse ready to bolt at any moment.

'But why, Betsy? Why Sylvia? Could she have done this herself? Why would she do such a thing as harm herself like that? The room was bolted. Nobody was in there.'

Betsy suddenly thought of the letter. With everything that had happened she had forgotten about it. She reached into her pocket and took out the pieces, laying it out on the table for Henry to see it.

'This is the letter I found it in the garden with her doll early this morning, just after we arrived in. I was going out to feed the cat. I don't know how she got it. I checked the postbox and it is still locked. Someone somehow gave it to her or shoved it in the door. I knew something terrible was up, when I saw her doll lying broken on the ground.'

Henry looked at the letter and then suddenly he looked at Betsy.

'Thank goodness you were here. The child could be dead, only you found her. I was drunk and asleep, my wife possibly sleeping some pills off. Christ, we would not have her only for you.' He gripped Betsy by the shoulders with such force that it almost frightened her.

'Hush now, the child is alive, that is all that matters,' she whispered.

He looked at the letter intently and then Betsy saw fear turn to black anger in his eyes.

'I will hunt down whoever did this until every breath is gone from my body and God help them when I do find them.'

Betsy did not like the way he said it.

'This is a matter for the gardaí,' she said. 'Goodness! Maybe I should have left the room as it was – for clues. But I have scrubbed it clean. Don't take this into your own hands, Mr Ward.'

But Henry was not listening.

'*I tell you, Betsy, they have no idea who they are dealing with!*' he said with fury. 'This letter was the instigator of what almost killed my daughter. *I will hunt them like the dirty vermin that they are!*'

Betsy regretted showing him the letter. Maybe it was shock and lack of sleep, but Mr Ward looked like a madman.

CHAPTER 14

There was nothing left to say, no angry words of blame. Just large unsaid silent words filling the black hole that had seemed to develop between them as they drove back to Eveline, leaving their daughter sedated in the hospital. It had taken all her strength to leave, but the Matron would not hear of her staying any longer. She saw the reaction of the Matron when she saw Sylvia's injuries. The cuts on her arms and legs that were so deep that they resembled stab wounds. Her face was swollen and red. It looked like she had been walloped or had hit her head and face against something. Blood was oozing from her nose. It was as if she was beaten. The Matron had blessed herself when she saw her.

When Sylvia came around the doctor asked her how it had happened. Sylvia shook her head, crying, then began chanting something in a language that Violet did not understand, as if she was in a trance. Then she began shouting. She cursed at the Matron and, when the hospital chaplain Father Keogh sat beside her, she spat in his face. Blood oozed from her eyes. Violet could barely breathe in shock at what was happening. Eventually she found her voice and screamed at the doctor to do something. He tried to calm Sylvia and gave her something to sedate her. Eventually she seemed to pass out. She awoke again but other than looking traumatised she had no recollection of anything happening. The Matron had summoned Father Keogh again. He was a thin stern priest who looked permanently dour. He took out a prayer book and prayed over the child, his face contorted as if in pain.

There had been an argument between Father Keogh and Doctor Norton, the hospital doctor who was looking after Sylvia. Violet could not really make sense of what they were saying. But the doctor did not agree to having the priest there and the Matron had to tell them to calm down. Eventually they had both left Sylvia as she slept and slept.

Violet grabbed Doctor Norton by the arm and begged him to tell her what had happened to her daughter. He was a tall man with a shock of grey hair that looked almost unruly, his clothes immaculately pressed and thin-rimmed glasses on his face.

He looked over his glasses at her, his eyes seeming tired. He was near retirement and he looked like he could do with sitting at home with a pipe and slippers.

'To be truly honest with you, Mrs Ward, I have never seen anything like it. But I am a doctor and I know there is an explanation for it. It is important to keep her calm and having Father Keogh here is not helping matters. He seems to believe there is some evil spirt at play.'

'An evil spirit?'

'Yes, so he believes. Mrs Ward, I have heard of strange things that have happened to people throughout the centuries, but I have little or no belief in such claims. I respect the fact he is chaplain of the hospital but your daughter is in my care and I will not have assumptions of some form of religious witchcraft influence my care of her.'

'Do you think someone did this to her?'

'No,. I believe she somehow did this to herself. How? I have no idea. She possibly had some sort of fit. A convulsion. All we can do right now is make sure she is as stable as possible. Some of her injuries right now are inexplicable. But, in my experience, in time we will find the explanation. There are new discoveries all the time. Your child may have an illness that we know nothing of. The child is traumatised, there is no doubt about that. We may need to look at getting some specialist treatment for her. We can see in the next few days how she is, and I can begin deciding. What exactly happened to her? Only time will tell. I will be back to see her later tonight. In the meantime, the Matron will keep a good eye on her.'

She thanked him but felt her blood run cold as she tried to block the images of her child doing this to herself. The image of the blood on the walls and on the mirror flashed before her. Her beautiful little girl. It was too horrific to deal with. She hoped she was strong enough to try. She remembered her mother's faith in God. She wished she had it. Was this something to do with her? When she was young, they said she was not normal. Had she somehow transferred something terrible to her daughter? Were the people of the town right, had she been cursed for writing what she had written? Was she being punished in the cruellest way?

Now she was in the car with Henry driving home. Home without Sylvia. She could not trust herself to speak. A sense of unreality overcame her when they arrived back. Could all this really have happened only that morning? She looked at the door, the same door through which Henry had carried out Sylvia in his arms, not knowing if she would live to make it to the hospital. Her legs gave way and Henry caught her and helped her into the drawing room where Betsy had lit a fire earlier.

It was late and Betsy had gone home. She wished that she was still here. Betsy was the nearest thing she felt she had to family.

Henry was looking at her. He too seemed to have aged since morning. He looked like he was about to talk. There was so much to talk about, but her voice seemed cut off from her throat. The image of her child lying on that bed with those horrendous marks and blood oozing from her little body came flashing like pictures in a film.

Flashes of her own childhood began to form images in her brain. She could see herself as a child, kneeling, inhaling the incense, the aroma of the wax candle, the slow swish of the vestments of the priest on Good Friday and the carrying of the Cross. Good Friday, when they were in the cold confines of the church and the only light was like a prism through the stained glass. At four o'clock, they were told the day would go dark, the earth would blacken at the death of Jesus. Violet was always in the church when this happened, but her mother had assured her that it did just that.

Guilt almost overpowered her. Why had she ever returned here? What had she exposed her child to? How she had at first agonised over leaving Ireland! She had missed the air, that clean air that could only be found there. She had missed the music, the haunting music that carried the voices of the ghosts of the past. She had missed the landscape even though the hills and the rivers at times

113

seemed to chime with a melancholy and a dark brooding. Most left Ireland for a new life, but she left it because she wanted to always love it, her true love, but if she stayed it would surely suffocate her. She knew that, even if she lived away, she could never truly leave Ireland. It would be forever with her, every day of her life. She must love Ireland from afar.

Religion had been the tapestry of her childhood – it was how her childhood was played out. *Heaven* and *hell* were words that she was familiar with. Hell where the devil awaits for all the sinners. She knew her people believed this. She did not know what she believed. Did hell really exist? Did the Devil and demons exist? Was that what was at play here? But never had she or her kind witnessed anything like what had happened to Sylvia.

She had heard of such a thing, small snippets of such a thing. The fear of the Devil getting into you. She remembered Confession in that dark wooden box when her heart would almost stop beating at telling the priest of how she had forgotten to say her prayers at night or given her mother trouble by disappearing to the lough. But as much as she feared the priest and all that he said, she was not sure what she believed. How could this good God that they talked about allow something like this to happen to an innocent child? They said he was all-powerful. Where was he now? Or was he there and just punishing her? Then he was surely a cruel God. What did it mean for her child to have such wounds? Henry had wanted Sylvia baptised and brought up as a Catholic. She had mixed feelings about that. She knew that her family would condemn her even more if she did not raise her as a Catholic but that hardly mattered now as they seemed to have washed their hands of her. But she had gone along with it for Henry's sake. Was this God's way of teaching her a lesson? Putting her in some kind of purgatory on earth? She had heard plenty about purgatory where Catholics were purified of their sins before they could enter the Kingdom of God. But if she was in some kind of purgatory on earth, where was her child? In a hell on earth?

She had brought Sylvia to Mass in London. She had made her First Holy Communion there. But theirs was not a very religious house. She had a holy picture in the hall. A holy-water font at the door and a small crucifix that was in the house when they had bought it. She never liked looking at the crucifix. Why stare at his ravaged body? She had put it in a drawer in the kitchen. They had stopped going to church altogether now and had rarely gone in London. Not like when she was a child. The missions and the rosaries and the prayers. There was a large picture of Jesus in the kitchen of her childhood – a picture of the Sacred Heart. Her mother had a blessed candle underneath and it was lit for prayers. Was this her punishment? How could a good God punish her through her child? But this God had sacrificed his own child so that the sins of the world could be forgiven. His son was crucified on the cross so that his followers could go to heaven. What was he doing to her child? She felt she was going mad. She pulled at her hair, bringing away clumps of it in her hand. What was happening to her child? How could she stop it?

Oh, how she wanted to run all the way to her home and beg her mother to help her! What would her mother say? Would she tell her that she had brought this on herself, by living the sinful life that she had and betraying her family by running away and bringing shame on them? Or would she be forgiving? If her mother denied her and shut the door, that would be too much for the heart to bear.

The nuns in the hospital had said little. But they had been kindly to her and made her drink some hot sweet tea. The wounds were bandaged now and they had left Sylvia sleeping peacefully, drained of everything.

Violet looked at Henry who was sitting opposite her at the fire. He was about to speak when there was a rap on the door. They both jumped. Henry got up to see who it was.

She recognised the priest's voice. Father Quill. Henry brought him in. Father Quill looked at Violet with deep concern etched on his face. Suddenly she wanted to rush to him and beg him to help her. There was an air of calm that emanated from him that she craved. She was hungry for that calmness.

'I heard what happened,' he said softly, his brown eyes searching her face. 'I needed to check you were alright.'

Violet looked away. His concern was enough to undo her.

'What did you hear?' Henry asked warily, standing behind him.

Father Quill turned around to face Henry. 'I heard that Sylvia is recovering but that she is very ill.'

'Were you told what happened to her?' Henry asked, his voice heavy with mistrust.

'I was told assumptions, that's all, Henry,' he replied carefully.

'By whom?' Henry asked accusingly.

'By Father Keogh – he called down to see me.'

Henry banged the mantelpiece with his fist. '*Oh, for the love of God, what did he say?*'

'I think you know what he said, Henry. He believes

something happened to Sylvia almost not of this world.'

'What do you believe – do you think that can happen, Father?' Violet whispered.

Father Quill looked back at her. 'I think that no one should jump to conclusions. We know little of the mind, especially here in Draheen. You hear of psychological problems, ones that we know little about. Tell me, was the child worried about anything in particular?'

'Hold on,' Henry said, pointing to a chair for him to sit. He went out of the room.

'Violet, please, know I am here for you,' the priest said. 'I am so sorry that this has happened.'

Violet looked away. His kindness was tangible. She didn't trust herself to speak.

Henry returned with the most recent letter that Betsy had found. He showed it to the priest while filling him in on the previous letter.

'Well, this certainly explains that she was deeply upset,' said the priest. 'Have you any idea who could have written such vile letters?'

'No, but I will find out, Father, and I will have no mercy in my heart when I do,' Henry replied.

'Henry, I know how angry you must feel but I think you'd better let the gardaí handle this,' Father Quill said warily.

'I tell you, Father – someone wrote that poison and almost killed my child. I will not rest until I find them and, when I do, I hope God has mercy on them because I certainly will not.'

Violet looked frightened at the outburst. She had never known Henry to have such anger.

'What should we do, Father?' she implored.

117

'I don't think there is much you can do. Hopefully the child will forget this in time and the wounds will heal. I gather this has never happened before?'

'Never,' Violet replied. 'Sylvia is a very sensitive little girl. It's unimaginable that such a thing could happen to her.'

'I think the worry of what was going on may have somehow brought it on,' Father Quill said.

'I'm frightened for her, Father.' Violet's voice was barely audible. 'When we went into the room, it was shocking, absolutely shocking.'

'I think you need to go to the gardaí with these letters, Henry. I beg you not to take this into your own hands,' Father Quill implored.

Henry stubbed out his cigarette, a flash of anger crossing his blue eyes.

'That I cannot promise you, Father. However, I will let them know. But my child is sick and I don't want to hear any more about evil demons. Do you hear me, Violet?'

He strode to the door and opened it. 'I think you should leave, Father.'

Father Quill got up and went towards the door.

'Very well, but if you need me you know where I am.' He looked over at Violet.

'We won't need you, Father.' Henry retorted. 'You can be on your way.'

'Goodbye, Violet. I will pray for Sylvia's recovery,' Father Quill said softly.

Henry banged the door after him.

Violet began to cry.

'Can we go back to London, Henry? I can't stay here.'

'*Christ, Violet, now is not the time for this!*' Henry shouted, walking up and down the drawing-room floor.

'But we can't stay here. In this house. What if there is something evil? How can you even suggest that we stay here? And if it is an illness they will know more about Sylvia in London than here in Draheen.'

'*We are not running anywhere. Do you hear me?*' Henry shouted.

'*Well, I have no intention of staying here once Sylvia can move,*' she shouted back. '*I will take my child away!*'

Henry grabbed Violet from the chair, pulling her up close to him. The alcohol from the night before was rancid on his breath, his blue eyes full of wrath.

'*You are not taking my child anywhere without me, do you hear me? I am still boss in my own house!*' he bellowed. His fingers dug into her arms.

Violet barely recognised Henry. His grip was so tight she winced in pain. She could almost feel the black anger emanating from his body. Terrified, she broke away and rushed upstairs.

She ran into the guest room and locked the door.

After about half an hour there was a knock on the door.

'Violet, I'm sorry. I am tormented with what has happened. I should not have spoken to you like that. I know I frightened you. Please forgive me.'

Violet slowly opened the door. Henry was sitting on the floor, weeping.

'You know how I feel about going back to London. I can't bear it.'

'What about Sylvia?' Violet cried.

'You can't blame moving here for everything that has happened. There is no evidence that this will all go away as soon as we leave.'

'Henry, you are my husband and I am begging you to

leave here with me as soon as Sylvia can travel. I cannot stay here. I simply have to go.'

Henry got up and wrapped his arms around her, holding her so tight that she felt she could barely breathe. At last he let her go. He cupped her face in his hands. But instead of comforting her it made her feel even more on edge.

'We will talk tomorrow – try to get some rest,' he whispered. He kissed her lightly on the lips.

She could taste the stale whiskey and tobacco.

The night passed with no sleep. As soon as dawn broke, Violet dressed in a warm cashmere jumper and high-waisted tweed trousers. She grabbed her jade-green coat. She had to get out of the house to think straight. Panic had set into her body since she'd seen Sylvia in that terrifying state, a panic that was not subsiding. She grabbed a red beret and fixed it on her head, tying a green silk scarf around her neck.

She walked out of the house, shutting the gates behind her.

She walked up the road and into the town and then up towards the woods. There was hardly anyone about. In the woods it was slightly darker, the mist rising from the small brook. Violet breathed the air, the smell of decaying leaves, the choking feeling that she had easing. She found a spot where the violets grew wild. It was barren now, but she knew that once the spring would come, it would be a burst of colour. She sat listening to the gurgle of the brook and the morning call of the corncrake.

Eventually she walked back, eager to get to the hospital as soon as they would allow her in. She would have to walk past the church entrance.

There was the usual group of women gathered outside the church – the same group of women that Betsy had talked about. They were all about the same age, possibly in their late fifties, They were heading in for morning Mass. They eyed her warily, as if she were a young wolf who was slyly watching their fat chickens. She could feel the hatred from them. What on earth had she done to deserve so much hatred?

'How is your daughter?'

Violet stopped and turned to a small woman with a headscarf tied tightly on her head and a dark bottle-green coat with large buttons, her cheeks full of red lines like spider's legs spread across her face. Her eyes had a yellow tinge to them. She recognised her from Betsy's descriptions as Nelly Cooke. The others were dressed similarly with heavy coats in shades of brown and black with their heads covered in dark-coloured headscarves.

They eyed her warily, waiting for her to pounce.

'How do you know about my daughter?'

'It's a small town. I believe they had to call the priest. Never before has the likes of this happened in Draheen.'

'I suppose you will be leaving as soon as you can?' Molly Walsh spat, her eyes examining Violet from head to toe.

Violet thought of the letter. It had to be one of these. But how on earth could she know which one? She studied them all.

The two Grey sisters that Betsy had told her about looked awkward and avoided any eye contact with her. But the other three stared at her without blinking.

'Are you happy with yourselves?' she said. 'You got what you wanted.'

'What are you talking about?' one of them said.

She was a large woman wearing a navy coat that was

bursting at the seams. Her grey hair was pinned up and her ankles were so swollen that they were falling out over her shoes.

Violet knew she had to be Agnes the Cat. Betsy had described her well. She looked at Violet as if she had crawled from the rat-holes of the woods. She knew instantly what Betsy meant about her having a look of pure evil about her. There was a terrible aroma of stale cat urine off her that made Violet want to retch.

'My daughter almost died, is that what you wanted? Is that what you wanted, answer me? Shame on you, shame on all of you!' Violet wanted to claw at their faces and watch the blood fall down their pious cheeks.

The woman she knew must be Agnes the Cat pushed the others away. She came within an inch of Violet's face, the stench of her so overpowering it almost made Violet throw up. But Violet held her ground and stared right back at her.

Agnes's eyes bore into Violet's, making her flinch.

'You brought this on yourself. You are not in London now. There are rules to live by when you live in Ireland and don't forget it,' she threatened. She pointed a finger in her face.

'If you know what is good for you, take your child and go back to London. We don't want your kind here.' She stepped back. 'Come on, ladies, Mass is about to start. We can pray for that poor child – she needs every prayer that she can get with a mother like hers.'

The others looked less venomous than Agnes, but they turned on their heels to follow her.

'*Well, what a fine Christian act this is!*'

Betsy was suddenly at Violet's side.

'Shame on you is right! I heard every vicious word. Go

on in and pray! Pray that God and his Blessed Mother will find it in their most blessed hearts to forgive your evil ways. Shame on you! Go in and fall on your bended knees!'

'Betsy Kerrigan, watch your tongue,' Agnes the Cat said. 'You'll rue the day you went to work in Eveline. Your mother would turn in her grave to see you stand with that woman. There was a cousin of Kevin Fleming who knew someone who went to see her filthy play. Dirt, pure dirt, making a mockery of the holy priests.'

'You leave my poor mother out of this! She was a good Christian woman, not like you, with your cruelty and your judgements. Go on, go in and pray and remember to go to Confession. The Holy Mother knows the truth of what you lot are up to. Go on. *Go!*'

Miss Doheny arrived up with a young girl by her side. Violet noticed that the girl must be barely thirteen or fourteen. She looked awkward and shy and half-terrified. Violet wanted to tell her to run, run as far away from here as possible, before these pious women got their claws into her.

'What on earth is going on here?' Miss Doheny said. 'Have you all lost your senses, making a holy show of yourselves outside of the chapel? Mrs Ward, you have created enough distraction for one morning, I suggest you go home. Ladies, Mass is about to begin. Good day to you, Mrs Ward. Betsy, I think you should take Mrs Ward home. She looks like she will be needing some smelling salts soon.'

Betsy linked Violet's arm and drew her away.

'Hush now,' she said as they walked up the street. 'Ignore those old crones.'

Violet looked back at the young girl beside Miss Doheny, her sad brown eyes gazing after her silently as if begging for rescue.

Violet walked on, Betsy holding her arm tightly.

Violet began to sob heavily. It was all too much. She had gone to the woods for some peace and instead had ended up in a fight outside of the church.

Back in Eveline's kitchen, Betsy sat Violet at the table and made some tea and toast for both of them.

'Betsy, I am so sorry to have brought all this trouble into your life. You don't deserve this.'

'I was only delighted to speak to those women. Who do they think they are? Oh, all holy Joes and not one bit of common decency between them. Did you recognise them from my descriptions?'

'Yes, I definitely recognised Agnes the Cat. I actually thought I was going to throw up. The smell is like something dead.'

'Agnes is pure mad. Her brother Mike Dillinger is mad too. He used to live with Agnes, but he killed one of the cats. Wrung her neck because she got up on the table and ate his dinner. Agnes threw him out. She was afraid of him, I'd say. Anyway, I think he is back living with her now or so Miss Doheny was saying. She banned him from the shop because she said he would frighten the customers. I think she is afraid to ban Agnes. Then there is Nelly Cooke. She is married to that yob of a husband – the Bullock they call him because he is forever in fights. Then you have the two Grey sisters, Kitty and Nora – sure, they are easily led and a bit soft in the head. Molly Walsh is the one with the slitty eyes. She is the biggest gossip in the town. I feel my heart will boil over with anger when I think that one of them may have written the letters. It's hard to know. But it must be them. It has to be.'

Violet was crying again.

Betsy reached across the table and caught her hand. 'Hush now, it will all be alright. Did you see that poor girl with Miss Doheny? I hope to goodness they don't get their claws into her. The poor girl has no one and someone thought it was a good idea to send the poor soul to work for Miss Doheny. She would be better anywhere. Even getting the boat to England.'

'She looks so young,' Violet said.

'I know and very frightened but, look, we have enough to worry about. But I am sure those women have something to do with those letters. I am sure of it, Mrs Ward.'

'We have no proof. Henry was going to the gardaí this morning but . . .'

'Well, let them try and sort it, but they'll have their work cut out trying to find the culprit. Those women will hide behind the Church. Poor Father Quill has no hope with that lot. They run rings around him. I just hope Mr Ward doesn't take it on himself to find the culprit.'

CHAPTER 15

A week had passed now, and Sylvia remained in hospital under sedation. When she was awake, at times she was back a little to herself and at other times she went into a trance, chanting words in Latin in a voice that sounded nothing like a child's voice. Violet was terrified to see her like that. Then there were episodes when Sylvia would stare into space for hours. When she came around she would have no recollection of anything and beg for Violet to take her home. But during these trances it was as if she was someone else. She would stare at nothing and smile a strange smile that made the hairs stand on the back of Violet's neck.

Then Violet was told that she had another terrible fit where she seemed to have an almighty strength and had pushed the nun who was attending to her wounds so hard that she fell to the floor. The Matron and two other nuns had to hold her down. They had given her extra sedation to calm her. It was as if her eyes turned inside out and blood began to seep from them.

The priest was fighting with the doctor. The doctor wanted to send her to a hospital in Dublin that would have some experience of the kind of thing that had happened.

The doctor had explained yet again to Violet that he had no time for the assumptions of the priest about what was going on with Sylvia. Father Keogh was convinced that some sort of darkness had grabbed hold of her. He wanted to get permission from the bishop to do some sort of cleansing ritual on her but the bishop said he would have to contact the Vatican and let them know and look for approval first. It terrified Violet. But after another episode where Sylvia tried to strike the priest he told Violet that he was certain that she was possessed by a demon. He wanted to try to exorcise it but he would have to gather evidence before the Vatican would give the green light for an official exorcism ritual. A priest that was experienced in such matters would have to come and perform it. The bishop would try to make the arrangements.

But the doctor told Violet that there were signs that Sylvia was suffering from a disorder called schizophrenia. He also told her of another disorder called multiple personality disorder. However, he also believed that the upset of the letters could have thrown her into an unstable mental state and that all of this could be simply a result of the trauma. A breakdown of her mental state. But he was not a specialist, and he wanted her to see a doctor who was more knowledgeable about such matters. Have her go through some tests. He felt that if it was ignored and the priest kept going with his wild assumptions, she could very well end up in a padded cell in an asylum or worse. He said he also had to be mindful of his staff. They did not have the facilities within the hospital to restrain her if the fits got worse. All they could do was sedate her.

Violet did not know what to believe and was terrified of either of them being right. She knew that Henry had no belief in what the priest was saying, and he had little confidence in the doctor either. He had told Violet that he wanted to take Sylvia home to Eveline. But the doctor had assured them that the child needed to remain in hospital until they had some signs of stability. The wounds were beginning to heal, but Sylvia was barely eating and, until they knew what the fits were caused by, it seemed far too dangerous to move her. Sedation seemed the only answer.

'They will have her completely mad yet!' Henry had cried to Violet in pure frustration.

In the darkest hours Violet wept alone, unheard. She wept for the estrangement she felt towards her own family. The family that had given her life and now wanted no more to do with her. She wept for her mother who had denied her. She knew her father would have no forgiveness in him – he was a hard man and had firmly shut the door on her. She was dead to him. Her mother would never go against him – it was this she wept for the most. How could she allow fear to rule her and allow her to turn her back on her child? She wrote again, but she vowed that if she got no reply she would never write another letter. She begged her mother to come to her. She told her of their troubles and what had happened to Sylvia. If there was some sort of terrible curse on her daughter, then her mother just might know what to do. She told her it would be the last letter. If she did not come to her in her hour of need, she would never hear from her again. She still had not posted it. It was a final letter. She could not beg anymore.

If she posted it, it would be delivered by Luke Wilkinson the postman. He would see that the letter was not from England but would recognise the writing of their wayward daughter.

She wept for the heather-covered hills of her village. She wept for the sheer beauty of a sunrise with the mist rising over Lough Deeravaragh, she wept for the brooks as clear as crystal and the sweetest blackberries in Westmeath. She wept for Henry as she heard him pace the floor and wept at that terrible void that seemed to have opened up between them. How she wanted to feel his arms around her and have him tell her that it would all be alright! She was shocked at the anger that had risen up inside him. When he was not weeping for Sylvia, he was going around like a madman, wondering who was to blame. She hated to admit it but when he was like that he frightened her. She had spoken to Betsy about it. They were afraid to tell the gardaí their suspicions about the women at the church. Goodness knows what Henry would do if he found they had written the letters.

If only Sylvia would improve enough to go to London. Move away from here and let the gardaí work it all out then.

She wept for her little girl most of all. With her hair as soft as spun silk and eyes like pools of pale-blue water and a rosebud mouth that could be on one of her dolls. She wept for the raw scars still on her little body. The big black bruises that had appeared and now were a dirty faded yellow. It was hard not to blame herself. Even when reason tried to convince her that it was not her fault, the dark thoughts of blame became overpowering.

She felt suffocated in the bedroom as if the air was thick. It was thick with guilt and she needed to escape it. The room was cold as she dressed and washed. She would have some tea with Betsy later, before she went to the hospital but, for now, she just wanted to get out into the woods. Her mind could think more clearly there.

129

She put the letter in a drawer hidden under her underclothes. She would post it later. Wrapping herself up as warmly as she could she lifted the latch of the back door and slipped outside.

The street was quiet. As she passed Miss Doheny's she looked up and saw the curtains twitch. Nothing escaped Miss Doheny's eyes. Violet wondered did she ever sleep – she was forever on guard. She wrapped her coat more tightly about her and walked swiftly on.

She began to plan. As soon as Sylvia was well enough, she would book a passage and return to London. She could rent somewhere to live. But deep down she knew it was not as simple as that. Henry could refuse to let Sylvia go.

She turned into the woods, the early-morning frost like jewels on the decayed leaves. She walked on, taking paths that were new to her, hearing the crackling of the dead twigs and the early-morning chatter of wrens and goldfinches searching for big fat worms, made harder by the frosted ground. It looked so untouched, as if mankind had not found it yet.

Eventually there was a clearing. She could see the old graveyard, forgotten now with sunken graves and broken stone walls. Suaimhneas Graveyard. Some early snowdrops were peeping out between the cracks. There was a stone wall surrounding it and within the graveyard a small section walled off with tombs inside. She looked at the dates. One was an Inspector General who had died in 1832. It read that he was respected and beloved by his family. Another was dated 1848. It was difficult to read. Sacred to the memory of three daughters. Another was dated 1838 and interred was Mary Jane who died in 1844 aged twenty-six. Outside of this small area were other gravestone slabs with the writing faded. She tried to make it out. Some seemed to date back to the late 1700's. There was a small wooden sign saying *Suaimhneas Graveyard*. What was it *Suaimhneas* meant? Oh, yes . . . peace.

There was an area with no gravestones. She had heard of it from Father Quill. It was a mass grave from the time of the famine. He had been saddened to see it and hoped that at some stage they could put up a proper memorial. It was a graveyard of typhus and hunger. Broken dreams and stolen lives, a hundred years buried. Names never recorded. There was a stillness emanating from it. A boneyard of the famine, the only remnant of their lives to show they ever existed.

A few ravens flew up that were nesting in a yew tree, startling her.

It began to rain and, with no raincoat, she took shelter under the trees. It was good to think, have time to think. She had to protect Sylvia and if that meant leaving Henry and going back to London alone, then that is what she would do. She would not do as her mother had and live in fear of going against her husband. Henry had changed since coming back to Ireland. In London she had never imagined that she would ever fear him but now, when that black anger took him over, it was as if she hardly recognised her loving and charismatic husband.

As soon as the rain eased, she began to make her way back. The sky was full of inky swollen clouds.

It had grown darker – the early-morning light had dimmed with the impending rain. She missed the turn back and found herself in another part of the wood near a brook that she had never visited before. She kept walking and ended up back at the brook again. She had walked around in a circle. She walked on again and this time she saw the tree that she had passed earlier – it was a strange tree half dead and half alive with a wren's nest in the middle of it. Then she saw a path that she was familiar with. There was another clearing at the end of that path. Relieved, she knew that she would soon be back on the path that led to the graveyard. She could start again from there.

It was then she thought she heard something . . . it was just a whisper, but it was a human whisper not a woodland animal. A whisper and the crackle of twigs breaking. She shouted out hello. If it was someone walking, they would make themselves known. But there was only silence. She began to walk again and then she could hear the whisper again. A fear gripped her. No one knew she was here. Maybe it was a hunter looking for rabbits or deer. She walked on again and then she began to run, her heart beginning to beat fast. She had missed the path again. They all looked the same. She could hear someone else breathe as if out of breath and then another whisper, then more twigs breaking . . .

She shouted out again but no sound came back. An image of Sylvia flashed in front of her – she had to get back. Sylvia had said they were in danger. The whisper was getting louder.

'*Who is it? Who is there?*' But there was no answer, just the haunting cry of a corncrake to answer her.

There was someone following her, she was sure of it.

CHAPTER 16

Betsy arrived, hung up her coat and went into the kitchen. She would get the fire going and then make some fresh bread. She was determined to make something today that might appeal to Mrs Ward. Ever since that first letter she was as bad as Sylvia for barely eating. She would make some sausage rolls with some light pastry and some milk jelly.

She had needed some supplies and had braved it and gone into Miss Doheny who had put her nose up in the air after the row outside the church yesterday. Betsy asked briskly for the supplies that she wanted, and Miss Doheny almost fired them at her. There was no stopping to examine each item and tell Betsy of its fine quality as she usually did. The shopkeeper didn't ask after the welfare of the Wards, but Betsy knew she was bursting to know. Eventually Miss Doheny could hold it no longer.

'It will be the bishop next will have to visit with all these goings-on. There is a cloud over Draheen since they first set foot in Eveline House. How is the girl?'

'She is stable and if there is any news of the bishop visiting, I am sure you will be informed, but I have no reason to believe he will.'

133

'The chaplain Father Keogh said he had never seen the likes of it. Nora Quinn who works in the kitchen of the hosptital said that she heard the bedroom of the girl was shocking. Indeed, strange happenings are occurring up in the hospital too. Nora Quinn said that the child had a fit up there and the poor nuns and Father Keogh nearly died with the fright of it. They had never seen anything like it. Nora Quinn said there was talk that it could be something dark, something terrible had got hold of the girl. I am telling you the day the Wards set foot in Eveline a darkness came with them and now the poor child has it.'

'I have never heard such nonsense. Mr and Mrs Ward are good kind people and their child is unwell and all this town has done is name-call and spread evil gossip.'

'What about her play that brought shame to the Catholic Church? She brought this evil on herself, that woman.'

'I know Mrs Ward and she is one of the kindest souls I have ever met. Her writing is nothing to do with me. You would not want to believe idle gossip or spread it, may I add. The child is very sick – it could be a sickness we know little about.'

'Well, that is far from what I heard. The fear of God was put into the priest when he saw her, that is what I heard from a very reliable source.'

'Aren't you blessed with your sources, Miss Doheny? I am sure the *Draheen Post* could do with you if you ever tire of the grocery trade. For your information the girl simply took ill, possibly some strain of food she may have eaten. If I were you, I would take care that your eggs and produce are the freshest as I am sure Mr Ward will want to find out the cause of her illness.' With that Betsy gathered up the flour, eggs, sugar, tea and packet of jelly and made for the door. 'I will ask you to put that on the bill for Eveline and

Mr Ward will be up soon to sort it out.' She bid good day to Miss Doheny who looked like she would simply explode at any minute with that last accusation.

Betsy cycled as fast as she could, not daring to stop in case anyone else decided to pry for information. So, the whole town was talking about the poor little mite and saying terrible things about her. Betsy knew it was something terrible herself, but she couldn't even begin to believe that it was some sort of evil spirit that had caught hold of her.

She caught sight of Miss Doheny's new girl walking up the street. She looked very upset as if she was crying. Betsy wished she had time to stop and talk with her. The poor child was possibly traumatised by working for Miss Doheny. She made a note to try to get to know the young girl and befriend her – there was a sadness about her, she seemed lost.

The kitchen was warming up now as the bread and sausage rolls were baking. She had a light soup on too and she had made a sponge cake that she knew Mrs Ward was partial to. Hopefully she could tempt her with something, or she would end up sick too. She gathered some trimmings of fat for the cat and went out to the garden to feed her. She was surprised that she was not sitting on the windowsill as she usually was looking for her breakfast.

In the garden, she was taken aback to see Henry sitting with his head in his hands as if he had been crying. She pretended not to notice as it would only be an embarrassment for him.

'Good morning, Mr Ward, I thought you were out – the gate is opened outside.'

Henry looked surprised. 'I wasn't out. Violet must have gone out for a walk. I wish she would at least tell me that she is going.'

'Well, it's going to bucket down soon, so she will come back when she sees the clouds. I will make some tea.'

She went back in and wrapped her fresh loaf in a clean tea towel to soften the crust and laid the sausage rolls on a rack to cool.

She had lots to do. She would make a stew for later and then give the drawing room and the guest room a bit of a dusting. She really wanted to rush to the hospital to see Sylvia, but the nuns were strict and would not let her in. She would go later and bring her up some of her dolls. She would buy some glue and try and put poor Petite Suzanne back together.

Henry came in and had some tea and some sausage rolls and then retreated to his study. The rain, as she had predicted, began to pound down. Mrs Ward must have taken shelter. Betsy lit the fire in the drawing room as sometimes Mrs Ward would retreat there to write, although she had not written any of her play in quite a while. A telegram had arrived from a large theatre in London looking to possibly perform her next play. But Mrs Ward had barely looked at it and Betsy had noticed Henry was made very agitated by its arrival.

Another hour passed with no sign of Mrs Ward. She would be soaked and end up with a chest infection – she had told her she was prone to them.

Betsy gently knocked on Mr Ward's study door.

'Sorry to disturb you, Mr Ward, but would you take the car out and look for Mrs Ward? The rain is so heavy she may not be able to return. She possibly went up towards the woods. I checked and her wool coat is gone, and it's certainly not any good for keeping out the rain.'

Henry came out and took his coat from the stand and his hat.

'I'll go. She is forever in those woods. It was hardly a morning for it.'

'It was brighter earlier, but I can't see it letting up any time soon,' Betsy replied.

He left immediately but after an hour he returned alone. He told Betsy that he had driven up the town and over to the entrance to the woods, got out and went along the usual paths Violet favoured, calling her name, but there was no sign of her.

'Is there anywhere else she could be?' he asked.

Betsy shook her head. 'Unless she popped in to see the doctor's wife or Father Quill. I will pop over and see – there is a bit of a break in the rain. She would not be allowed into the hospital this early and she hardly walked that far.'

'I can drive over,' Henry suggested.

'I will be as quick walking. I'll run now before the next heavy shower.' She grabbed her coat, hat and umbrella.

She walked down the main street and discreetly looked in the windows of shops. There was no house except the doctor's house that Mrs Ward would be in – it shamed her to think so few had made her welcome. But the doctor's wife Heather was a bit worldlier than most and had been a good friend since she arrived. She was an Englishwoman who was known to go to Dublin and stay for a week and bring home half the clothes from up there. She was Protestant like her husband and sang with a kind of operatic voice at all the services. The doctor's wife had been very friendly and intrigued by Mrs Ward, constantly admiring her fashion tastes and fancy clothes. Yes, she had possibly gone there – she would just knock on the door and ask. But the doctor's secretary answered the door – Mrs Wilson, a very severe woman who always looked like she was doing something very important. Mrs Wilson informed her that the doctor's wife was on a shopping trip to Dublin. She raised her eyes to heaven as she said this.

'I am sure we will need to send a special car to carry home the shopping alone. Is that all you're here for? I must go – I have a room full of patients to attend to.'

Just then the doctor came out of his surgery and when he saw Betsy he came over and enquired about Sylvia. He said he would drop up to the hospital the following day to see how she was doing.

That left the priest. Betsy bit her lip as she stood and considered that possibility. She did not like to say to Mrs Ward that people were beginning to talk about her great friendship with Father Quill. Mrs Ward had enough on her plate without hearing more gossip. Yes, she should check there.

At the priest's house she met Mrs Masterson his housekeeper who told her that the priest was out on calls. She was a good woman who had lost her husband when she was only married a year. She had become the housekeeper for Father Cummins and remained on for Father Quill.

'You look worried, Betsy – when did you last see her?'

'Well, I arrived earlier this morning and she had already gone out for a walk – she was gone before Mr Ward was up too. We presumed she had taken to the woods – she loves the woods and often goes there – but the rain was so bad Mr Ward went to look for her there. He couldn't find her. Maybe she is back and I am just making a fuss – she might have taken shelter in the woods till the rain passed and not heard Mr Ward when he called for her.'

'Look, why don't you go back and check if she has come back – she may just have wanted some time alone. Father Quill is due back soon and is heading out to the hospital to relieve Father Keogh – if she is there, I will tell him to let her know that you are worried. And, of course, we'll contact you or Mr Ward at Eveline.'

'She has never walked all the way to the hospital in the rain, surely?'

'It's a worrying time and you are good to be concerned but she is most probably, as I said, just having a bit of time on her own,' the woman said gently. 'She may be back home by now.'

Betsy hurried back to Eveline, hoping Violet might be there tucking into some food but there was no sign of her.

Henry then drove up to the hospital and asked the nun at reception. But no, she had not been there either. It was heading for midday now and she had been possibly gone from seven. Henry began to drive around and Betsy walked up and down the town again. Miss Doheny might know. She hated having to tell her anything but she would just have to go in and ask her.

'I see Mr Ward driving up and down the main street with a strange look on his face and looking all around the place?' Miss Doheny remarked.

Her new girl was washing the windows, as if in a trance.

'Make sure they are spotless and for goodness' sake put a bit of elbow-grease into it!' Miss Doheny scolded. 'Honestly, I do not know what has got into her today – she is away with the fairies. Caught her outside crying and sobbing. It's just not working out – I will have to get in contact with my cousin and arrange to send her back.'

'She does look very pale,' Betsy noted.

'Well, it's not from work,' Miss Doheny said in a tone of annoyance. 'So, what is Mr Ward driving around like a mad thing for?'

'Perhaps he is testing the car out in case it needs anything fixed. Was Mrs Ward with him, I wonder, or maybe you saw her on the street perhaps?' Betsy asked casually.

But Miss Doheny's ears were pricked for any morsel of news.

'Indeed, I did not. I saw her out this morning before Mass. She was walking up towards the woods. She was certainly not in Mass. She goes walking in them woods instead of praying. You were not at Mass yourself this morning, Betsy?'

'No, I had errands to run. I will take six of those lovely fresh eggs, please, Miss Doheny.' She thought she'd better buy something, or it would raise Miss Doheny's suspicions even more, but her heart was thumping. Maybe Mrs Ward had fallen in the woods and hurt herself. She grabbed the eggs and walked down the street back to the house.

Mr Ward had just arrived in.

'Miss Doheny saw her go up the town towards the woods before early Mass,' Betsy said. 'She could be in the woods having fallen – maybe unconscious, God forbid – and you did not see her. We need to drive up here again and look for her, sir.'

'Let's go,' he said, looking distraught.

In the woods, they walked the path Violet normally took, calling her name all the way. Betsy knew all the paths well and had often talked to Mrs Ward about them, so she knew which ones she frequented and they tried those first. But there was no sign of her.

They took the path to the holy well and eventually arrived at Suaimhneas Graveyard where in desperation they decided to split up and search separately following less frequented paths.

Eventually they met again at the graveyard.

'Surely she wouldn't have left the paths for any reason, alone as she was?' Henry said.

'If she did and collapsed somewhere among the trees and bushes, we'll never find her, sir,' said Betsy.

'Not without a properly organised search,' said Henry. 'We need to return to Eveline – perhaps we'll find her there. If not, we'll have to organise a search party.'

'Yes, sir,' said Betsy, her voice trembling.

They were about to leave when Betsy spotted it: a green silk scarf that had fallen into a puddle. Mrs Ward's scarf. She picked it up and then she saw it. Fresh blood was spattered on the underside of it.

'Is it Violet's scarf?' Henry asked in horror.

'Yes, it is. Mrs Ward bought it on her last trip to London.' Betsy was in tears.

'We must keep searching, Betsy – she must be hurt and could not get home.'

They set out again, moving more slowly the better to view everywhere they could, calling her name till their voices were hoarse.

Fear began to engulf Betsy. She sensed a strange atmosphere in the woods.

'We'd better return,' said Henry. 'I must inform the gardaí.'

'Leave me at the church, sir. I am going in to say a prayer and light some candles. She might even be there.'

'Unlikely,' Henry said, tight-lipped.

'Please God let her just turn up back at Eveline – maybe she's already there – maybe she had a bit of a fall and someone found her and has taken her home. Please God let her be at Eveline.'

CHAPTER 17

Betsy had lit candles, prayed and gone back to Eveline in hope and fear. But there was no sign of Violet. Henry had left her a message saying he had phoned the hospital again and the presbytery – to no avail. He was now going to the Garda Station.

Betsy went upstairs and checked the bedrooms. Everything looked normal. Nothing was out of place. But she noticed something significant – Mrs Ward's handbag was lying on a chair. She hadn't taken that so it was extremely unlikely she would have gone to the hospital or anywhere far afield. Or indeed to the shops – though perhaps she might have taken some cash in her coat pocket? But her walking shoes were gone. Everything pointed to the fact she had gone out for a short walk.

An idea suddenly came to her. She could be in O'Hara's Hotel. Even if she had no handbag and no money, someone could have invited her to go in for a drink or a meal or just to talk. But how could she have stayed so long there? Nevertheless Betsy went out again and hurried along to O'Hara's Hotel. But, no, Violet had not been there that day.

Deflated, she emerged and walked aimlessly along the street.

Suddenly she was confronted by Miss Doheny outside her shop.

'What is the matter with you, Betsy? You're like a woman losing her marbles. You're making a show of yourself, walking around looking like death. What's going on?'

'It's Mrs Ward, she never came home,' Betsy blurted out.

'What do you mean, she never came home?' Miss Doheny asked, eyebrows arched, eyes widening.

Betsy was glad to talk to someone, even if it was Miss Doheny – she was going out of her mind with worry.

'Remember you saw her this morning? Well, it seemed like she was going for an early morning walk, she tends to do that. She is forever walking about the woods and she possibly wanted to get out of the house. But she never came back. Myself and Mr Ward have walked all over the woods and I found her silk scarf with a bit of blood splattered on it but nothing else.' She had no idea why she was telling Miss Doheny, but she was so worried about Mrs Ward that she didn't care if there was more gossip. 'She's not at the hospital either.'

Miss Doheny beckoned her to come into the shop.

'I am closing up now anyway. Come on in and I will make a cup of tea for you. You look like you need one.'

Miss Doheny locked the shop door and then opened the hatch to allow Betsy through to the house. This brought them into a hall with a narrow stairs. Up the stairs to the right was a small parlour. Miss Doheny went into an adjoining room and set about making some tea. Betsy looked around at the red-velvet seats. A black-and-white photograph of a couple was on the wall. An oil heater smelled of paraffin. There was a radio on a table and some

143

copies of *The Far East*. Betsy was familiar with the magazine which was run by the Missionary Society of Saint Columban. There was also a bible, a prayer book and some red wool beside it with a pair of knitting needles. A Sacred Heart lamp was lit and a rosary beads hung over a small mirror. Miss Doheny arrived in with a wooden tray bearing a china pot of tea, two china cups and saucers, milk, sugar and a small plate of fruit cake.

Miss Doheny poured the tea. Betsy took her cup and poured some milk in. She took a sip and put it back on the table.

'But where could she have gone?' Miss Doheny asked as she sipped her tea. 'Has she run away?'

'Run away? Why would she do that?' But, even as she said it, she realised it was a possibility. Mrs Ward was so unhappy. But no, she would never leave Sylvia behind. 'And leave her daughter? No, never. She is out of her mind with worry about her.'

'But maybe she took herself off for the day?' Miss Doheny said.

Betsy shook her head again. 'With Sylvia lying ill in the hospital? No. I checked and her handbag is still in her room so, wherever she is, it must be nearby.'

Miss Doheny handed her a plate with a slice of fruitcake on it.

'It looks lovely, but I am too worried to eat. Thanks for the tea though.'

'So where is Mr Ward now?'

'He has gone to the Garda Station.' Betsy was barely holding back the tears.

There was a knock on the shop door and Miss Doheny looked out from the parlour window.

'Well, speak of the devil! Garda Flynn is at the door. Stay there and I will see what he wants.'

Betsy could hear the conversation at the door.

'Can I have a word, Miss Doheny?'

'What about, Garda Flynn? But you better come in or I will be the talk of the town with a garda at my door,' Miss Doheny said crossly. 'Wipe your feet.'

'It's about Mrs Ward,' the garda said. 'Her husband has just been to see me. She's missing.'

'I know. Betsy Kerrigan is upstairs.'

'I'll have a word with her.'

Betsy heard footsteps on the stairs and Miss Doheny led Garda Flynn into the room.

He had beads of sweat forming on his red forehead.

'Any news, Betsy?' he asked.

'No, not a sign. I have told Miss Doheny everything.'

Garda Flynn sat down and took out his notebook from a worn brown satchel. He then took a pencil from behind his ear and dropped it on the floor. It landed beside Miss Doheny who shook her head before picking it up and handing it to him. He cleared his throat.

'Miss Doheny, can you tell me what time you saw Mrs Violet Ward this morning and indeed if she looked in any distress?'

The garda was a very large man who barely fitted on Miss Doheny's small chair. He looked clearly uncomfortable and out of place in the small parlour and Betsy was worried that the chair would literally crumble under his weight.

Miss Doheny was looking at the chair too and Betsy reckoned she was thinking the same thing. Poor Garda Flynn seemed to be getting larger on the chair with the scrutiny of Miss Doheny, his face was getting redder and the droplets of sweat had turned to a layer of thick sweat that was beginning to shine on his forehead.

'I saw her walking up the street well before morning Mass – towards the woods,' Miss Doheny said.

He wrote this down and then looked intently at her. 'That is the last sighting of Mrs Ward and her husband is greatly concerned as this is not in her character to go off and not come home. But if that's all you can tell me I will be off, unless there is anything else that I should know?' He stood up, took a handkerchief from his pocket and wiped his brow.

'I assure you I know nothing that would concern you,' Miss Doheny said, clearly cross at the assumption.

'Very well, I will be off. You know where to find me if there is anything else. I am organising a bit of a search party in the woods, in case she went off the path and came to grief.'

With that he put his notebook away and the pencil behind his ear and bid them goodbye.

Miss Doheny escorted him down and out onto the street.

Betsy got to her feet as Miss Doheny returned.

'I'd better get back. Thank you for the tea, Miss Doheny.'

'Well, I am afraid I have not much faith in Garda Flynn solving any mysteries around here. The man is quite incapable,' Miss Doheny remarked, throwing her eyes to heaven.

Twenty people assembled for the search party including Henry and Betsy. With torches and two dogs and armed with long sticks they began the search. Old Ned Rigley gave advice about the different paths as he was one of the oldest people in the town and had the most knowledge of the woods. An early evening frost had set in. Betsy kept up aspirations to Saint Agnes as she walked. After two hours they all reassembled. It was quite a large wood but they must have covered every part of it with their torches. Every tree and bramble had been poked but there was nothing.

Then a young man let out a shout that they had found something. He held up a key with a gold-plated keyring. He shone the light on it as it was now very dark.

Betsy gasped as she instantly recognised it. It was the back-door key to Eveline.

'It's Mrs Ward's key. She always carries it!' she exclaimed.

Garda Flynn looked very concerned at this.

Betsy felt her stomach churn. It looked like Mrs Ward had gone to the woods and there the trail had gone cold. But how? She listened in disbelief as Garda Flynn thanked everyone for the search and informed them that he would need to contact his superiors and launch an official proper investigation into her disappearance if there was no sign of her. He would also contact all hospitals in the county.

Henry looked gravely unwell, listening as if in a trance.

Then Betsy thought of Sylvia. How on earth could they tell her? In her heart she had believed that they would find her before nightfall and here was Garda Flynn sounding all very different than he normally did, talking about official investigations. Please God she would turn up soon and it would all be cleared up as a misunderstanding. She could not bear to think that it could be anything else.

Back at Eveline Betsy made something to eat for Mr Ward, but it lay untouched. He remained out searching and walked all over the town of Draheen, even driving out all the roads leading out of the town, including all the small boreens. He was gone the entire night and when Betsy arrived the next morning, he was only returning. He looked like an old man and she could hardly believe it was him. He needed to shave and wash.

Somehow, she convinced him to eat a bit of soda bread and a boiled egg,

'You need your strength so turning away food is going to help nobody,' she scolded.

'I need to see Sylvia, but what on earth will I tell her?' Henry said.

'I will visit her and there is no need to say anything yet. I'm sure Mrs Ward will turn up. There could be an explanation for all of this. You need to sleep – you will fall down with the exhaustion and the shock of it all.'

Somehow she convinced him to lie down with the promise that she would call him in an hour or two or if there was any news. Two hours passed and she could hear him back up again. She was making a pot of tea when there was a knock on the door.

It was Garda Flynn. Betsy brought him into the kitchen.

'Any news?' he asked abruptly.

'None whatsoever and we are going out of our minds with worry. Mr Ward was out searching all night.'

Henry appeared beside Betsy. 'There is no trace whatsoever, Garda.'

Garda Flynn looked at Henry then at Betsy, then back to Henry again. He cleared his throat.

'I have checked all the hospitals in the county and she has not turned up in any of them nor do they have any unidentified patients. And I have contacted my superior about the matter. I will let you know what the next procedure is.' His voice had a new air of importance.

'Please find her, Garda. Please just find her,' Betsy said in almost a whisper.

'We will do all we can. Let me know if there is anything whatsoever that you forgot to tell me. But I have a couple of questions while I have you.'

He took out his notebook from his satchel and his pencil from behind his ear. He licked his finger and flicked to a fresh page.

'Is it true that yourself and Mrs Ward were up at the hotel the other evening?' he said almost accusingly to Henry.

'Yes, we were. What has that to do with it?' Henry asked, confused.

'Is it true that Mrs Ward came home alone afterwards?' he asked, staring at Henry.

'Yes, it is. We had a disagreement. It's not a crime to have an argument with your wife, is it?' Henry replied sharply.

'May I ask what it was about? This argument?'

'I can't see what it has to do with this. But my wife was very upset about those letters that our daughter had received and, well, she was talking about going back to London. I disagreed. There is no point in running away. That is why I showed you the letters, to see if you could find out who had sent them.'

'The morning after this argument you were seen walking down the street after sleeping in Peter Binchy's house. Is this true?'

'What has this to do with it?'

'Can you please just answer the question?'

'Yes, I had too much to drink and slept on the settle bed at Binchys'.'

149

'I see.' Garda Flynn was writing in his notebook. He turned to Betsy. 'Is it true that you were seen helping Mr Ward on the street the next morning, Miss Kerrigan?'

'Yes,' said Betsy, a feeling of dread coming over her.

'Where were you before that?'

'I was at my cottage and I was going to morning Mass and then I saw Mr Ward,' Betsy said, feeling sick to her stomach.

'Were you there when Mrs Ward came home from the hotel the previous evening?'

'Yes, I was.'

'So, how was she that evening?'

'She was upset and cold – she had gone down to Rothe river.'

'The river?' said the garda, looking up from his notebook and looking intently at her. 'Why the river?'

'Well, she liked the river. She would sometimes go there.' A dreadful possibility had sprung into her mind but she lowered her head so Mr Ward could not see her expression.

'Mr Ward, was this a normal thing in this house?'

'What do you mean?' Henry asked.

'I am simply asking if it was normal procedure for both of you to go out, have a row in public and then for your wife to walk home alone and for you to remain in a pub and become intoxicated and not be able to get home?'

'Garda Flynn, what kind of questioning is this? This has nothing to do with Mrs Ward not coming home,' Betsy said, alarmed.

'I would advise you to be careful what you say, Miss Kerrigan, and to tell me the truth. If you are covering anything up it is better to tell us now because the truth will be revealed.'

'*My wife is missing! Can you please try and find her and stop this farce?*' Henry shouted.

'I am conducting no farce, Mr Ward, and I would ask you to come up to the station in the afternoon as my superiors will certainly want to talk to you.'

With that, Garda Flynn turned on his heel and left.

CHAPTER 18

'My God, that gobshite thinks I have had something to do with all this!' Henry exclaimed. He could barely think straight. He held his head in his hands, trying to make some sense of what was happening.

He had searched their bedroom in case there were any clues as to her whereabouts, going through letters, her dressing table, her coats. He had searched the guest room and her writing bureau. He had sent a telegram to London to some of their friends, asking them to contact him if there was any news of her, he had contacted their friends in Dublin. But nothing. Nobody but Miss Doheny had laid eyes on her.

He could see that Betsy was barely keeping it together. He knew she cared deeply for Sylvia and for Violet. They had formed an almost sisterly relationship. Betsy was busy trying to keep some normality in the home. But there was nothing normal about what was happening.

Not so long ago they had arrived in Eveline to make a good life here. Instead of that, it was a living nightmare.

He went in search of Betsy. She was in the kitchen trying to glue back Sylvia's doll's arm and piece by tiny piece glue her broken face.

'She loves this doll so much. She keeps asking me to bring her in I can't bear to tell her what happened. She has no recollection of it happening. That is the only good thing.'

'Betsy, did Violet say anything to you that I should know about, anything at all you need to tell me?'

Betsy shook her head, fighting back the tears.

'There is no more to tell than you know already.' Her voice high-pitched. 'Only that she was tormented with the fact that she wanted to move lock, stock and barrel back to London and I got the impression that she was intent on going. But she was out of her mind with worry over Sylvia, and there is no way she would have left. I have a terrible fear about what has happened to her. I cannot believe she would leave even for a day without Sylvia – sure the Matron has had a hard job keeping her out of the hospital.'

'I need to know Sylvia is alright – will you go up and reassure her that all is well? There is no sense worrying the child yet. God knows it will set her back. I need to go back out and look for Violet but where will I look? She is not in the woods and I don't believe she left to go on a trip as her handbag is here. The fact her key was found is terrifying me. Please, God, don't let something bad have happened to my wife, I don't think I could bear it. I just don't know what to think. Part of me thinks something terrible has happened and another part of me is wondering has she run away. I just hope we are not too late when we find her. I am going out to look though I don't even know where else to look.'

'Mr Ward . . .' She didn't want to voice her fear. 'Have you searched along by the river?'

'No! I should have thought of that. I never checked there.' A dark shadow seemed to pass over his face. 'I'll go there now.'

153

* * *

Three hours later, Henry was walking back to his car after following the river for miles. All in vain.

During that time, the conversations that he had with Violet over the past week or two had kept going around and around in his head. Could there be something he was missing? He thought of the letters – if only they had not arrived this would never have happened. Garda Flynn had hardly reacted when he showed them to him.

'Some prankster, better to ignore them,' he had advised, much to Henry's annoyance.

'It's hard to say that to a young impressionable girl,' Henry said. 'Whoever is sending them has made sure that they get into her hands.'

He was just getting into the car when Garda Flynn arrived, his face red from riding his bicycle. He put the bicycle up against a tree and walked towards the car, stopping to hitch up his trousers.

Henry remained sitting inside.

The garda produced his notebook and pencil, then looking up from his notes he took on an air of pure importance.

'My superiors are here, and they want to speak with you. You must come straight away to the station, Mr Ward.'

'Are they organising another search party?' Henry asked.

'Yes, but they want to talk to you immediately. It is of the utmost importance that you come now. They are waiting for you.'

'I thought they would be organising a search for Violet

– why do they want me?' Henry said, eyeballing Garda Flynn.

'My superiors want to see you immediately – that is all the information I can give you at this point,' Garda Flynn repeated, a layer of sweat forming on his brow.

'Very well, I will go there now.'

Henry had a sick feeling in the pit of his stomach. He expected it was common enough to mistrust the husband of a missing woman. Garda Flynn was not very good at hiding his suspicions. He was already looking at Henry as the evil husband. Henry was not too concerned about Garda Flynn's suspicions or theories. The biggest case he had solved lately was who was stealing the milk bottles on Galley Street. For days, when the residents went outside to collect their milk, it was gone. Garda Flynn had hidden in one of the resident's kitchens with full view of the street. Over a big slice of warm soda bread and butter he spotted Seán O'Driscoll sneak the bottles away. He ran after him and tripped over George Fitzgerald's half-blind dog and broke Eileen McCarthy's winter roses. Eileen was not too impressed and had let him know exactly what she thought of him. So, a missing woman was sure to send him over the top.

Superintendent O'Neill was a tall thin man with very bushy eyebrows that looked like they had been cut quite bluntly. He was drinking a cup of tea and chain-smoking Woodbine cigarettes. He was picking Garda Flynn's cat's hairs off his plainclothes immaculately pressed dark trousers when Henry arrived in. There were some crumbs on the table from Garda Flynn's early breakfast and he pushed them off onto the floor as if they were contaminated. He looked at Henry through slits of eyes that showed very little emotion.

'I believe you were searching the riverbank when Garda Flynn located you. Any sign of your wife?'

Henry knew from his tone that Garda Flynn was not the only person who suspected that he had something to do with Violet's disappearance.

'No, nothing.'

'In fact, Garda Flynn and colleagues already searched along the river. He wondered about the possibility of . . . eh, her taking her own life?'

'No! Never!' Henry was horrified. 'With our daughter in that state in hospital? Absolutely not!'

'I see.' The Superintendent sat back in his chair and stared at Henry.

'I believe your wife wanted to move back to London and you refused. We have several witnesses who have made a statement that you had threatened her at the hotel as to her plans about taking your child back.'

'What has that evening got to do with this?' Henry asked.

'I am simply stating the facts, Mr Ward. You threatened your wife who left the hotel very upset, you drank almost until morning and were not seen until you were seen with your housekeeper, barely able to walk. That same morning your daughter became seriously sick. Your wife has not been seen since she went for a walk very early yesterday morning. Is that correct? She was seen by a Miss Doheny who I am told is a very reliable witness. Is this a regular thing for you, Mr Ward, not to be able to make your way home?'

'I needed to let off a bit of steam, that's all. There was so much going on – I was trying to get the builders into the building that I had just bought, Violet was upset over the letters that our daughter had received and, as far as I was concerned, she was having a kneejerk reaction about running back to London.'

'But you were having none if it?'

'Of course not. I wanted to find out where the letters had come from and try to put a stop to it. My wife loves Eveline House, she just found it harder to adjust to living in Ireland again.'

'But you had told her that under no circumstances would you move, or indeed could she take her daughter. Have you contacted anyone in London to see if she is there?'

'Our child is sick and she would never leave her. They have a bond that is incredible – she would never do this to her.'

'Did you contact anyone in London, Mr Ward?'

'Yes, I did – and Dublin. I have contacted everyone she knows.'

'What about her family here in Ireland?'

'They have not spoken to her in years, not since she ran away when she was seventeen.'

'So, she has run away before?' the Superintendent asked, his eyebrow arching.

'She was very young then. I am telling you she would never leave her child.'

The questions continued for over an hour.

'Look, I have answered everything that you have asked me, but my wife is out there possibly hurt and all that you seem to be doing is interrogating me. Either arrest me or let me go and look for my wife.'

'You may go, but we will talk again soon.'

Henry grabbed his coat and left, banging the door.

Back at Eveline, Betsy met him at the door, looking frantic.

'There is an outbreak of influenza in the hospital. They

want us to bring her home. Either that or move her to Dublin. I have promised to look after her and let the doctor know if she has any more fits. He feels that she is a little more stable and might be safe at home, but he wants to send her to some specialist in Dublin as soon as he can arrange it. He has heard about Mrs Ward. I told him that I can look after her if you agree, the doctor will look in on her night and day, but with this influenza hitting the ward it's better to have her home. Mr Ward, I had to tell Sylvia that Mrs Ward had to go away for a few days. I had to say something.'

'How is she?'

'Frail but making sense. The fits seem to have subsided. She is very anxious though.'

Henry was glad to see that Betsy had Sylvia's room fresh and clean with new linen and a bunch of wildflowers in an earthenware jug. There was no remnant of the nightmare that had happened. She had washed all the walls and taken some of the rugs from downstairs that were bright and cheery and put them on the floors. She had found a pretty satin quilt for the bed. All Sylvia's dolls, including Petite Suzanne with her glued-back face, were sitting on the bed waiting to greet her.

It looked a million miles away from the scene that the child had left. He had thought about moving her to the guest room but now thought better of it – the room was lovely and moving her would only serve to remind her of what had happened.

Betsy had said that the doctor had warned that she was to be watched night and day. She suggested that she would move the settle bed into Sylvia's room.

'I know there will be gossip about me sleeping at the

house but I am past caring what they say. It's the little one that is important.'

Henry spent the rest of the day searching for Violet. He returned and went to the hospital to see Sylvia. Betsy was sitting beside her, giving her some soup. They would collect her when the doctor was sure she was stable. Though they had her sectioned off from the other wards, it would still be hazardous for her if the outbreak got worse.

Suddenly it all became too much. Henry went to speak but could not. He fell on his knees beside the bed, crying. Slowly Sylvia sat up and reached for him. She put her small arms around him. He hugged her tightly as if his life depended on it.

CHAPTER 19

There were door-to-door searches, the woods were searched for days, the guards brought in dogs and searched from morning till night. Henry was brought in for questioning again. Betsy was summoned to the police station. She told them everything she knew. Draheen was full of strangers searching for Violet.

The gardaí went to her home place in the midlands to see if she had turned up there, but there was no sighting of her. Her mother and father were still alive. Her mother had wept when they told her but had said little else.

Violet had well and truly vanished.

It made the national news. **PLAYWRIGHT MISSING IN DRAHEEN.** There was talk in the newspapers about a possible abduction. Speculation about a ransom note.

Henry didn't think this at all likely. He was a man of means but not to the extent that anyone would risk kidnapping his wife for money. However, he went and spoke to the police about this possibility. They dismissed the notion, saying he would already have heard from kidnappers if that were the case. He left the Garda Station with a deeper feeling of dread. He felt they had decided they already had their suspect: him.

There was a vigil held in the church in Draheen. Father Quill made a special plea to all the parishioners.

'Please, I beg you, if any of you know anything at all about her disappearance, speak now.'

Betsy saw the 'church ladies' deep in prayer, the hypocrites!

They stopped her on the way out as she went to bless herself at the holy water font.

'Any news at all of poor Mrs Ward?' Agnes the Cat asked. Her face had a reddish-purple hue to it and her eyes bored into Betsy for any morsel of news.

The others stood close beside her.

Betsy turned around to them, her face hiding nothing of what she thought of them.

'Poor Mrs Ward is it now? That's not what you were calling her a week ago when you stopped her at this very place and insulted her so much that I was ashamed of our town. Don't give me your sympathy now. You wanted rid of her. You got your way with your prayers and your vicious tongues – you got what you were looking for. It's absolution you should be seeking. You sicken me. Get out of my way.'

'Watch your tongue, Betsy Kerrigan!' Nelly Cooke spouted. 'We may have told her that Draheen was no place for her kind but, sure, what do you expect – she was writing evil stuff!'

'You should have minded your own business, frightening the poor woman when her child was so sick. You don't fool me with your prayers and your novenas. There are more Christian thoughts in a pagan. Get out of my way, the lot of you!'

'How dare you speak to us like that!' Agnes the Cat accusingly pointed her finger almost into Betsy's face. 'Can you tell me what you were doing helping Mr Ward up the street and him in a drunken stupor all wrapped around you? You seem to have got very close to Mr Ward while his wife is missing!'

'*How dare you, you evil woman!* Get out of my way or I will surely slap the lot of you. Never mind scrubbing the altar, it's your mouths and your dark hearts that need scrubbing. What are you all looking at?'

She could feel her body shaking and had to fight to control herself not to slap Agnes across the face. It was all too much. First poor Sylvia, then Mrs Ward going missing and now accusations that there was something sinful going on between her and Mr Ward.

'You pagans, with your vicious tongues! Don't ever let me hear you spread your evil gossip again or, God forbid, I will throttle the lot of you!'

'Ladies, I think that is enough disgrace for one day,' came Miss Doheny's voice as she suddenly appeared at Betsy's side. 'Draheen is already in the news. We don't need the women of the town fighting like drunks at a wedding. Shame on you! Betsy was doing her job as you all well know and if I hear any of you spreading any other rubbish, you'll have me to deal with and I'll report you to the priest. *Eighth, Thou shalt not bear false witness against your neighbour.* Are you so ignorant you don't know the Commandments? Hold your head up now, Betsy, and I will walk with you.'

Betsy was taken aback to see Miss Doheny take her side – she was not expecting an ally in her. They walked up the town together with Miss Doheny staring back at anyone who dared to look at Betsy.

'Go back now, Betsy, and I will get some supplies sent up to you. How is the little one?'

'Weak and forlorn. We are meant to bring her home this

162

morning because of the influenza breakout. I just hope she has not already picked it up.'

'Don't worry – the nuns will make sure the room she is in is sparkling and free from any germs. Try not to let those women get to you. I know what people are like, I have had my own share of it over the years. Oh, I know what people say about me. But life has a funny way of putting you in a box, especially a town like Draheen. I know you are a good Christian woman, Betsy, like your mother before you, but you are in muddy waters. Be careful, I don't know what the end of all this will be, but I fear it's not going to be good.'

'Why do you say this?' Betsy looked intently at her.

'As I say, I know you and your people before you. When I heard them accuse you of something unchristian between you and Mr Ward, I knew it had all gone too far. But it's not good. There is no sign of that woman and I have a terrible fear that there is not going to be.'

'Please, Miss Doheny, you would not say that if you didn't know something.'

Miss Doheny beckoned Betsy to come into the shop. Then she stood at the door in case anyone arrived up – they would be looking for stuff shortly.

'I overheard something, that's all. It has me very concerned for that young one.'

'Go on, what did you hear?'

'I think they are going to arrest Mr Ward. They have it that he had a fight with Mrs Ward and threatened her. They have asked for signed statements. I had to give a statement about seeing her go to the woods. Then there is the scarf with the blood on it that you found.'

'But what are they going to arrest him for?'

'They think he has murdered her and hidden her body.'

'Oh sweet Jesus! No!'

'Well, there is no trace of her. He did threaten her.'

Betsy had to sit down on the one chair in the shop. A weakness overpowered her. This could not be happening. Going to arrest Mr Ward for murder? He could be hanged for this. What on earth would happen to Sylvia?

'There's more, I'm afraid,' Miss Doheny said gravely.

'More? What could be worse than this?'

'They think you might have had something to do with it. You heard those women – but it's not just them – there are rumours flying around that you were having relations with Mr Ward.'

Betsy retched. Miss Doheny grabbed a rag and handed it to her. She had eating nothing yet that day as she had been fasting to receive Holy Communion at Mass.

'It turns out that several people noticed you walking him home that morning. To be honest, it did look bad.'

'So, they think that we have done murder together!'

'That is all I know. There are two sergeants, a plainclothes garda and the superintendent and of course Garda Flynn who can't keep his mouth shut. They are all up in that station. I have it on good authority that they are hoping that Mr Ward will slip up and lead them to where he has hidden her. But make no mistake, they will make the arrest. Soon. They have a warrant to search the house but they are biding their time.'

'I must go.'

'You never heard any of this from me, right?'

'Right.'

'Be careful, Betsy. You are a good woman. We have had our differences, but I know that you have not had any hand in this terrible thing that you are wrapped up in.'

'I have to go.' Betsy went to leave but at the door she

turned back to Miss Doheny. 'Thank you, Miss Doheny.'

With that she was gone. Her heart was racing.

Back at the house she lit the fire and put the kettle on. The kitchen was warm and, as she cradled a cup of tea, she could hear Mr Ward coming out of his study.

'I am going up at ten to collect Sylvia. Are you alright, Betsy? You look a fright.'

Betsy was not sure how much to tell him. He looked like a man who could barely take any more, but she felt she had no choice.

'I heard some rumours.'

'Go on.'

As much as she could, she repeated what Miss Doheny had told her.

Henry sat down and ran his fingers through his hair, his eyes staring into space.

'Garda Flynn had me down as the culprit straight away. If they arrest me and charge me, they could hang me.'

Betsy began to cry. Henry looked at her.

'Betsy, do you think I had anything to do with Violet going missing? I need to know.'

Betsy wished with all her heart that she believed that he didn't. But she couldn't help recall the terrible anger that could rise up in Mr Ward. Yet she knew that he loved his wife. She could hardly tell him that she was more or less sure but that a tiny part of her worried that the guards were right in their suspicions that he did have something to do with it. It was hard not to notice the rows that had begun since he had bought that building. But she couldn't really believe he would hurt Mrs Ward. Not intentionally anyway. But could there have been a moment of madness and he had harmed her? She couldn't allow herself to think about it. All that mattered was the child. She swallowed hard.

'I can see why people think it but I know how deeply you care for Mrs Ward. Oh, Mr Ward, I feel sick with worry! What will become of Sylvia if they arrest you?'

Henry began pacing the floor, up and down.

'Mr Ward, what are we to do?' Betsy implored.

'I need to get Sylvia. I will need to leave here with her, vanish from the house. If they arrest me and they can't find Violet, I will either rot in jail or die from hanging. Sylvia will end up in the madhouse with no mother or father. It will be the end of us.'

Betsy was shaking. How could this all be happening? 'Maybe if I talk to them, tell them that I know you didn't do anything.'

'No disrespect, Betsy, but from you say they think that you might be trying to cover up for me. I daresay they think you and I were coming from your cottage when we were seen together – after all, the Binchys don't actually know what time I left their house.'

Betsy began to cry.

'Betsy, I am sorry.'

'It's Sylvia – what is to become of her if they arrest you and maybe me too? You must leave and take her with you. You must leave now – they won't delay in arresting you. We must protect Sylvia.'

'I don't want to drag you into this any more than you are, Betsy. You'd better leave now – you can tell them that you handed in your notice.'

'Where will you go, how will you manage? She needs so much care. What if she gets one of those fits? She could die if she is not cared for properly.'

'I don't know, I don't know, but I think I need to leave now. If not, it will be too late and any chance of leaving here with Sylvia will be lost. I just cannot bear to think about what could happen to her.'

Betsy saw a moment of her life flash in front of her, a moment that would change everything forever.

'You can't do this alone,' she said. 'The child needs so much care. I am coming with you. I will help you to look after her.'

It was madness but there was no choice. Miss Doheny was right – they would make an arrest soon, and then it would be too late. This was their only chance. What if he had murdered his wife? She wished she was sure that he played no part in it. How could the guards be so sure? She wondered did they know something that she didn't. But what would be the end of Sylvia? With no home to go to she could end up in one of those terrible places. There was no way they would let a spinster adopt a child. And from what Miss Doheny said she could end up behind bars too for some sort of conspiracy. There was no other way.

'When they find Mrs Ward, we can come back. It's all we can do,' Betsy said.

Henry grabbed Betsy by the shoulders.

'You don't have to do this, Betsy.'

'I do. I love the child like my own. She needs me.'

Henry stood up and looked around him.

'Right, we need to plan. We won't wait until later. When we collect Sylvia we will go. They could be following us, but we will have to chance that. You pack some clothes and I will get what money and jewellery that I can put together.'

Betsy ran to her house and packed a few bits. She grabbed

the box that contained her brother's letters, some photographs and her bible. As she stood in the small kitchen she dropped to the floor and did the only thing she felt she could do. She prayed.

'Please, my God, forgive me. But I must protect this child. I feel it is your will. I beg you to help me protect her. Mary Most Holy Mother, please guide me and hold my hand. Let me not fear any evil, knowing I have you by my side.' She grabbed her rosary beads and put them in her pocket. With her heart breaking for her little home she walked out.

She was back at Eveline within the hour and quickly packed up some clothes and things for Sylvia and Mr Ward.

'We need to leave, Betsy.'

Betsy could hardly think straight. She packed some food and drinks and some blankets for Sylvia and put them into the boot. She watched Mr Ward lock the door of the house the same as if it was any morning.

It was ten minutes to ten when they left. Miss Doheny was out talking to a woman on the street as they drove up the town. She gave Betsy a nod of acknowledgment. The young girl that worked for her was there too. She kept staring at them. Betsy looked at her. She couldn't say what but there was something about the girl that worried her. The poor girl looked so forlorn. She regretted that she could not have made some time for her. Hopefully the girl would be alright. But Miss Doheny had surprised her in the end. Without her warning, they would not be aware of what the gardaí were planning. Hopefully she would look after the young girl.

At the hospital Sylvia looked as pale as a ghost. But she

was up and waiting. The nurse gave instructions for taking some medicine and told them of an appointment with a specialist that had been made in Dublin in two days' time. The nun over the ward said a prayer for her recovery and bid them good morning. The doctor would call to the house the following morning to check on her. The influenza was spreading like wildfire. Hopefully Sylvia had not contracted it.

They walked as calmly as they could to the car, Henry carrying Sylvia. He lay Sylvia down on a blanket on the back seat with her head on Betsy's lap, and arranged another blanket on top.

Henry had just got in when Father Quill arrived.

Betsy prayed he would not notice the agitation on her or Mr Ward's faces. He asked how Sylvia was.

'Frail,' Betsy said.

'I am sure she will be glad to get home. Won't you, Sylvia?'

The little girl nodded.

'We'd better be off, Father,' Henry said rather nervously.

'I might call over tomorrow to see how you're all doing. After morning Mass.'

'Thank you, Father,' Betsy replied.

'God bless you now and let me know if I can help in any way.'

He raised his hand and blessed Sylvia.

Betsy barely kept it together. She waved to Father Quill as Mr Ward slowly drove down the avenue.

At the gate, instead of turning left for Draheen he turned right.

They drove in silence for thirty minutes. Betsy could feel her heart pumping. She could barely breathe in case they were being followed. Sylvia had fallen asleep.

'I think we are clear for now,' Henry said. 'But as soon as word gets out that we are gone there will be roadblocks and searches for us. I am going to drive straight to Dublin. There is a sailing this evening. If they don't try to make the arrest today, we might just make it. Once we get to England we will go into hiding for a while. I know someone who will help.'

Betsy was crying. 'Her dolls! I had fixed her favourite doll. I forgot them, I forgot so much.'

'She will be back, Betsy, one day she will back.'

Betsy looked at the child and the enormity of their situation hit her like a slap of a shovel. They would be very lucky not to be caught. What on earth would happen if they needed medical care for Sylvia? She looked so frail.

And what if Mr Ward had murdered his wife like the guards were so convinced of? She could barely breathe with fear. Had she just got into a car with an innocent man on the run or had she put herself and the child in a car with a murderer? She reached for the rosary beads from her pocket. It was her mother's. All she knew was that she had to protect this child. It was as if her whole life was leading to this moment. Silently she began to pray.

PART 2

CHAPTER 20

Eveline House, June 2019

Emily O'Connor scrolled through the property section of the Sunday papers. She was searching for a house that could work as a studio to showcase her bridal gowns, with a room to use as a workshop. But a house that could also be a home.

The commissions were building up and the small terraced house in Stoneybatter on Dublin's northside was beginning to be smothered in her work. She adored her home but, as beautiful and quaint as her two-up two-down red-brick terraced house was, she needed something bigger.

She cut a slice of lemon drizzle cake that Sebastian had made. Her son had just gone back to Barcelona where he had moved to a few weeks previously. She loved that her son cooked, but the downside was that she was constantly eating and the pounds were starting to pile on.

'You need to watch yourself, Emily. You don't want the middle-age spread to be setting in early,' her mother had warned her the last time Emily and Sebastian had arrived down to Dunmore East for a visit.

Sebastian had come to her defence.

'Granny, Mum is voluptuous.'

'Is that what it's called today?' her mother huffed.

Her mother's house in the quaint village of Dunmore East was still the same as when Emily had grown up there. The precious china in the cabinet and the religious statues on every available counter, mantelpiece and wall. There were statues of every saint imaginable. Some had pride of place. Like Saint Therese or Saint Martin. Amongst the Communion photos and the Confirmation photos were pictures of more saints. Her friends used to tease her and ask her if they all came alive at night?

A large statue of Our Lady was in the hall with memoriam cards of those gone placed beside it. A large candle was lit when special prayers were needed. Her mother was very devout, and it had caused many an argument over the years.

When Sebastian had announced that he was an atheist, her mother made a special trip to Lough Derg on a pilgrimage to pray for him. She said three novenas and then made a trip to Lourdes on his behalf. But despite their different beliefs grandmother and grandson were very close. But her mother did have another love. That was Daniel O'Donnell the country singer. She had a large picture of Daniel over the mantelpiece next to the Sacred Heart picture.

For her eightieth birthday, Emily and Sebastian had taken her to stay in a Kilkenny hotel where Daniel was playing. She met him afterwards and he had serenaded her with the song 'Sweet Sixteen'. It was a momentous occasion. One of the few times that her mother looked truly happy.

Emily kept scrolling through the papers, but nothing drew her attention. She had to fight with herself not to have another slice of the mouth-watering cake. She had tried every diet going but her sweet tooth and the late hours that she often worked ensured that each diet was destined for failure. Recently she had even tried a water-fast diet and almost fainted. After that she resigned herself to the thought that maybe she was not meant to be thin. She was about to give in and have another slice when she saw something that stopped her in her tracks. It was an article about an upcoming auction of a house.

It was a house in a town called Draheen not far from Dublin city, out the N11 with the backdrop of the Wicklow Mountains. Emily realised that it was the same town that her mother had lived in for a short time as a young girl back in 1950. Emily tried to remember the name of her employer. Yes, it was a Miss Doheny. It was a live-in position. But she had only stayed a year and then had gone to Kerry and eventually went to work for a priest in Kenmare as a housekeeper. That was before she had met Emily's father Donal O'Connor who was from Dunmore East, at a dance in Listowel.

Her mother Peggy had not had an easy life. Peggy's father was a drunk and her mother ended up in the local asylum. Peggy at the age of eight was sent to live with her Aunt Katy who had little time for children. Katy shipped little Peggy off to Draheen on her fourteenth birthday to work in a grocery shop.

It wasn't that she ever talked about her time there. But through snippets of conversations over the years Emily had put a picture of her mother's life in Draheen together.

She had brought her mother to Draheen many years ago and she was almost sure they had stopped outside of the very house that was now up for auction. Her mother had kept staring at it. Emily remembered the wrought-iron gates. It had looked old and forgotten with clematis over the doorway. But it was quite a quaint house.

On that visit they had looked for the shop that Peggy had worked in, but it no longer existed as a drapery store. It was converted into a very hip shoe shop that stocked all the designer brands. They had gone in and as Emily had looked at the gorgeous shoes it was as if her mother was surrounded by ghosts of the past.

They had driven on to Greystones and got fish and chips and ate them looking out at the sea. Her mother had been quite melancholy and had said little about how she felt about revisiting the town all those decades later. There was so much about her mother that Emily didn't know. All she did know was that she had not had it easy. Peggy's mother had died in the asylum, so Peggy had no family except for Emily and her brother Jack. Their father had died when they were both young.

Emily read the article. It was a country house set on its own grounds. It said it was within walking distance of the main street of Draheen. It was intact but unlived-in for decades. It was open for viewing today to the public and would be auctioned with the remaining contents in ten days' time. There was a very low reserve on it, and it needed a quick sale. Emily checked the time. The viewing was on in an hour.

On impulse, she decided to go. She rushed upstairs and dressed, then glanced in a full-length mirror. She was wearing a teal silk dress which complemented her long red curly hair. She made most of her own clothes and had bought the silk at a knockdown price in Barcelona. She had inherited her father's freckles and over the years had eventually begun to embrace them.

She fed Striker the big black cat that Sebastian had rescued as a kitten, grabbed a light cream jacket and headed for the town of Draheen. She tried to tell herself that it was out of curiosity, but a nugget of excitement began to develop.

It was a Sunday morning and traffic was very light. With her satnav on she should arrive in plenty of time. She was not used to doing anything so impulsive, but the article had really intrigued her.

As she was driving out, she noticed that Sebastian had left his favourite scarf in the car from when she had dropped him to the airport that morning. It hit her that he was gone, a tug at her heart. It was hard to believe that he was now twenty-three.

'Mum, I'll be back soon. Dad and Bella will soon tire of all my messy ways. Love ya.' He grinned as he gave her one last hug before he left to catch his flight.

He was staying in his father's house for now. His father Michel lived very close to Barcelona and Sebastian had always had his own room there.

She had to hide her shock when he first told her that he had got a job as an architect in Barcelona. But it was the city of Gaudí. Sebastian had always had a fascination with buildings and architecture. He adored Barcelona, the home of his father. A city with dazzling buildings that displayed and evoked Gaudí's art. On her last trip there, Sebastian had insisted on showing her his favourite parts. He had a huge interest in Modernism. All the Gaudí buildings had to be visited. They had breakfasted every morning on delicious omelettes and aromatic coffee in the quaint coffee shops.

She had dreaded him leaving. But she knew his father would adore every hour he had with his son. Barcelona was Sebastian's second home, with tons of cousins, uncles and aunts. He had stolen all their hearts.

Discovering she was pregnant at seventeen was horrendous and announcing that she was pregnant from the Spanish student who was staying up the road was a nightmare. She was months gone before she had told anyone. It was 1996 and she had just finished her Leaving Cert and managed to get a place in Limerick College of Art and Design. She knew her mother would be devastated. She had worked so hard to give them a chance of education, taking on cleaning jobs even when she had arthritis flare-ups that made her almost cry with pain.

Her mother had not cried or got upset. It was as if she almost expected things not to go easily for her.

'You made your bed, Emily, now you have to lie in it,' she had said with little emotion. She had given her the money she had saved for her to go to college. Jack her brother, two years older, had been a straight A student but then had gone to college and got heavily into drugs. He failed every exam, eventually being turfed out of college.

Her mother managed to get him into a rehabilitation programme the same year that Emily fell pregnant. Emily had thought of adoption or travelling to England for a termination. But in the end, she left the small cottage in Dunmore East with the money her mother had given her and got a dodgy flat in Harold's Cross in Dublin and raised her son alone.

She wrote to tell Michel the Spanish student. She didn't ask him for anything. She just thought he had the right to know. But he wrote back telling her that he had told his parents and they wanted to be involved. They formed a long-lasting friendship that somehow had withstood the last twenty-three years. He had visited every chance he could get. Even when Michel married the gorgeous Bella, they always included Sebastian. They had two children Andre and Rachel, who both adored their big brother.

Now it was Michel's turn to have his son live with him. Well, at least in the same city. He planned to find an apartment. But Emily knew that Michel and Bella would spoil him so much that he would not want to leave their house.

Emily and Sebastian had dinner the night before he left, in Mi Thai, their favourite Thai restaurant in Stoneybatter. Over a large glass of Rioja, she tentatively told him of her plans. She had told him she wanted to sell their small terraced house.

'But where would you go? You love our house and you are so close to the neighbours. Stoneybatter is home.'

It was true. When she had bought the tiny terraced house, it was not the trendy place that it was today. A brother of her father's had died and shocked her by leaving her a house in Dunmore East. She had sold it and bought the rundown house that was now their much-loved home. Turning the key to her own home was something she would never forget. Sebastian was only four and they had lived in that same rundown flat in Harold's Cross from the day she had arrived home from the hospital.

She had spent hours stripping back the years of paint in their new home. Fixing the doors or grabbing a piece of furniture at a flea market. Making the tiny garden a little haven. But the tiny terraced houses with the redbrick charm had become part of a new trendy place to live and the

179

prices had soared. A ten-minute walk from the city centre and served by the Luas, it was full of historical sites, but had a new sophisticated air. She knew her little house was worth a lot more today. She had also managed to save some money over the years and had a nest egg that she hoped to use to help set up her own shop and studio.

'I adore it here but as you know I would love to have somewhere to work, a studio, and somewhere that customers could come and try the designs. I would love a house that I could do all that within the walls. But maybe outside of Dublin.'

'I love our home, Mum, but it's you who makes it home. If you want my blessing, you have it. Just be sure it's what you want. I'm so glad you are finally getting to do what you were always meant to do. Be a designer. I can see it now – *The House of Emily!*'

'It's funny, I still feel unsure about calling myself a designer. Maybe if I had started years ago?'

'You *are* a designer, a talented one and a qualified one. You just went around a few roundabouts before you got there. You are no longer the local lady who works all hours doing alterations. It's the next chapter, Mum.'

All the days of working at dressmaking in her little kitchen had paid off.

Ten years ago, Julie her best friend was getting married and asked her to make her wedding gown. She had made dresses and skirts before but nothing as ambitious or expensive as a wedding dress. Julie persuaded her and bought the material. A beautiful silk for the dress and some Carrickmacross lace for a veil. Emily was terrified at the cost of the material, afraid to cut it despite the fact she had attended lots of courses on beading and embroidery. She had done a course on lacemaking and had worked with it, making Communion veils and the like.

Julie was slight in build, so it should be nothing that would drown her. Emily put hours and hours into the creation. Inspired by the elegance of the past, it was totally romantic. Every night when Sebastian was asleep, she worked on the dress. Doing everything herself. Handstitching fragile embellishments like tiny crystals on the edging that would catch the light. During the day she was still busy with her normal work.

Finally, after months and months of working on the dress, it was completed. A floor-length sheath dress with a boat neckline and delicate long sleeves. It moulded itself to Julie's body perfectly, the lace vintage-style veil giving an ethereal elegance. With Julie's long dark hair swept up, she looked stunning. The dress was a sensation. The veil glittered with delicate stitched gems and pearls. Emily cried. She could not believe she had created something so beautiful. She knew at that moment that this was what she wanted to do. She went back to college as a mature student and completed a degree in design. After that she had not looked back.

It was quiet on the motorway and it was not long before she passed Greystones and then almost missed the turn for Draheen. She drove on and into the town. There was a lovely early-morning buzz with many having Sunday breakfast outside.

It seemed much more polished than the town she remembered with lovely cafés and artisan food shops. Flower baskets abounded and gold-embossed shop signs.

As she turned and drove up the hill on the outskirts of the town, she saw the house. It looked every bit as enchanting as she thought it would. Although quaint and charming, it was not too big. She could feel her belly fill with butterflies. This could be it.

She knew it was premature, possibly ridiculous, but her gut told her she was meant to find Eveline House.

CHAPTER 21

She parked on the street and grabbed her bag, locked the car and walked up the street to the entrance to the house. There were lots of cars around. The viewing was attracting a lot of attention. Her heart sank.

At the entrance was a wrought-iron gate. It was open and at least forty people were waiting inside to view. Mottled grey cobblestones led up to the house. Looking back, Emily could see the town. The cobbled path was lined with yellow and pink roses, thistles and weeds mingling to welcome them as they walked up the steps to the front door. A horse-chestnut tree stood to one side of the house, shading it from the June sunshine, next to a stone wall that was almost white with a wild rambling rose.

Two women dressed almost identically in white linen trousers, bright colourful tops and sandals, stood in front of her as they lined up waiting to go in. They were giggling and quite excited at the prospect of the viewing.

Looking at the crowd, Emily began to think the house would go for a lot more than the reserve price.

'Can't believe we are at last going to get a peep into Eveline,' one of the ladies in front said to her friend.

'I wonder will we see any ghosts?' her friend said, giggling, then turned around and nodded hello to Emily.

Emily was intrigued by their conversation.

'I don't mean to intrude, but is the house supposed to be haunted?' she asked.

'There is a story that it is, but sure you couldn't believe that,' the smaller of the two women replied. 'My mother used to say that it was. But sure, she also said that my eyes would go crooked if I told a lie. All with a pinch of salt, my dear. It's a very old house. My mother said that she remembers hearing of lovely roses in the rear garden. I love roses. All kinds of roses. So, I am very much here to see that. If I happen to see any ghosts, I will be sure to say hello.' She laughed.

'I have walked by those wrought-iron gates all my life and never saw a soul inside or out,' her friend said to Emily. 'There has always been a bit of talk about the house being haunted but sure that's only old folklore. When I was little, I used to run by it though just in case anything peeped out of those windows. Especially on Halloween – some of the other children would hide near the gates and jump out and scare the daylights out of you.'

'You are both locals. It seems a lovely town,' Emily said.

'It is. Lots of strangers living here now. And lots of lovely coffee shops and boutiques. You should have a stroll down,' the smaller woman said.

'Half of Draheen is out for a look at Eveline,' the other said. 'Who could resist a peek at it? It's a fine Sunday too so it will draw a good crowd. I have always tried to imagine what it is like inside. I hope there are no mice – never mind the ghosts!'

Emily felt relieved. It seemed most people were here out of curiosity.

'I read that it has been deserted for decades,' Emily said to them.

'It said in the advertisement that the auctioneer felt it was like walking into a time capsule,' the taller one replied. 'Even the newspapers strewn on the table were from the day it was last lived in back in 1950.'

'Imagine!' the other said. 'I can't wait to see it. My sister was meant to be here – we always wondered what it was like inside, so I have promised to take lots of photos.'

'Take a video and send it on WhatsApp,' her friend advised.

The door opened and a man in his fifties, dressed in a spick-and-span dark suit and shiny black patent shoes, came out. His grey hair was cut very short and a pair of glasses hung on a chain on his neck. A young woman with a sleek black ponytail and slight figure, dressed in a tight red dress and high black court shoes, handed out some promotional material to everyone.

'Feel free to have a look around,' the man said to everyone. 'If you have any questions you can ask myself or Karen here.'

The people trooped in and stopped to look at the stairs and hall.

A black-and-white tiled hall welcomed them. A carved stairway sat in the centre of the hall. Four heavy dark wooden doors led off the hallway. There were some oil paintings on the walls and areas where paintings had been removed, leaving large rectangles of a darker burgundy wallpaper. To the left was a large drawing room. Heavy gold drapes made the room appear dark and the aroma of years of dust hung in the air. A large white marble fireplace dominated the room. The floor was faded but Emily recognised it was pitch pine.

There was a small study off the room with a writing desk and a large chair. Books on jewellery-making and goldsmithing were scattered around. An inkwell that once contained what looked like black ink sat on the desk with some dip pens beside it

It all looked authentic as if you had stepped back in time. In fact, to a time long before 1950. It also looked like whoever had lived there had just left.

There were photos on the marble mantelpiece. A stunning black-and-white photo of a woman with large expressive eyes who looked strikingly like Vivien Leigh. There was another of the same woman with a tall handsome man in a wide-legged suit and a small child with curls holding her hand. The child's other hand was clutching a doll. They were standing beside a Morris Minor car. All smiling.

Why would someone leave such beautiful photographs behind? Emily wondered. A dusty polished oak phonograph sat in the corner with some old classical records. There was also a more modern record-player with a stack of records featuring singers such as Ella Fitzgerald, Bing Crosby and John McCormack. Two wing-backed fireside chairs in chocolate brown were placed beside the marble fireplace with throws that looked of Indian origin trailing on the backs of them. The material was faded and frayed. Books lined a complete wall. There were gaps with dust lodged where books had been removed at some stage.

Emily took a book down, a draught of dust catching in the half-light by the window. A butterfly flew out and took her by surprise. A beautiful golden butterfly with purple-and-pink wings. Luckily the window was open, and the butterfly escaped into the garden. The book was the complete works of Yeats. Under the window was a dark wooden bureau with a Queen Anne chair. There was an inkwell of pewter filled with dark-blue ink that had dried up completely, some dip pens and a fountain pen beside it, and what looked like a very old typewriter that had now gone to rust. At the other side of the room was a chaise longue in a dark-red velvet. It was faded and stained but Emily could see how beautiful it must have looked. A pale-blue floral wallpaper had started to peel away in places. Yet the room somehow looked lived-in, as if you could light the fire, sit and read. A glass cabinet held lots of Waterford crystal glasses and a sherry decanter that was stained and looked as if the sherry had simply evaporated but had left a dark burgundy stain behind. There was also a silver tray with glasses and goblets of all shapes and sizes.

In the next room, there was a chesterfield and a coffee table, an old radio and a table and chairs, a china cabinet with some gold-embossed china and another fireplace, this time with a large painting of the same lady. Emily could not take her eyes off the painting. Its colours were vivid. The woman really was stunning, her skin fair against dark hair and ruby lips. But whoever had painted it had caught a poignancy about her. She had a faraway look and her dark hair was loose about her face, falling in curls like those of the little girl in the photo on the mantelpiece. Her delicate neck was adorned with pearls. She looked like a movie star of the golden era of Hollywood.

Up the stairs were framed posters of plays and recitals. All performances from London in the forties.

Emily stepped into the first bedroom. It was grand, beautiful and haunting all at once. A large boudoir-style bedroom with a four-poster bed and gold-embossed wallpaper as a backdrop. The paper was peeling badly. There was a Queen Anne dressing table and mirror with ornate bottles of perfume and bottles of potions. A lady's vanity table and a large lady's and gentleman's wardrobe was at the other side of the room.

Emily had worked in a local antiques shop in Waterford City for the summer before she got pregnant, so she had some idea of the era of the furniture and items. It was there she had fallen in love with all the things of the past, seeing how each item almost held the memory of those who had owned it, each item telling its own unique story, of the different lives it had lived. It had been a discovery of sorts.

It had said in the advertisement that some of the more valuable items had already been bought by two auction houses and that all the remaining contents were being sold as one lot with the house. Emily could see that items had been removed, like the paintings in the hall. Rugs from the floor she reckoned had also been removed. Parts of the pitch-pine floors in the drawing room looked darker or less dusty. But there were still so many wonderful things remaining.

People were picking up the items and examining them. Emily felt protective of the objects. She wanted to tell the people to stop picking them up. They really did seem like they belonged to someone – someone who had just stepped out. The wardrobe lay open and she could see an array of beautiful dresses – it seemed strange that they had not been removed. They seemed so personal and were certainly designer vintage.

One was a jade-green silk dress with appliqued pink roses along the neckline and tiny little gems that she realised were all handstitched on. It was stunning. A pale-pink taffeta dress hung beside it. Blouses of silk and fitted skirts that Emily thought must have only ever fitted someone with the tiniest waist. Fur stoles that had unfortunately got eaten by moths. A cashmere wrap in the palest of pink. There were hatboxes with a selection of hats. Some with little jewels and crystals pinned on.

One woman who was unashamedly taking photos of everything on her phone remarked that whoever bought it would possibly then have an auction of the items.

Emily stepped into another bedroom with pink rose wallpaper that had turned mottled and faded. In places it looked scraped away. Her eyes were drawn to the four-poster bed with a faded cream pink canopy and a pink faded satin bedspread. It looked dusty and moths had certainly made a bed there. But what stopped her in her tracks was an array of dolls that were lying on the bed with their heads on the pillows. They looked almost ghostly as if they could come alive. She counted nine dolls, each with beautiful clothes and hair that had become a nest for cobwebs. There was a beautiful doll wearing a silken cream coat with pearl buttons, but her face looked like it had been broken and glued back together.

On the floor was a doll's house that looked faded and tired and a sad-looking rocking horse whose hair looked like it had got the mange. There were faded children's books on a little locker.

The man in the fancy suit who had allowed them in came over to her.

He pointed to the dolls which were drawing great attention from the onlookers. 'A bit eerie, I thought when I saw them – it's exactly as I found them. I am sure some collectors would pay something for them.'

'Yes, it seems strange to be selling everything as one.'

'Those are the instructions from the banks.'

'It's all so strange – as if its owners had just walked out.'

'This house somehow got forgotten through the years.'

'I am very interested,' Emily heard herself say.

'Well, it's a good solid house. We have had a surveyor have a look. There is a reserve. But it's at a knockdown price for a quick sale. There is some interest but the fact that it is to be auctioned might set a lower market. Put in an offer or see you at the auction. It should be interesting.'

'Why does it have to be so quick?' Emily asked.

'Time is money, I expect. It has sat here for decades with the deeds gone missing. They turned up lately and, as the house had a mortgage that was not repaid, it is now the bank's to do with what they want. The bank doesn't have any interest in any items unless they are of significant value. They just want rid of the lot. It's not worth the hassle for them.'

'I see. Well, hopefully I will see you at the auction.'

'Come early to get a seat – I have a feeling we will have lots of onlookers.'

She nodded in agreement. It felt more like a day out for the local ladies of Draheen. There was also a group from a local historical society taking photos and making lots of notes.

Emily walked around the rest of the house, her belly full of butterflies. There were three other bedrooms and one looked like it had been used for painting. There were some beautiful pictures on the walls – watercolours of woodland animals, flowers and woods. Possibly done by a child but certainly a talented one. The old paints and brushes were left there as if just waiting for the child to come back.

There was a large bathroom upstairs with a standalone bath. A shelf that had lots of potions and lotions all either rancid or empty. Emily picked one up. It was a vanishing cream of some sort and had a stamp from Harrods of London. There was a tiled mosaic on the walls of the bathroom in gold and green.

The two large drawing rooms downstairs could easily be turned into a studio and a workshop. Back in the hall she went through another door that led to the kitchen and a pantry. Her eyes fell on a faded green dresser filled with now-vintage treasures of delph, china and odds and ends. All sorts of old-fashioned crockery and pots and pans, some gone to rust. But some looked very much untouched. It was remarkable how intact it all was. It could easily be turned into a kitchen and living space.

There was a smaller bathroom with baby-blue cream floral tiles downstairs. The floors of pitch pine were so beautiful she could only imagine what they would look like when they were brought back to life. A thick carpet runner in green and gold lined the carved staircase and had luckily not been removed for the sale.

The advertisement had said the house needed new wiring and plumbing and a heating system put in. But the structure and roof were sound. Emily felt protective of the house. She could see how it could work. The first drawing room as a studio to display and try on the designs and a workshop in the other drawing room or parlour. The kitchen was big enough for her to make into a living area. Upstairs three of the rooms could be bedrooms – one for her, one for Sebastian and a guest room – and the other two could be used as maybe an office or a storeroom. It all needed work. But it was perfect.

Then she stepped into the rear garden. It was completely wild but was surrounded by a stone wall with a wild white rose rambling across it. The garden had a clear view of the Wicklow Mountains. A pink rhododendron was in full bloom and wisteria wrapped itself around the back of the house. The smell of violets filled the air. She was sold in that moment. If the house went for anything near the reserve, she would have enough but if it went for more it might be too much for her and she knew she would be gutted. Her instinct was that this was the house. She knew she had utterly fallen in love with Eveline House.

CHAPTER 22

After eventually leaving the house she realised she had the whole day with no immediate plans. There was loads of work waiting for her, but it could wait. She decided to drive down to Dunmore East to visit her mother Peggy and Jack her brother who was living there with her. She had not seen her mother since her last visit when they had argued about Sebastian going to Barcelona. Her mother did not approve of Emily giving her blessing to Sebastian and made her feelings known.

'You should put your foot down and let him stay in Dublin where you can keep a good eye on him.'

'But it's his life, Mam, he is a grown man. I can't stop him, and I would not want to.'

'Well, I suppose that is what comes of all this in the end. If his father was at least Irish, this would not be happening.'

Emily had to restrain herself from storming out. Her mother never lost a chance to give her a dig. Yet, despite her mother's misgiving about how he was conceived, she knew she adored him and would miss him deeply.

Sebastian used to travel down to see Peggy every second weekend before he moved. In truth he had a much better relationship with her than Emily did. He played cards with her for hours, devoured the soaps with her as they drank huge amounts of tea together.

Emily stopped for a coffee along the way and had to fight to resist the tempting pastries. She bought some fruit to eat instead.

Her mind was in overdrive thinking of Eveline House. It was as if it had cast a spell over her. She would make an appointment with the bank and one with an auctioneer that she knew. See what could be done. Philip Doyle was an auctioneer and his son was friends with Sebastian. He had told her that he could have a buyer for her house if she ever decided to sell. Stoneybatter was home but something in her yearned for a different type of life and she knew it began with moving. The idea of being near to Dublin but in a town really appealed to her. Draheen had looked like the ideal town to begin her new chapter.

She took a detour and stopped at a Sunday market to buy a few things for her mother. Some freshly made brown bread, a jar of local honey, some free-range eggs and a coffee cake with walnuts and pecans that smelt divine. Some fresh strawberries and new potatoes.

As she drove into Dunmore East, she never failed to love how familiar it felt. The smell of the sea air, the scent of the saltiness and the glimpses of the waves. It really was so quaint. But it was the coves that she really loved about her home village. How many summers had she spent gallivanting with her friends off through the rocks to Stony Cove and Badgers Cove with big bags of salty chips and the odd can of beer? Only coming home when the moon was beginning to shine on the water. Stealing her first kiss. Sharing her secrets and her woes.

She had many happy memories. It was a haven. She had

thought of moving there but the truth was she knew she would find it hard to live so close to her mother. She was never able to talk to her. She was well in her eighties now and Emily felt guilty for not wanting to spend more time with her. Perhaps it was the age gap as her mother was quite set in her ways. She felt bad for Jack. Her mother could not be easy to live with. Knowing he was there took the burden off her but she knew that wasn't fair. It was just the way it was. Her mother was in good health for her age. She'd had a slight stroke a few years earlier but had recovered mostly. It would be easier if they were close. She knew her mother loved her in her own way, but it was as if her melancholy affected everything. It was not depression. It was more of a feeling of disappointment with life that emanated from her.

Peggy lived near to the village in a little cottage.

Emily parked on the road and walked around to the back door. A large black-and-white cat lay in the sunshine and five kittens scrambled away into the garden shed when they saw her.

She could hear the radio as she went into the little hall and then into the kitchen. Her mother was sitting at the small round kitchen table listening to the one o'clock news where a man was rather dramatically reporting that a local councillor had opened a new supermarket in Waterford City. Her mother looked up in shock when she saw Emily come through the back door.

'Emily!'

'Hi, Mam. Thought I would surprise you.' Emily smiled as she came in and dropped her bits and bobs on the table.

'My goodness, Emily, you never called to say you were coming!'

'It was just an impulse thing. I wanted to surprise you.'

'But I have nothing ready and it's lunchtime,' her mother said worriedly.

'I'm not even hungry, Mam. Don't be fussing. I was on the road earlier and I decided to take a trip down. Sebastian left last night so I just thought it would be good to call down.'

'Jack and I had a rasher sandwich earlier and we were leaving the dinner till a bit later.'

Her mother was not letting up about the food.

Emily noticed the dark circles under her eyes. Her skin was paler than usual. Her grey hair was cut in a sensible short style. She had never been a good sleeper. Emily remembered often hearing her awake, praying in the middle of the night.

Peggy had changed into her customary grey skirt with a cream blouse, her Sunday clothes back in the wardrobe for next Sunday. She went to morning Mass every day but she had separate clothes for that. Sunday clothes were different.

She was forever worrying about having food ready and having plenty to eat in the house. Emily reckoned that it came from the times when she struggled to feed them as children after their father died. The fear of her children being hungry never left her. Also, Emily knew that as a child her mother had been left hungry at times.

'I brought you a few things and don't be worrying about dinner. I told you I'm not hungry, but I would murder a cuppa. I'll put the kettle on. I have a coffee cake here and it is dying to be eaten.'

Her mother got up and Emily noticed that she had become a little feebler than before. Her arthritis was beginning to worsen. Although it was June her mother had an electric Duplex heater plugged in.

The kitchen had not changed much since Emily was a

child. The holy pictures had become more plentiful and were dotted literally everywhere. All the statues were arranged on the dresser with some good cups and plates. The countertop was clear except for the toaster and the microwave. The rusty-orange tiles had holy pictures stuck to them with bits of sticky tape. The Formica presses were painted magnolia every year. The walls then got a coat of magnolia at the same time. A small round table, with four chairs and an oilcloth with green flowers and a faded yellow background, was in the centre. There were about six geraniums trailing at the windowsills.

She filled the kettle while her mother took out some mugs, the milk jug, the sugar bowl and some small plates with the willow pattern on them from the press.

Emily looked over at her as she began to cut the cake. 'Were you at Mass?'

'The priest is away in Lourdes. We have some stand-in called Father Tim if you don't mind. There is not an ounce of religion in this one. Not an ounce. Trying to finish it as quick as he can so he can go off with Mary Caldwell and Vicky Henderson to the golf club. He should never have been allowed to be a priest. He nearly fired the Holy Communion at us he was in such a hurry. No sermon whatsoever except to say that there would be a field day next Sunday and a golf tournament for the parish. I tell you I have no idea what is going to be the end of it all.'

The priest she was referring to was young and not her mother's cup of tea. Peggy did not approve of priests not wearing their priestly clothes outside of the chapel and had told Emily that she thought it shocking to see them dressed in denims and T-shirts and they had no right at all to be going around in shorts.

197

'The other day I was down at the post office collecting my pension when up comes Lily Boland's brother, the priest home from Africa. As bold as you like with a bike and dressed in a pair of those terrible tight shorts that they insist on wearing. I had to look away. It was enough to put me into hospital. Our Lord never meant his followers to wear those things. Disgraceful.'

Emily tried to hide a giggle. She would have loved to see her mother's reaction to the priest in his tight cycling shorts.

'How's Jack?' she enquired as she made the two mugs of tea. 'Is he here?'

'Up at least. He is looking at some film in the sitting room. He is forever looking at films of course, it drives me mad. He pulls over the curtains and makes it look like no one has got up out of the bed. I have no idea what anyone must think when they see the sitting-room blinds shut in the middle of the day. Especially when it is a Sunday. Not that that matters to him or you.'

'Look, why don't we get out for lunch later? My treat. Hopefully we can get Jack to agree.'

'Highly unlikely. He doesn't go anywhere anymore. Sleeps, eats a little and collects his dole.' Her mother shrugged her shoulders in defeat. In fairness she had tried everything with Jack, but his life was merely an existence.

Emily felt a stab of guilt. She had done little to help him.

'I'll make a coffee and take it in to him.' She knew how he liked it. Strong and sweet. 'Well, you and I can go anyway. Maybe into The Granville in town. You never know who you might meet in there.'

She placed the mugs of tea and the plate of coffee cake on the table.

'I don't want you spending your good money when I could put on some potatoes here,' said Peggy, 'and I have some gammon steaks.'

'I insist and we will bring Jack back something if he's not up to it.'

Her mother signed. 'Jack is not up to anything, Emily. Nothing.'

Emily felt another stab of guilt. Her brother's life had really crumbled. Jack had been clean for years, but it was as if his binge of drugs had stolen his life anyway. He had never really recovered mentally.

'I'll see if he wants to come. By the way, you'll never guess where I have just been?' Emily busied herself making the coffee for Jack.

'Where?'

'I have just come from Draheen. In Wicklow. The town you worked in for that Miss Doheny in 1950. Well, can you remember that house we saw when we visited years ago? The one on the edge of the town? It's called Eveline House. Maybe you can't remember it. Gosh, it must be ten years since we were there.' She hesitated. She knew her mother did not like anyone doing anything impulsive. 'Well, it's up for auction and don't be shocked but I am thinking of selling up and buying it. It's going for quite a steal and my house is in quite a good catchment area so should be worth quite a bit –'

At that moment her mother's mug of tea fell from her hands, crashed to the floor and broke into smithereens.

Emily swung around. Her mother's body was slumped on the floor.

CHAPTER 23

'*Mam! Mam!*'

Peggy's eyes flickered open.

'*Mam, are you okay?*'

'It's alright. I just got a weakness.'

Emily helped her up to sit back in the chair.

Emily had no idea what had just happened. She was forever worried that something could happen to her mother when she wasn't around. She was on medication, but her last check-up had been fine.

Her mother slowly seemed to come back to reality. But she was clearly shaken.

'Just sit, Mam, and try to relax. I think we need to get you to a doctor.'

'No!'

'But, Mam –'

'It's just a bit of weakness. Stop fussing.'

'I am hardly fussing – a minute ago you were in a heap on the floor.'

'Emily, I'm fine. I just have a touch of vertigo. I have my tablets upstairs. I'll take some in a few minutes. There's no need to go to the doctor.'

'I'm not so sure, Mam. I would prefer if you got checked out.'

'No, Emily, I'm fine. It's just vertigo. A bit of a dizzy spell.'

But her mother was staring ahead as if she had seen a ghost.

'You should be taking it easier, Mam. I wish you would come up to me in Dublin for a few days. Have a proper break. You have not had a break in so long. Or I could take you away for a few days, even to the sun. It would help your bones.'

But her mother wasn't listening.

'What were you saying about Draheen and that ... that house?' she asked.

'Oh, nothing, Mam – never mind.'

'No, tell me, what were you saying about it?'

'I was telling you about the house I saw – it's called Eveline.'

'I know what it's called,' her mother said quietly.

'Well, I'm thinking of selling and moving to somewhere outside of Dublin. Somewhere I could work and show off my designs and live. So that house in Draheen is up for auction. It's a bit strange, to be honest, as whoever lived there left the same year you were there – 1950 – and never returned. It was as if they had just walked out. Are you okay, Mam?'

'Yes, go on,' her mother whispered.

'It's as if time has stood still all these years, Mam.' She took out a brush and pan and began to sweep up the broken mug. 'So weird. There was this bed with all these dolls lying on it. As if the child playing with them had just stepped out of the room. There are portraits of the family that lived there. She was really beautiful and he was really handsome. They had a little girl. A very pretty little thing. But you must have known them – at least to see?'

'No. Never. They had left by then.'

'If I sold my house, with the money I have saved I could possibly buy it. Well, that is if it goes for the reserve. I know it seems very grand. But if I were to rent a shop and workspace it would be huge money, so this way I can do everything under the one roof and it's not far from Dublin so it's quite central. It needs work but they want a quick sale which might work in my favour. It's just gorgeous and perfect for what I want. What do you think? I spoke to Sebastian before he left last night. I wanted him to have a say in it. I never expected to see a house so soon. It was just pure luck that I was looking this morning and saw it was being viewed today. Anyway, Seb is cool with it all and he has given me his blessing to sell.'

'Why Draheen? Why go to Draheen?' Peggy said accusingly.

'Well, it just came up to be honest. I had never thought of it. You say that as if I looked there on purpose. Is everything alright, Mam? You seem upset. Mam, you're trembling!'

'After all these years! Why now? Why go to that town?' Peggy cried.

Emily was taken aback. 'Why not? Why does it upset you so much? I know you worked in the town but I never knew you had much feelings about the place. It's very trendy now, not like it was when you were there all those years ago.'

But her mother was not listening. She closed her eyes.

'Mam are you alright? Would you like to lie down?'

'Yes, I will lie down. I'm not feeling that good after all.'

Emily helped her up. 'Come on, a lie-down will do you

a world of good. I'll go in to chat to Jack. Drag him away from whatever movie he is stuck into.'

She helped her mother into the hall. She really was quite shaken. They slowly mounted the stairs.

At the door of her bedroom Peggy stopped and turned to Emily.

'Emily, you shouldn't buy that house,' she said. Her face serious and full of concern.

'Why would you say that?'

Her mother looked distant. 'Draheen is a strange town. The people of it might not welcome a stranger.'

Emily shrugged. 'But times are different today, Mam. People move around all the time. It's not far from Dublin so I would think there are loads of people living there that are not originally from there. Don't be worrying. I am only looking. It would be good to get out of the city.'

'Yes, but Draheen is not an ordinary town. It is not like any other town.' With that she opened the door and walked slowly to her bed.

The bedroom was papered in tiny pink flowers and her dresser held more holy pictures and statues, a bible, prayer books and a blue rosary beads. A picture of Emily's father.

Her father had been a kind man, a quiet man who had worked hard for his family. Emily had many happy memories of fishing and swimming in Dunmore with him. They never had much money, but they never noticed. When he died his loss was great. With no proper insurance or pension, times had been very tough for Peggy. Emily knew she had worked so hard for them.

Her mother took off her cardigan and slipped out of her shoes. Emily turned down the blue bedspread and helped her mother to lie down.

'Can you pull the curtains, Emily, please?'

'Mam, maybe I should call a doctor – you really look terribly pale and you're trembling.'

'No, I just need to lie down. Turn on the electric blanket. I do feel cold.'

'Yes, that will soon have you warm,' she said soothingly. 'I will just pop down and bring you up some tea.'

She was just going out the door when her mother spoke again.

'Remember what I said, Emily. Draheen is no ordinary town. I really think you should forget about that house. There will be other houses but not Eveline. Not Draheen.'

Emily went out and down the stairs. What was that all about? She knew her mother worried constantly about everything. She didn't like any change. She was sorry for mentioning Draheen. She was dying to know what she was talking about though. Why was she being so mysterious and tight-lipped about the place? If anything, it made her even more intrigued about Eveline House and Draheen.

CHAPTER 24

The next day Emily had a busy morning. She had a commission for a silk wedding dress, and she had literally spent months getting it perfect. Her client Rosa was a tall thin Swedish blonde who had fallen in love with Ireland and an Irishman. She was coming for her final fitting today and Emily was praying that it would be perfect. It was a bias-cut silk sheath that was minimalistic, understated and incredibly elegant. It was timeless and possibly Emily's favourite creation to date. But she was nervous. The fitting had to be perfect.

Rosa arrived on time and Emily barely breathed until the dress was on. Then she allowed herself to breathe again. It moulded her body perfectly.

After she left, Emily put the dress away. She would deliver it later to Rosa's apartment as she wanted to make sure absolutely nothing happened to it on the way.

Around midday she made some calls. First to the auctioneer she knew who lived in Stoneybatter and then to the bank. The auctioneer was very confident that her house would raise enough funds and he already knew of people who would be interested. Next, she made an appointment with the bank in Harold's Cross. They would see her in the afternoon. She had held an account there since she first moved to Dublin. She had managed to build up some funds that would be enough for a sizeable deposit if she was to secure the house. Also, she would need to borrow some money to renovate it. Her meeting went well. Her accounts looked healthy, so she was assured that all looked good for her to go ahead. The auctioneer had given her a name of a surveyor to check out the house. She rang the surveyor and he said he would contact the auctioneer and see the house as soon as possible.

She knew it must all sound a little ludicrous. It was the first house that she had really visited but it had absolutely stolen her heart. She held a belief that things were just meant to be and for some reason she knew she was meant to find Eveline. It was a beautiful house, but it needed rescuing.

So, if the reserve did not go too much higher, she felt she would be able to put an offer in that just might be acceptable. She would possibly have to borrow more than she had anticipated to make it habitable, but it could all be managed.

She tried not to get too excited because she knew she would be deeply disappointed if she didn't get it. But the more she thought about it, the more perfect it seemed to be.

Emily had worked hard on her designs, developing a website and a social-media platform. She was showcasing two of her dresses at a very prestigious charity-ball fashion show in Dublin and she knew that if it was a success it could be huge for her. There would be lots of what she now knew as 'influencers' there.

She had a beautiful lace creation that she was going to showcase at the ball and a pink chiffon dress that looked so delicate and ethereal it was fairylike. The ball was in a few weeks' time and she was finishing off the two dresses every hour that she could.

But through word of mouth the commissions were coming in too and her head was buzzing with designs. Bespoke wedding gowns were big business and she had found a niche that suited her. Her designs reflected the glamour of old Hollywood.

Her mother had recovered later yesterday evening and had got back up out of bed. Neither of them mentioned the house again. Jack had broken his film binge to eat some dinner. Her mother was not up to going out. Emily had cooked mashed potatoes, cabbage and gammon steaks. She made a bread sauce with some cloves to go with it.

She had noticed how incredibly pale her brother had become and his teeth had deteriorated terribly from his endless cups of coffee and the cigarettes. But it was the melancholy that emanated from him that concerned her most. He was so handsome when he was younger with a thick head of black curls. But the drugs had stolen so much from him.

She had mentioned her mother's strange reaction to Draheen and Eveline House.

Jack had just shrugged. 'You know Mam. It's all *Angela's Ashes* when she talks about her young days. Having no money and having to go out to work when she was only fourteen. A kind of Dickens novel. Sure, she was only a youngster when she went to work in that shop. She worked long hours I am sure for little money. She probably resents it all now. Seeing the youth of today, it was so different in her day.'

'She does seem to have a bit of ill feeling about the town. I won't mention it anymore.'

'Well, good luck with the house, sis. Don't worry too much about Mam's reaction. No matter what you would have suggested it might not be right. Imagine being able to even think about doing that. I'm proud of you, sis.'

Emily had given him a hug. She knew he was genuinely glad she had done so well.

Their mother arrived in then and insisted they all say grace.

'Jesus, Mam, no one says grace anymore for feck's sake,' Jack said.

'Well, while you are under my roof you will.'

Her mother knew where to strike to hurt Jack. Jack was thirty-five, yet she spoke to him as she would to a child.

Emily knew there was no point in antagonising her. They said grace and had their meal. Then they ate more of the coffee cake which proved to be even more gorgeous than it looked.

'You should watch what you're eating, Emily. The older you get the harder it is to lose it.'

Jack flew to her defence. 'Emily looks just fine, Mam.'

'I am just saying you don't want to let the weight get out of hand.'

Emily could not answer her as she was munching on her second slice of coffee cake. But at least her mother was back to herself. Giving both of them grief. The house in Draheen was forgotten. For now, anyway.

Thinking back now, she should have looked in her mother's house while her mother was asleep. Maybe there was something there from her time in Draheen. She would have a snoop the next time she was down. Mentioning the town had possibly triggered some difficult memories. But one thing for sure was that Draheen of 2019 was far removed from the town her mother worked in.

She rang the auctioneer to see if she could have another viewing the next morning. He agreed.

CHAPTER 25

In the early morning the house looked even more beautiful. She noted that inside the entrance you could easily get about three parking spaces. In her mind's eye, she could imagine a sign in gold lettering: *Eveline House of Bridal Designs*. She laughed. She was not used to getting so carried away.

The auctioneer arrived right on time but, just as he let her in his phone rang. He apologised and went back outside to talk to someone.

Emily walked in alone. There seemed to be so much she had not seen before. The dusty Waterford crystal chandelier in the hall, the rose-pink ceramic doorknobs, the ornate cornices and architrave and the dark bog-oak stand with a black gentleman's umbrella hanging from it. The scent of the past like a forgotten story lingering in the air.

She took the door that led into the kitchen. On the dresser she picked up two frayed and dusty cookbooks and a little box with handwritten recipes. How precious, she thought. Even though no one had lived in the house in so long, she could imagine how homely it would look. The range was a cream Aga and she had googled them and was amazed to realise that it could still possibly work.

There was even a calendar with a photo of a fox from 1950.

Next, she went outside into the rear garden. Even in the early morning it was so sheltered by the stone walls it looked beautiful. She spotted some yellow roses the colour of crushed lemons peeping out amongst the weeds and briars at the bottom of the garden. There were red and pink roses too. A real rose garden. And, of course, the wild violets that seemed to scent the air like perfume. With some work it would be a wonderful haven.

The auctioneer was still on the phone outside when she came back into the hall.

She went into the large drawing room. She gently took down the portrait photo of the man and woman with the young girl. What was their story? Where were they now? Why had they left their photos behind and everything else?

The auctioneer startled her when he arrived back in and she jumped.

'Sorry, didn't mean to startle you.'

Emily put the photo back on the mantelpiece, her eyes lingering on it.

'The family simply disappeared,' he stated. 'The woman disappeared first. Some say that something happened to her, others say she was having an affair and ran away. Then the father and child disappeared one day with the housekeeper and were never seen again. All a bit of a mystery. There were lots of stories, but nobody really knows what happened.'

'What kind of stories?' Emily asked curiously.

'Well, there was an investigation into the mother's disappearance. She was a playwright and there was a bit of a stir about it at the time. It was, I am sure, very unusual for a woman to go missing and of course she was quite a

211

striking woman. I am sure the papers were all over it and she was well known in London. But nothing ever came of it. She never turned up. And, of course, the father and daughter had disappeared too. The deeds of the house remained with the bank as just beforehand it was mortgaged, but there were never any payments made on it. They had also bought what was the old bank but there was money owed on that too and never paid. The house and the building returned to the bank. But the deeds of the house were lost and possibly forgotten for years. That is until recently. Now they want rid of it. It's the way they work.

'Is that all you know about the family?'

'Well, from talking to people that seems to be the story. I do remember my father talking about her. He said she was like a movie star and looking at that photo and her portrait she was. The family name was Ward as I recall. Are you still interested?'

'Absolutely. Tell me what Draheen is like.'

'Draheen has changed beyond recognition since I grew up here. It was very much the small town, and everyone knew everyone, but the fact it is so close to Dublin has changed it completely. Today it is a very up-and-coming town. A little pretentious maybe for me, lots of fancy coffee shops selling queer coffee and it's hard to get a ham sandwich without someone trying to sell you some strange vegan thing. But it's perfect for Dublin. A kind of village in a town close to our city centre. It's a perfect location and I think, if the banks took their time, they could ask a lot more. But they don't want the hassle of doing up the house, of course.'

'My surveyor is coming tomorrow to have a look at it, if that is okay?'

'He telephoned me. That will be fine.'

'How old is the house?'

'It is dated back to 1850 as far as I know. I am not sure of much history before the family lived in it. I think though it was sold in 1949 to the family from the bank. A family called Boyne built in originally. They had a mill out the road although there is little left of it now with the new motorway. But there are no Boynes now living in Draheen. It must have been the last of them. Just to mention, there is a basement too. There was an entrance to it beside the stairs but over the years it was blocked off and it would need a builder to knock down a wall to get into it. But it could probably be used as storage or something in years to come.'

'I wonder why it was blocked off?'

'Our surveyor reckons it was blocked off to retain heat. It was possibly used to store coal and would suck the hot air out of the house when it was opened. There is an entrance to it outside. Come on and I'll show you.'

They walked to the back of the house and near the rear garden he pointed to the wall of the house.

'It looks like someone was thinking of breaking the entrance into it again but then never bothered to finish it and just blocked it up again. It could be reused as I said for storage but would need renovation.'

'Okay, thanks for telling me. I am sure my own surveyor will advise me.'

She spent the next half hour going around the house while he talked endlessly on the phone. She was sure this was the house. She could picture what she would do with it. She was intrigued by what he had told her about the family. It sounded like there had been some scandal.

She went back upstairs and into the bedroom with the dolls. What on earth would she do with all this stuff if she did get it? It might be old but somehow she knew it was precious to someone at some point. Very precious. She picked up the doll with the broken face. How terribly poignant she looked there in her faded silken coat and broken face, her hair matted and full of cobwebs. Emily vowed to somehow get the doll restored if she bought the house.

Afterwards she decided to grab a coffee in a gorgeous coffee shop that was completely pink. It was called the Pink Chocolate Box. It was also a chocolate boutique and the aroma was just divine. She could not resist one of the handmade truffles with her latte.

She had seen a sign for a woodland walk. She still had some time before she would have to get back to Dublin. She changed into some runners and drove to the woods.

There was a church and then a little further on a sign and a car park. *Blythe Wood*. How brilliant to have all this on the doorstep. She headed off for a walk.

It was a heavenly wood covered in buttercups and daisies and a haze of wild hawthorn. There were lots of people having a lunch-time run or bringing their skinny lattes and sitting on the few benches scattered near the entrance, basking in the early June sunshine.

She walked on admiring the trees and the aroma of wildflowers. She walked towards a little manmade pond deep in the woods. There was a family of wild ducks that looked rather tame swimming peacefully around. What a perfect little place!

As she walked on, she saw a sign for a graveyard. *Suaimhneas Graveyard*.

Intrigued she followed the small wooden arrows. She arrived at a clearing and a metal plaque with the name. The graveyard looked ancient and some of the headstones dated back to the famine and before it.

There was a plaque erected on a stone wall in another area. It seemed to be a mass grave.

It read:

To all those who died during the famine of 1847.

Let them never be forgotten.

Erected by Father Quill and the parishioners of Draheen, 1951.

There was a slight eeriness about the place.

Then there was another area which was walled in. It contained three tombs. The writing on them was too worn and difficult to read.

Suddenly she just wanted to get back to where the trees were not so dense.

She walked away and came upon a little holy well with medals and pictures and prayers hanging from a hawthorn tree. There was a little seat and she sat down. The sun was sending shafts of light between the trees. She closed her eyes to shade them from the sun and then like a thunderbolt a memory hit her.

She had been here before. She had no idea when it was, but an intense feeling of déjà vu hit her. She tried to think hard. But it had left her as quickly as it had appeared. It was an intense memory, but it was fleeting though very unsettling.

She walked on back into the full sunlight and sat on a seat. It hit her again – that same feeling that she was here before. Could her mother have brought her here when she was younger? She had never remembered being brought here as a child and when she had brought her mother to the town a few years previously they had never ventured down here. She tried to dig into the recesses of her mind, but nothing emerged. Just a feeling of this not being the first time she was here.

The sun was bright, and the light sound of birdsong should have made the place perfectly peaceful, yet an uneasy feeling had crept over her and she moved back to the car.

Once back on the road she tried to shake off her strange feeling of familiarity with the woods and instead concentrated on how perfect the house would be for her. It would take work and commitment, but she knew it could be so beautiful and the location was perfect. She had spotted some stylish boutiques in the town and a bespoke jewellery shop as well as a very expensive lingerie shop which could work well for her gowns as sometimes finding the correct lingerie for underneath was an issue. Soon the feelings that had surfaced in Blythe Wood had faded and her head was buzzing with all she had to do.

She had just finished a commission for a lace veil for a bride and she had a consultation with a new client who seemed to have a million requests about how her wedding gown would look.

She checked the time – she had lots of time to get ready for her client who judging from her phone calls would demand lots of attention.

She arrived home and set up for her client's arrival in the small sitting room which was now completely converted into a showroom and design studio. It was decorated in French vintage with distressed floorboards, cream walls interspersed with a delicate embossed wallpaper in cream and lilac and ornate mirrors. A vintage-style wooden screen allowed for some privacy. A chaise longue in dove-grey and a small glass coffee table completed the room. But as pretty as the room looked, Emily knew it was only a temporary solution. A new workspace was now critical.

She had water and glasses ready when the bride arrived in with her mother and three bridesmaids. Emily counted herself a good judge of character when it came to her clients and she knew instantly this was going to be tough. She was right.

Jenny Wright handed her a folder of cuttings of wedding gowns. There were hundreds of photographs. She then put three of the photographs in front of Emily.

'I want it to look like this at the front and at the back like this and as tight as this.'

Emily studied each photograph.

'I want you to make my dream dress. A complete showstopper. Nothing else will do,' Jenny stated rather grandly.

'Jenny, you are always a showstopper,' one of the bridesmaids said. 'Gosh, my head is on fire! Does anyone have any paracetamol?'

Emily noted she looked a bit ill.

'No cocktails for you, Tanya – you are a lightweight!' another girl shouted as she plonked herself down on the couch.

Emily looked at the photographs and tried to hide her distaste. Each dress was horrendous.

'I want my bust to look as big as possible,' Jenny said. 'Remember Pippa Middleton's butt stealing the show from poor Kate? Well, think more Kim Kardashian when it

217

comes to my creation. I want it to be completely backless. Right down to the top of my butt.'

Emily was floored. She was trying to carve out her name as a designer and she wanted to be able to be proud of her dresses. This looked like nothing that resembled her designs.

She tried to put it as delicately as possible. 'My designs are very much inspired by the elegance and glamour of the forties and the fifties. I am not sure I am the right designer for your creation which looks wonderful but again much more contemporary than my designs.'

But Jenny was not so easily put off.

'I have done my research. You can name your price and double it. I have spoken to a couple of brides and they have told me that you are one of the most up-and-coming designers. I want you to make it. Don't worry about the cost or if you must spend extra hours because it is so unique. I want this dress and I want you to make it.'

Emily looked at her. She had a pout on her lips that was certainly helped by an excess of lip-fillers. She was dressed in the tightest pair of designer jeans with a white T-shirt showing a large bust and a perfectly spray-tanned midriff. Her very long curled eyelashes framed blue-green eyes and her dark mane of black shiny hair was pushed up with a pair of sparkly dark sunglasses. Her teeth were brilliant white made even whiter by an alarming amount of dark make-up. Emily tried to imagine her with less make-up and thought that if she could really see her she would probably be very beautiful without all the glam.

Emily knew that Jenny Wright believed that her world would be perfect if her dress was perfect. Unfortunately, Emily knew life was not like that. However, this was what Jenny wanted and believed and she said to name her price and that was bait that even Emily could not refuse. She had to fight with her conscience. Should she tell her the truth and say that she did not like the look of this dress and thought it was anything but glamorous? But then Eveline House came into her mind and all the money it would need.

'Leave the photographs with me and I will come up with something incorporating your requests but with a design that reflects me as a designer. That is all I can offer.'

'You make me look fabulous and we have a deal. Is this where I will be coming for my fittings?' Jenny enquired, looking around the room.

'Actually, I am hopefully moving to a permanent studio,' Emily replied. It was out before she really thought about it.

'Where?'

'Draheen. In Wicklow.'

'Oh yeah, it has a fab cocktail bar out there and a cool lingerie shop.'

They discussed the fabrics and the embellishments and did some measuring while her friends grabbed lattes in the nearby coffee shop. When Emily mentioned the cost, she was more than happy with Jenny's reaction.

'Cool. If it costs more, don't worry. Do not spare on anything!'

'I will be in touch when I've worked on the design,' Emily said as she waved her off. Her mind was already in Eveline and the studio that she would create.

CHAPTER 26

The day of the auction loomed, and Emily arrived and took her seat. Her surveyor had given her the okay. He had agreed with everything the bank surveyor had said. He was concerned that it would need a complete rewiring. Also the cost of heating the house and making it somewhat cost-efficient was a concern. He had added that to survey the basement the entrance wall would need to be knocked but care had to be taken as the house was old and any reconstruction would need careful planning. But the roof and walls were sound. He had given her a written report and she had sent it to Sebastian to have a look at. Sebastian had looked at it in detail and given her the thumbs-up.

She felt a bit sick. But she knew she was sick with dread in case she didn't get it.

The auction room began to fill and soon there was barely room to stand. It didn't look good.

As it began the auctioneer stated what the reserve was. Nobody put their hand up.

He went slightly lower and still nobody bid.

Emily looked around, waiting for the moment to bid.

The auctioneer went lower again with no response.

When he went slightly lower again Emily's hand went up. It was as if it was attached to someone else. She wondered what all the people were doing there if they were not putting in offers.

Someone else offered something a little higher. The auctioneer asked again for the reserve price and she put her hand up.

To her astonishment no one topped it. He called it again and asked if there was another offer. He said he had to check if the offer was acceptable. He went out of the room. It must have been only a few minutes but seemed a long time to Emily. She was jittery with nerves.

Then he arrived back and asked if there were any other offers. There were none.

Then with a bang of his hammer the house was sold.

Eveline House was sold to Emily O'Connor. She felt faint. Strangers were congratulating her. She wondered who they were. There was only one other bidder. He didn't exactly look crestfallen at missing out on the house. She signed the contract and organised for the deposit to be paid immediately.

She walked out, celebrated with a tall latte and rang Sebastian.

'You crazy momma! It sounds magic. I can't wait to see it. I will be home in a few weeks. I want to see this Eveline House.'

Her house was put up for sale and, true to his word, her auctioneer had an offer within two days that she was more than happy with. It was a first-time buyer who was home from Dubai and did not have to wait for mortgage approval, so it was all guns blazing ahead.

The next few weeks were a blur with packing, auctioneers and work.

Sebastian arrived home the last weekend that they had their home. She was due to get the keys to Eveline in a few days.

'We were very happy here and we will be in Draheen,' Sebastian said, giving Emily a big hug.

That was it. She didn't feel any guilt, just sadness at leaving her neighbours who threw a little dinner party for her and Sebastian.

Her mother had not taken the news well. She had arrived down to tell her. She knew the news wouldn't be well received but she was not prepared for her mother's reaction.

Her mother rarely raised her voice. She could be cutting at times with her choice of words but rarely did her voice level change.

'*You did what?*' she almost screamed at Emily.

Emily was shocked. 'I told you I was thinking about it. It's perfect for what I need. It saves me hiring a separate studio.'

Her mother was pacing the floor, all the colour gone out of her face.

'You must go back. Or ring them. Tell them it was a mistake, that you had no idea what you were doing. How on earth did you afford it?'

'My house was worth quite a bit. It's all to do with location, I am told.'

'Do it now, Emily. Tell them you need to withdraw your offer.'

'Why on earth would I do that? Mam, what is wrong with you? Why are you reacting like this?'

'I told you to stay away from Draheen and that house. But you refused to listen. I am telling you to do as I tell you. No good will come of it. Why would you do this to me?'

'To *you*? What am I doing to *you*? Mam, I have no idea what is going on with you. You are making no sense. Why are you acting like this?'

'*There will be no luck to come of buying that house!*' her mother cried.

Jack arrived in after collecting his dole. He looked at Emily then at his mother.

'Is everything okay? Mam, are you okay?'

'I need to lie down.' Her voice was barely a whisper.

Jack helped his mother up the stairs.

Emily put the kettle on, her thoughts in turmoil.

When Jack came back down they sat at the table and she filled him in.

Then it all became too much – the stress of buying a house, selling her home, work and now this strange reaction from her mother. Emily started to cry.

'I feel dreadful. I seem to have stirred something up. Maybe she is right, and I should never have bought the house. I knew she was against the idea but I didn't think she felt so strongly about it. My goodness, I never heard her raise her voice like that. She seemed so fearful when I said it.'

'Maybe there is something else going on with her. To be honest, she seems very irrational most of the time lately.'

'It can't be easy for you, Jack, living here.'

'It's my lot.'

'But it could be different. You can still do so much with your life.'

'Thanks, sis, it's nice to know not everyone has given up on me.'

The moment hung in the air.

'I'd better bring her up some tea,' Jack said.

There was no more mention of the house and, when her mother eventually got up, she seemed withdrawn. As if in a trance. She retreated again to her bedroom quite soon and Emily could hear her praying for what seemed like hours. She decided to stay the night.

But the next morning her mother was even more distant. She walked up to the church for morning Mass and stayed for about three hours.

Emily went to find her. Her mother was on her knees with a rosary beads, staring at a statue of Saint Martin. Everyone knew how devout Peggy O'Connor was.

Peggy got up and they walked back. Her body was hunched. Emily tried to get her to talk but it was useless.

Peggy had some tea and toast and then headed back to the church.

Eventually Emily knew she'd better make tracks back to Dublin. She told Jack she would be back in a few days to see how Peggy was then. But she felt a terrible guilt leaving. Well, there was no going back. The deal was done.

Hopefully Jack was right and it was something else that was bothering their mother. She would try to convince her to go to the doctor and maybe have some tests done.

Four days later Emily drove down to Eveline with the keys. There was so much to do. Getting workmen – painters, a carpenter and an electrician. As she turned the key, she felt a sense of surrealism knowing this was now her home. She walked around, admiring everything as if it was her first time. It really was a charming house with a sense of the past that was almost tangible. Then she set to work. She knew where she wanted to begin. She had wanted to work on the master bedroom.

She began clearing out the wardrobe. She had wanted to do it alone. She felt she owed it to the woman whose beautiful clothes were left hanging there. They were exquisite but because of being left there for so long were very dusty and stained. She put some gloves on and began. She adored the jade-green satin one and after putting a sheet over the bed she laid it down on it. The stitching was superb and the embellishments all of course done by hand. She decided to try get the dresses cleaned and then she would decide what to do with them. She certainly did not want to part with them. She should keep them as an inspiration for her work. In fact, she suspected she would end up keeping most of the personal belongings. She couldn't imagine just dumping them. A thought struck her. There was a heritage house in Draheen that might be glad to accept such vintage items.

She moved over to a chest of drawers and looked at the ornate bottles of perfume. There was a vintage bottle of Chanel No 5 and, when she opened it, she was amazed that there was still some of the precious liquid inside.

She pulled out the drawers of the dressing table. There were some underclothes folded in the drawers, still intact. Mostly all made from the finest silk and lace. She was about to close the drawer when she saw the edge of an envelope. She pulled it out. A faded cream envelope with elegant handwriting on the front of it.

It was addressed to a Mrs Doreen Clarke in Whitewater,

County Westmeath. It was not sealed. It wasn't really hers to open but she knew she couldn't resist.

She sat at the dressing table and began to read it.

Eveline House
January 12th, 1950

Dearest Mama,

I am making one last bid to reconcile with you. I know in your eyes I have deeply disappointed you. But I beseech you to try to forgive me for the sake of your granddaughter.

Sylvia is the most precious thing in the world to me. I have never known a love so pure.

But Sylvia is ill. Very ill. An illness that frightens me so much that at times I cannot breathe. We live in a town as I have told you in my previous letters that has not welcomed me.

Someone sent poison letters and Sylvia was the first to find them. Calling me a witch and threatening us. The writer of the letter warned us to leave Draheen.

But, dearest Mama, my poor Sylvia has a very strange illness. She is so little and what has happened to her has my heart broken into bits of tiny glass. We found her almost dead. Her body was full of cuts and wounds. Her body bruised. Yet it seems that somehow she harmed herself. I fear something terrible has happened to her. Something evil has somehow grabbed hold of her and I am so very frightened for her.

The doctor thinks it could be some psychological disease, but he does not know much about it. He wants her to see some special doctor in Dublin. But

*the chaplain of the hospital is sure that her wounds
are not of this world. I am so scared for her and I beg
you to come to Draheen. I feel you are the only person
who could somehow help me. I don't know why.*

*If you could just try to be here. I know you have
a deep faith and I feel that will help. Please, I beg
you. Come to Draheen. I fear for her life.*

*I cannot write again after this if you do not come.
So, if I do not hear from you, this is goodbye forever.*

Your ever-loving daughter,

Violet

Emily stared at the letter. She threw it down. What had she
just opened? A fear gripped at her.

Why was it not posted? It had raised a thousand
questions. Something fell from the dressing table and made
her jump. She didn't believe in ghosts, but a very unsettling
feeling descended on her.

She put the letter in her bag and grabbed her keys. All
thoughts of cleaning and sorting out the house had left her.
What the hell had gone on with this family? Well, she had
to find out. It dawned on her that she should have done all
this before she bought the house. But she was too busy and
the auction was so rushed. This woman had disappeared.
She should have researched it. The auctioneer had said that
there was an investigation. Why had she not checked it
out? She felt foolish. Well, she would have to know now.
She locked the house. She had seen a Garda Station as she
was driving into the town. That would be her first stop.

A young garda was signing passport forms for a family. She
waited for her turn and then tried to explain.

227

'My name is Emily O'Connor. I have bought Eveline House. The old house just outside the town. I am afraid I did very little research on it before I bought it. I believe a family lived there. Could you tell me anything about them? I believe there was an investigation into the woman who went missing who lived there?'

He looked a bit dubious as if he hardly knew what she was talking about. He went to talk to an older garda behind the glass screen. The older man looked up at Emily, then got up from his desk and arrived out to talk to her

'Good evening – I believe you are the new owner of Eveline House,' he said.

He was a small stout man with a bald head, and he stood with his hands behind his back.

'Step into my office here for a minute,' he said.

He opened an adjoining room that was just as grey as the station and ushered her in.

'Take a seat, please.'

He sat down opposite her. The desk was covered in brown files and empty used coffee mugs.

'Yes, I am the new owner. Could you tell me any history that perhaps I should know about it? I believe the former owner went missing. Have you any details on it, please?'

He looked at her as if weighing up what he was going to tell her. He scratched his bald head and sat back in his chair.

'Well, there was a family who lived there called the Wards. They were Irish but had been living in England. They hadn't been in Draheen very long when she was reported missing and an investigation was opened. It is a cold case.'

'What does that mean?' Emily asked.

'Well, there was never any satisfactory findings. The

case remains open in case any more evidence is found. The woman was never found. But that is about it. The father and daughter disappeared after that. With the housekeeper – a local woman.'

'Was there any idea as to what happened to Mrs Ward? Did she run away perhaps?'

'That is a possibility. There are hundreds of possibilities. But it was investigated as a possible murder case.'

Emily felt the colour drain from her face.

'In fact, they did try to arrest her husband and the housekeeper, but they had both disappeared the evening beforehand. There were searches, I believe, even in London but there was never any sign of any of them again, including the child. The gardaí at the time had circumstantial evidence but a body was never found. As I said there were many theories. But nothing really proven. The case remains opened.'

Emily's mother's words came back to her – to leave the house well alone. She tried to find her voice.

She thought of the letter in her bag. Would this be new evidence? But she decided not to divulge it. At least not for now.

'Can you please tell me where I could get some more information? I would like to know a little more as I now live there.'

'*The Draheen Post*. Their offices are over on Market Square. Talk to Gerry Hynes. He's the editor and a journalist. He knows most things about the town. He has written several articles on the missing woman. I can't give you any more information on the case, but Gerry can certainly give you some history on the house. He is quite the historian.'

Emily thanked him and came out to her car and rang the *Draheen Post*. She asked to speak to Gerry Hynes.

'Hold on a minute,' a young girl replied. 'I think he's here. Who will I say is looking for him?'

'I am the new owner of Eveline House. I am just trying to find out the history of it and I believe he might be able to help.'

'Oh, grand, Gerry is actually here now,' she said cheerily.

Emily could hear her relaying her query to him.

'Good morning, how can I help you?' came a male voice.

'Hello. I'm Emily O'Connor, the new owner of Eveline House. I was aware there was some history about Eveline, but I was unaware that it was quite a story. I would love to know a little more.'

'I can do better than that. I have lots of cuttings from the papers of that time. I researched it. It always intrigued me. Drop over to the offices. I would be delighted to tell you about it. And – welcome to Draheen.'

CHAPTER 27

Gerry Hynes was a tall thin man with a very thick head of grey hair and a grey neatly trimmed beard. He was dressed in a dark suit and rimless glasses. He brought her into a very orderly office and went to a drawer and within minutes took out a file.

'I am of the old stock. I still like to rely on a filing system. I don't trust that cloud in the sky. It's possibly my age, hard to change old habits. Take a seat. So, you want to know about the family that lived in Eveline? What do you know? It's been a subject of curiosity of mine for many years. I did a little investigative journalism on it, but it always ended at a closed shop. But someone in this town knows exactly what happened to the Wards of Eveline House. That is a fact I am sure of. Tell me, how much do you know about the Wards already?'

'Next to nothing, really.'

'I see. I wondered if the auctioneer had given out all the details of Eveline before the sale.'

'What do you mean "all the details"?'

'Well, about the Ward family.'

'To be honest, it all happened so quickly, and I was

caught up with work. I didn't really research who lived there. There are some beautiful portraits of the family and I know they kind of just left but there was something about her going missing first? I went up to the Garda Station before coming here. The garda told me to contact you. He said that the case was still open pending any new information. What do you think happened to the family?'

'Well, that is the thing – no one really knows. It seems that Violet Ward upset the people of the town by moving here. You do know that she was an up-and-coming playwright but banned in Ireland? It was a very different Ireland of course in the 1950s. Any books or plays that were written were heavily censored. Ireland was fiercely dominated by the Catholic Church and some of the townspeople did everything to make her aware of how unwanted she was. Even though the play was not performed here, everyone knew the content – not that they understood it or the intention of the playwright – and that very much upset the priest and the people of the town. Her presence here to some people tarnished the reputation of the town. Then there were letters that the child received that threatened them if they did not leave. These letters began a whole spiral of events. They were supposed to be quite vindictive, and there was supposed to be a terrible incident where the child had some sort of fit and almost died. There were even rumours that she was possessed. Sure, you can imagine the hullabaloo that would have caused. Some say this was codswallop and she had some sort of mental illness like schizophrenia but things like that weren't very well understood by the general populace back then.'

'So, when did this woman go missing?' Emily asked, almost afraid of what he was going to say.

'One morning when her child was still very ill in hospital on January 12ᵗʰ 1950. Early that morning, Violet Ward went for a walk. Some say she went to Blythe Wood and a scarf and a key were indeed found there. They had search parties out. But to this day she was never seen again.'

Emily could feel her breathing deepen. She had written that letter the day she had gone missing. She tried to steady herself.

'What do *you* think happened to her?' she asked.

'There were certainly suspicions that her husband Henry done her in, I am afraid. That he was having an affair with the housekeeper. But if he did, he did a good job of hiding any evidence. Then he disappeared with the housekeeper and the child before he was to be arrested. The police went to the house to arrest him but there was no trace of him. There were supposed sightings in England and extensive searches here and in England, but they were never found. They searched the house of course but found nothing. There is, of course, the basement at the house and they thought that he had hidden her body there but again there was nothing there. They thought then that he had perhaps moved the body. But, to be honest, from all the research that I have read I think it was more complex than that. I don't think he was having an affair and wanted his wife gone. It does point to him being guilty but who knows? He was meant to have quite a temper. Perhaps a moment of madness. But there was no concrete evidence. He would most probably have hanged for it though if he was caught. With or without a body. The housekeeper too.'

Emily sat back, weak with this news. Gobsmacked.

'I gather you never knew all this before you bought the house?'

'No. Not at all.'

'That auctioneer is a shrewd operator. He knew that if news got out about the house it might put people off, so a quick sale was decided on, I suspect. I saw the advert in the Sunday paper. It never mentioned any of this of course.' Gerry Hynes was shaking his head.

Emily thought back to all those people who had packed the auction room yet did not buy the house.

As if reading her thoughts Gerry said, 'The auction attracted quite a crowd. You see, they thought perhaps the daughter, Sylvia, might turn up. "The Jeweller's Daughter" as she is referred to by the locals.'

'He was a jeweller?'

'A very well-respected goldsmith and jeweller. Both parents came from humble beginnings, but they did very well. He had a workshop in the town and had plans to open a large jewellery shop.'

Emily felt as if she had opened a door and had no idea how to shut it. It was hard to face that she already had misgivings about buying Eveline. It was not like her to be so impulsive. She should have given it more thought and she should have for once listened to her mother. Maybe the house was cursed with bad luck or something. But it was far too late. The deal was done. Suddenly, her little house in Stoneybatter looked far too appealing and she wished she could wave a magic wand and reverse what she had done. She had an ill feeling about it all and that garda was very cagy earlier. Telling her nothing.

Gerry Hynes was looking through some newspaper cuttings.

'I gather you never heard of the old rubbish about the house being haunted either?' he asked.

Emily felt her stomach lurch. Could this get any worse?

'When I first arrived, some women joked about it at the viewing. I really didn't take much heed. I thought they were saying that just because it was locked up for so long.'

'The folklore is that the ghost of Violet Ward is searching for her daughter and can be seen through the window on certain nights. A very popular story around Halloween let me tell you!' Gerry said with a laugh.

But Emily was not laughing. She felt her stomach churn.

'Of course it had a bit of history before the Wards bought it too,' Gerry went on. 'It was belonging to the Boynes. Now they were a colourful family. The last one who lived there was a kind of herbalist. She died in unusual circumstances.'

'What kind of unusual circumstances?' Emily asked, her voice a whisper.

'Oh, well, she was found almost dead. She died shortly afterwards. Some said she poisoned herself. She was not the full shilling, shall we say. Then it was closed for a few years before the Wards bought it.'

He opened a folder and pulled out even more faded newspaper clippings. He spread them on his desk for Emily to see.

'I have a bit of a collection on the Wards as you can see. Here, have a look at these – there's something I need to attend to – I will nip out and be back shortly.'

'Okay.'

He went out of the room.

Emily tried to pull herself together. Did her mother know about this? Is this why she was so upset about her buying it? But why hadn't she warned her? Why hadn't she spoken up when she was so opposed to her buying it? Why never talk about it when they visited before?

Of course her mother had said that she arrived in 1950 and had never known the Wards.

She leafed through the clips. She didn't believe in ghosts, but it still freaked her out to think that something bad could have happened in Eveline. But truly, thinking of the house she couldn't believe that. It was a happy house. She had felt a lovely energy the moment she had stepped inside. Tentatively she began to look at the newspaper clippings.

A picture of Violet Ward. It looked like a very professional photo. Emily surmised that as she was a playwright there would have been some publicity photos taken. She was so like Vivien Leigh it was uncanny. Another photo of Violet and her husband at a charity do in Dublin. They were very debonair. A family portrait with their daughter with a doll in her hand. Emily looked at the doll. She was sure it was the doll with the broken face. The child was utterly beautiful. Almost angelic. The cuttings of the articles were there in black and white.

Playwright Missing in Draheen. Suspicion of Murder. A photo of her husband with a tormented look on his face, getting into a car and trying to shield his face with a newspaper.

Woman Vanishes without Trace. Another picture – this time of her at a theatre in London. It said it was taken the previous year in 1949 at the premiere of her play.

What Became of the Jeweller's Daughter? A photo of the child Gerry had called Sylvia.

Then Emily picked up a clipping that made her gasp for breath.

GIRL BEATEN UP IN BLYTHE WOOD.
A young girl called Peggy McCormick who works

for Miss Doheny was left beaten and badly shaken in Blythe Wood. She somehow made her way to the church where she was found partly conscious by Father Quill. But for his quick discovery of her, the young girl would surely have died.

Emily felt the blood drain from her head.

A photo showed a young teenage girl sitting beside a nun. Her head was wrapped in a bandage and her face looked battered.

Gerry arrived back in. 'You look like you have seen a ghost!'

'This girl in this photo? What do you know of her?' Emily whispered.

Gerry studied the photo. 'Oh yes, the poor girl who worked for a Miss Doheny. What was her name? Oh, look, it says it there. Peggy McCormick. Well, the story is that she knew something about the disappearance of Violet Ward. But it seems she was beaten up quite badly and almost left for dead in Blythe Wood. Nobody ever knew who gave her the beating. It may not have had any connection to the Ward family. She refused to speak and the gardaí thought she was a bit disturbed. They said her mother was locked up in an asylum so it was possibly in the family. Poor girl. I think she was from Tipperary or somewhere. She never returned to Miss Doheny's shop. She was sent to a convent to be cared for by the nuns. I have no idea where she went after that. Doheny's grocery shop had been there for generations but shortly afterwards Miss Doheny closed it and went to live with her sister in Dublin. It was all quite soon after the family disappeared. I don't know what became of the young McCormick girl. She could have ended up anywhere.'

Emily knew she had to get out of the office. She got to her feet. 'Sorry – I need to go – all this has been a bit of a shock.'

'Yes, indeed.' He got to his feet. 'It is a shocking story but a very intriguing one. I do hope you settle into Eveline. It's good to see it opened again.'

'Thank you so much,' Emily managed to say.

He escorted her to the door. 'No problem and, if you want to know any more about it, let me know. But I should warn you – the people of Draheen don't talk much about it. It threw a dark shadow over the town that they soon wanted to rid themselves of. They wanted to keep their reputation as a good Christian town intact. Most that remember it are now gone. As a young journalist decades later, when I first got interested in it, I found it was a closed shop. Swept under the carpet.'

'I understand.'

'Well, good luck in Eveline.'

'Thank you – I really appreciate your help.'

Emily tried not to shake as she left and walked to her car. She sat in and, trembling, put the key in the ignition. Then, like a bang, another memory hit her hard. She was in Draheen before with her mother. She remembered the well and Blythe Wood. There was the aroma of wild garlic everywhere. She had hopped and skipped and chased the butterflies that seemed abundant in the pretty woods. She was very young. Jack was with them. She remembered playing but also remembered her mother crying and crying. No wonder her mother was shaken when she had mentioned Draheen! But why had she lied and said that she knew nothing of the Ward family?

Her mobile rang. It was Jack.

'Sis, you must come. Mam has gone in an ambulance. I think it's her heart.' He sounded petrified.

'Oh my God.'

'Sis, she looked bad. Really bad.' Jack's voice was hoarse.

'I am on my way.'

Emily tore down the motorway. What had she done? She felt responsible. She wanted to throw the letter she had found out on the motorway. It was as if she had opened up a nightmare. Her mother had been beaten and left for dead in Blythe Wood. No wonder she wanted Emily to have nothing to do with Draheen! Did she know something about what happened? Emily felt sick thinking of the first Sunday when she had mentioned the house. She didn't listen to her despite her obvious distress. Now she could die.

'Please don't let her die!' Emily cried. She would never forgive herself.

CHAPTER 28

Emily drove into Waterford City. She went over the bridge, turned right and followed the road for the hospital.

Jack was outside the entrance to the A & E, having a cigarette. He had a baseball cap on, a black leather jacket and black jeans. He looked up with relief when he saw Emily, putting the cigarette out in a cigarette disposal bin and going towards her. Emily was shocked at his appearance. His face was grey and it was as if he had aged years since she saw him last. To her shock there were tears in his eyes.

'I was watching a movie. I hadn't come out to the kitchen for hours. She was on the floor. I thought she was dead. Emily, she might have cried out for help and I didn't hear her. She could die and it will be my fault.'

Emily put her arm around him and tried to comfort him.

'Jack, of course it's not your fault. It was lucky that you did find her. Where is she now? What's happening?'

'She's in ICU or some high-tech heart-unit place. They said they would know more in a little while.'

'Come on and I will see if I can talk to anyone,' she said.

They found a nurse who said a doctor would speak to them shortly. Emily grabbed them both a cup of tea from a machine while they waited.

Eventually a doctor arrived. Young and hassled-looking. He sat down beside them where they were sitting in the corridor.

'Your mother has had a stroke, but she is now stable. We will know how badly affected she is in a few hours. I am sorry but that is all I can tell you now.'

Emily thanked him and they began to wait.

Hours passed and it was not looking good.

Emily decided to call Sebastian.

'I'm sorry, love. I wasn't sure whether to call you or not,' she sobbed.

'Of course you were right to call me. I will get the next plane home and don't worry about collecting me. Don't leave. I will get there as soon as I can. How's Jack holding up?'

'Not good to be honest.'

'Tell him I am on my way. Love you, Mom. Talk later.'

She felt another stab of guilt. She was going through the motions and trying to comfort Jack who was eaten up by guilt. But unknown to Jack it was she who felt responsible. She was devastated to think she had somehow brought her mother to this. But telling him would make it even more real. But she couldn't let him think it was in any way his fault. If it was anyone's it was hers, not poor Jack's.

They slept on the seats in the hospital and eventually at about five o'clock in the morning the doctor told them that she was more stable and had begun to come around. They could see her one by one for a moment or two.

'You go first, sis,' Jack offered.

Emily took a deep breath and went in.

Her mother was hooked up to a machine that was monitoring her heart and her vital signs. There was a drip into her vein.

'Oh Mam!' Emily cried.

'It's alright. I'm still here,' her mother whispered.

Her breathing became laboured then and a nurse asked Emily if she would allow her to rest.

The tears were rolling down Emily's face.

Outside Jack looked terrified. Emily gave him a hug.

'It's okay, Jack. It's okay.'

'She could have died.'

'Jack, Mum was upset with me for buying Eveline House. She had warned me not to. This is not your fault. If it's anyone's it's mine. I obviously opened up some old wounds.'

The nurse overheard them and approached.

'I know how upsetting this is. But it's important for both of you to know that your mother's illness is not your fault. She is one of the lucky ones. She is still with us.'

Emily could have hugged her. Whether it was true or not, Jack and herself needed someone to tell them that. If not, they would be destroyed with guilt.

'Thank you,' Emily whispered.

'Go in for moment and see her,' Emily encouraged Jack.

When he came back out he looked calmer.

'She's sleeping. I need a fag. I'll be back in a few minutes.'

He walked out, head bent.

Sebastian's flight landed the following morning and he got a taxi straight to the hospital. When he saw Emily, he ran up and grabbed her in a big bear hug.

He sat with Peggy and she could see how much he meant to her mother.

Even Jack seemed a little lighter now that Sebastian was home. They took turns staying with her and at no point did they leave her.

Emily had to reschedule some of her appointments. The painter, the electrician and the plumber were due to begin working on the house so she had to put them off until she got back.

The days passed and her mother got stronger. She never mentioned Eveline or Draheen.

It wasn't until Sebastian had persuaded Emily to go for a bite to eat in Dunmore East that she told him what she had found out. She had not said anything to Jack.

'*Holy fuck!*' he said when she finished. 'Sorry, Mam, but that is quite a story. Poor Gran. It makes sense somehow. There was always something so sad about Gran as if she saw life as something to get through. I love her dearly as you well know, but let's face it she would never have been the happiest person. She always seemed to be quite sad. Well, except when she was at a Daniel O'Donnell show. All those statues and prayers. Maybe that's why she's so holy. It's her salvation from all this. Poor Gran!'

'I feel it's all a bit of a mess. I wish I had never seen that advert for Eveline. Then perhaps she would never have had the stroke,' Emily said, tears flowing down her face.

'You can't think like that. Let's go up to the house in the morning and have a snoop around. Jack will be fine with Gran tomorrow. You always say things happen for a reason. I think you were meant to find Eveline House. It's all very strange about Gran being there, but it might not be connected at all.'

The next morning, they left for Eveline as dawn was breaking.

Emily had filled Jack in on everything the evening before. He had taken it well.

'Look, sis, you were not to know. Maybe we will have to stop blaming ourselves,' he had said.

Sebastian walked into the house.

'Wow, Mom, it's just gorgeous!'

He walked around admiring the drawing room, the carved staircase, the study, the parlour. Then he walked into the kitchen area.

'What do you think, seriously?' Emily asked him. 'You're an architect after all.'

'Mom, you are a clever lady. It's an incredibly beautiful house and I think you got it for a steal.' He gave her a massive hug. 'Stop worrying – all will be okay in the end.'

Sebastian looked in every nook and cranny.

'Okay, I love it but there is something about it. Maybe it's what you have told me already influencing me here. But it is an old house, it is bound to have secrets held within its walls.'

'Yes. Whatever the secrets of the past, I still love the house.'

They spent the next couple of hours looking at colours and fabrics. The renovation was going to cost more than her nest-egg could cover, but she had gone to the bank and it would mean taking out just a small loan.

'Do you have a name for your business yet, Mom?'

'No, not yet. But I do need to come up with one for my website. Any ideas?'

'How about simply "Emily O'Connor Bridal Couture, **Eveline** House". On a beautiful sign on the way in. In gold, of course.'

'You think my name rather than something made up?'

'Mom, people will want an Emily O'Connor creation. Think Vera Wang. You need your name up there and you do create a design from scratch to suit each bride.'

'I think you nailed it,' Emily said with a grin.

'Great. Let's check out somewhere nice for lunch. And I have to see the shop where Gran used to work. See if we can find any clues. This Blythe Wood – we'll have to check that out too. Come on!'

'Yes, let's do that. I wouldn't dare go to the woods again without your company.'

'You know, Mom, I have a feeling that the truth is about to come out about the history of Eveline House. Hope poor Gran is up to it.'

'I know. It's as if a door to the past has opened and there is no going back.'

PART 3

CHAPTER 29

Chatham, Cape Cod 2019

The dream visited Sylvia again.

She could see the staircase and her mother standing at the top. Her white delicate hand resting on the banister with her diamond ring and wedding band on her ring finger. Her gold bracelets catching the light. She is dressed in a silk jade-green dress with pearls resting on her delicate neckline. She is calling her, her voice soft like velvet. 'Sylvia, Sylvia, where are you?' Her voice fading. Her dark hair has a silver comb with jewels resting in it. In the dream Sylvia is calling back to her, but it is as if her voice is choked, silent.

The air has the hint of a yellow sparse flower called wintersweet. Betsy likes to put them in the earthenware jug on the coffee table beside the chaise longue.

Then the dream shifts down to the parlour. The fire is lighting, glasses shine ready for drinks. She can see from an outside lamp that light flakes of snow are falling like confetti.

Then the dream moves to the kitchen. Betsy is like a busy bee getting ready with trays of canapés and shooing the cat from the window by throwing a sliver of sheep's liver outside for it to devour.

Then that fades and an image of her father appears. He is in Blythe Wood. The air is filled with the scent of rotting twigs and rotting earth. She can see the ravens nesting in the high trees. Her father is weeping and falls to his knees. His hands cover his face. She tries to reach him, but she can't. Then the wood is full of blood, a river of blood gushing down between the trees but when she looks it is coming from her own body. The red blood is thick and is beginning to congeal. The wood is now thick with the congealed blood. She cannot walk through it.

The image changes again. She is back in her childhood bedroom in Eveline. Petite Suzanne has a blue satin bonnet and a cream silk coat with pearl buttons, the doll's original red coat and hat set aside. Her hair is pinned up under the bonnet. Her other dolls are laid out on the pink satin quilt. The air has changed and has a hint of jasmine and a memory of roses. She reaches out to pick up her doll, but the doll slips through her fingers. She tries frantically to save her but then she hears the crash. Her doll's face has shattered into a million smithereens. The pieces floating like dust and catching the light from the open window. Floating away. She desperately tries to catch the fragments but like dust they disappear.

Sylvia awakes from her dream with a start.

It was dark in the bedroom. The light was on in the hall, throwing a low golden hue near the door. The light bedspread felt heavy on her fragile bones. The window was slightly opened, and she could hear the sea. The soft hum of the water ebbing and flowing. Instantly it began to calm her.

It was what had drawn her here all those years ago to this house. It was far from anyone that she had ever known, and it was near the sea. She felt her brow – it was warm. She pushed her hair away from her face. Her body felt weak as a kitten's but her mind as clear as crystal. Her mouth was dry.

Her eyes became accustomed to the light. She switched on her bedside lamp. She looked over at the dressing table. Her dresser full of bottles, potions and some medication.

She called for Max. It had frightened her. Why now, why would it all come back and so clearly? So many years she had dreamed of her mother but why now all these years later should it be so clear? Why was the memory so strong? Her mother forever young and beautiful in those memories. Her elegance and grace and the way her eyes had a glint of melancholy. But she could still feel the love that she had from her, a love so very pure that it had lasted the test of time.

Eveline was still in the recesses of her mind. She could never forget that house. The scent of violets from the garden. The Christmas roses peeking from the kitchen window where Betsy always had some hot cocoa for her. A house so full of memories that she had tried so hard to close the door on it. But in the darkness of the night the door could open. But it had not happened for a long time. She had managed to keep it away. Filling her days and always trying not to remember.

Max arrived in and flicked on the light. He was dressed in a blue T-shirt and pyjama bottoms, brown chestnut hair falling over one eye.

'I'm sorry, Max, it was just a dream. I'm sorry for waking you.'

'It's okay, I was only half asleep anyway,' he said, yawning. 'I'll pour you a glass of water. I could do with one myself. It's the heat.'

She was glad not to be alone. How could she still remember? But, in the dream, it didn't seem like years. She had tried to push the memories away for so long. It had haunted her nights and her days, always wondering. Her mother's voice was still intact in her memory, her perfume, the way she walked with a slight tilt of her chin. Her voice like velvet.

She had loved to watch her put on her make-up and paint her lips scarlet. She looked like one of her dolls. Her beautiful clothes, the silks and chiffons, the fur stoles. But Eveline was clear too in her memory. Yet she knew that her mother had not always worn fur stoles and chiffons or lived in a house as charming as Eveline. She had often told Sylvia of her life in Ireland as a child where she lived with her family. And she had told her of Lough Derravaragh and how at sunset the lough glistened like glass.

No, her mother was not brought up with fine clothes, but her elegance and grace were something that she was born with. She could see her in her mind's eye sitting at her writing desk in Eveline. Her dark head bent in thought, her pen writing her beautiful words. The scent of the woodsmoke from the fire mingling with the smell of polish from Betsy waxing. The memory of flowers and the Christmas roses that were abundant that winter.

'You look like you've seen a ghost,' Max said.

He helped her to sit up and then gave her a glass of water.

Sylvia smiled wearily.

'To be honest, I kind of did, but it was just a dream, a dream about a very long time ago.'

Max looked intrigued. 'What was it about?' Or is it for telling?' he asked with a grin.

Sylvia looked at Max. Max was like her own. His parents had lived beside her when she moved to Chatham in Cape Cod. Max was a writer. His parents had died in a car crash years before. He had lived in New York for the last few years, got married and divorced, but had returned to Chatham and had come to an arrangement with Sylvia. He would live with her and help her and in return he had a home with her. For now, it suited them both perfectly. Max meant a great deal to her and somehow she knew she did to him too.

Max had very little family and Sylvia had none, none that knew she existed at least. That was the strange thing. It was relatively easy to disappear. Chatham was a million miles from Draheen. Nobody had ever heard of Sylvia Ward the jeweller's daughter. She had simply become Miss Sylvia. Max's parents had christened her that when they first met her. She knew it was because when they tried in the beginning to engage with her she remained reclusive, not even allowing them to know her surname. So they had begun to leave muffins and flowers on different occasions on the balcony – always labelled '*To Miss Sylvia*'.

Slowly she began to form a friendship with them and with their young son Max. She was guarded about her past and they never intruded on it. The name Miss Sylvia stayed with her and that is how she was known to everyone in Chatham.

She had wanted to move to the sea. She felt, if she was ever to find some peace, living by the seashore would have to help.

'So, come on, spill the beans! What were you dreaming about, some old romance?' Max winked.

'Not quite. I was dreaming of a house that I lived in as a child. It's funny, you think you cannot recall something and then, somewhere in the recesses of your mind, it is as if you are there, dreamlike. The mind is a funny thing, isn't it?'

'What was it like? This house?'

But as much as she trusted Max, she hesitated.

'It was a very beautiful house with a garden of roses. It was not a large house, but it was a very charming house on the edge of a small town. There was a horse chestnut to the side guarding the house and we had a large black cat who liked to climb to the top and sit there viewing for a poor mouse.' She could feel Max's inquisitive eyes staring at her. 'I'm tired now, Max. Thank you for the water and for coming in to me. Why is it that only in the dead of night does the past comes back to haunt us. I will sleep now – go get some rest.'

'Okay, Miss Sylvia, I get the message – no more questions. You are a mysterious lady. I will see you in the morning with your morning coffee,' he said, smiling.

Max could not be kinder to her. Indeed, in ways he was like a son.

When his parents died he was only seventeen and he had almost killed himself with grief. He had gone out that night and had not come home. It was almost six in the morning and his parents were becoming frantic with worry. They had tried to find him and drove all over the town looking for him. But there was an accident with an oil spillage and his parents crashed their car and were both killed instantly. Max could not forgive himself and blamed himself for their accident.

But it was Sylvia who had somehow prevented him from going into total despair. She had got him some professional help and took care of him until he somehow began to stop blaming himself. She knew he still did but somehow he had begun to live with it. It amazed her how strong the human spirit could be. At times she had not wanted to go on herself but, somehow, she did.

She drifted then into a dreamless sleep and awoke to the bright light of Chatham through her window. She loved to see the light coming in and rarely pulled her curtains. Every morning the sky was different, blues, violets, pinks and yellows slicing the sky.

True to his word, Max arrived in with some freshly brewed coffee, some yoghurt and fruit.

'You spoil me, Max.'

'Some people are worth spoiling,' he said, grinning as he opened the window and let the morning fresh air fill the room.

The walls were painted an off-white and the wood panels a gentle blue. It really was a pretty bedroom with soft cream throws and a pale-blue rug on the white wood floor. Sylvia liked to think the house was like a cool summer breeze, a balm to her senses.

'I thought, after you are dressed, we could take a stroll along the beach. It's a beautiful morning,' Max suggested.

Sylvia was about to say no, but she knew that he would not take no for an answer. Maybe he was right, and it would do her good. It might blow the remnants of her dream away. It had been so vivid. But now in the morning light she knew it was only her mind playing tricks on her. The ghosts of the past had left her for now.

CHAPTER 30

It took her quite a while to get washed and dressed. But thankfully she was still able to do everything for herself. Her bathroom had a walk-in shower and afterwards she dressed in some cool linen trousers and a fresh pink blouse and cardigan. She had a cane that she used to help her to balance as sometimes her balance was not as it should be. She sat at her dressing table and for a moment the years drifted away. Her eyes were the same as her mother's. But in her memory her mother was forever young. She combed her silver hair and put some cream on her face, then sprayed her favourite French perfume. Aromas affected her deeply. This perfume had a light hint of rose.

Max linked her arm as they walked down to the seashore. The smell of the saltwater was as healing as it always was. They watched the gulls swoop for their breakfast. The white waves looked pure and, yes, the cobwebs of her dream were drifting away with the sea air. She didn't talk. She needed to clear her mind.

After the short stroll she sat in the shade with some iced tea that Max had made. She was still tired from the night before and could feel herself drift into a light sleep. Just as she felt herself drift, it hit her. The scent of wildflowers. Wildflowers that grew in Ireland in winter. At first, she thought it must be her imagination. She was in Cape Cod and it was summer. But the scent was so strong, as if she was in an Irish garden. The same aroma that scented Blythe Woods. She looked around. She was not sure what she expected to see. There was no one there and as quickly as it had arrived the aroma began to disappear. But a strange sense had come over her. She had tried to forget the dream of last night. In the cool light of day she had hoped it was just like Max had said – just the heat playing tricks on her mind.

Her mother had loved the intoxicating aroma of flowers and had been like a child when she first saw Blythe Wood. Like a memory locked into her soul, the image of her mother was as clear as day. She became unsettled sitting there. Normally she would be content with a book or magazine on art, flicking the pages and enjoying the breeze. Her mind was always full of art. It was a way of life. It was how she viewed life. Trying to see the beauty but sometimes only seeing the pain. The sea now inspired all her work – the gulls, the waves, the lighthouse. The colours of the sea depending on the light. Luckily Chatham had quite the tourist trade and her paintings sold very well in the galleries there and the surrounding different towns of Cape Cod. She tried to settle but she couldn't, the aroma of earlier had given her a feeling of unease.

She had a room converted into a studio. A large table stood in the centre and all her paints and brushes were on custom-made shelves. Glass at the front looking out on the ocean. Each time she painted it, it was different – the texture, the depth, the darkness and the light. She liked to take inspiration from the colours. The signature on the end was simply *Miss Sylvia*. It provided her with a good living and her paintings had allowed her to be independent financially.

But today her mind had drifted away into the past. She felt uneasy. She called for Max to bring her inside. She could walk but the balance problem had made it difficult for her to manage alone.

She also had a lady who called in once a day. Doris. A large lady full of fun and laughter who Sylvia adored. Doris would leave her house like a new pin and manage to put some lovely homecooked dish in the stove before she left. She did the laundry too. But mostly it was the wonderful energy this beautiful African lady brought to Sylvia's life every day that gave her such unexpected joy. She was like a bloom of energy that dispersed light as she went, leaving little petals of energy as she whisked through the house.

Max came and helped her in. Sylvia noticed that he was gone so brown from the sun. He lived a quiet life. Too quiet, Sylvia thought. She had lived her life alone. But she hoped that Max would one day find a love that brought joy to him – someone that he could share his life with. He had so much love and kindness in him. Sylvia worried about him. He too had had too much heartache for one life. But he wore it lightly, his face always ready to break into a smile, hiding any pain underneath.

'Max, I need you to do something for me.'

'Your wish is my command, kind lady,' he said, teasing.

'I need you to go on your laptop and look something up for me.'

'Okay, what's on your mind? Some ancient artist? Some new handmade paper that costs a fortune?'

'I want you to look up a house for me. A house, can you do that?' she asked cagily.

'Miss Sylvia, you can actually *see* a house these days on the internet if you have a code. But do you know the address? Maybe I can google the street.'

Technology astounded Sylvia. But no, she was not ready for anything like that. It could be demolished for all she knew and, if it was, she did not think she could bear it. She was about to tell him she had changed her mind. It was a spur of the moment idea brought on by that dream last night.

'Okay, so where is this house?' Max asked her, his hand on the laptop.

'In a town called Draheen in Ireland.' There, she had said it.

Max looked quizzically at Sylvia.

She had guarded her past for so many years, even from him. But something was pulling her there. It was more than the dream. It sounded silly but the aroma of wildflowers was like a message to her very soul. It had to be her imagination, but it had been intoxicating.

'There was a house there. It was called Eveline. I am not sure if it still even exists. But could you see if anything comes up?'

Max did as he was asked and within minutes he looked up.

'Okay, I have something.'

Sylvia could barely breathe. She closed her eyes.

'Just tell me what it says.'

'I can show it to you. It's an article that I found about an auction.'

'No, just tell me,' Sylvia whispered.

'Alright. It says that Eveline House was locked up for

259

nearly seventy years but was recently sold as a going concern. That's all I can see. But I can dig a bit more? Gosh, it looks really quaint. Very charming.'

'Does it say who bought it?'

'No.'

'Okay. That's all.'

'Would you like to talk about it? I can keep searching and see what else comes up.'

'No, Max. But thank you. That's enough for now.'

'Are you okay? You look like you've had a shock.'

'I am just not ready to talk about it yet, Max. It's something about my past.'

Max wrapped a blanket over her legs. He knew not to pursue it.

'Right, Doris is off today on that shopping trip. I can only imagine what she will buy. I am off to rustle something up for us for dinner later.'

'Thank you, Max.'

'I will be in the kitchen or in my study. If you need me just holler,' he said softly.

That night sleep would not come. Eventually Sylvia awoke and switched on her bedside lamp. Max had left a glass of water for her. She took a pill from the drawer. She had to shut out the memories. They were back to haunt her. They frightened her too. She did not want to become unwell. But the door had been opened again.

The next morning, she sat at her dressing table and began her routine. Brushed her hair. Her face was pale despite living in the sun. She looked at her hands. Old hands. Yet she didn't feel old. At times she was still young, still searching for answers. She opened a drawer and pulled out a photograph. It was of her mother and father. They looked so happy with their whole life ahead of them. He was so handsome and she was incredibly beautiful. Then she fingered Betsy's rosary beads. Poor Betsy, what would she have done without her? How precious her mementos were to her!

There was a knock on the door.

'Coffee!' Max called.

'You are a dear. Come in.'

'I am going to meet with my agent today. To see if he can give me some direction. But I will be back in the late afternoon. Is there anything you want from town?'

'No, but I do want to ask you something.'

'Go on.'

'Would you help me find out something about my past?'

'Is this something to do with that house we looked up?' Max asked gently, sitting down on a wicker chair.

'That house was my home once upon a time. It was where we lived. I have run from it for too long. But something tells me it is time to go back and face the truth. Whatever it is. No matter how painful.'

'What are you talking about, Miss Sylvia?' Max asked, intrigued.

'Max, you have often asked me where I came from. I know you thought I was English. I suppose I am in a way. I was born in London to Irish parents. But I did live in Ireland for a short time. I once lived in that house that I asked you to look up.'

'Miss Sylvia, can I ask why you never wanted to talk about it before? Your past has always been such a guarded thing with you. Are you sure you are cool to talk about it now?'

'I have never told anyone what happened, Max. To be

261

honest it was too difficult to process. When I was only eight years old the life I knew changed forever. But for some reason it is as if the past has come back to me. Draheen was a town full of secrets. Secrets that now need to be unearthed. But I am very frightened of what the truth might hold.'

'Are you alright? You look a little unwell?'

'I am okay. I am not sure I have the strength right now to tell you all of it. But I want to at least try and find out what happened. Will you help me? I need to contact the people of Draheen.'

'Of course I will,' Max said softly.

'I lost so much in that town. I was only a child when we drove away from it but in some ways, I never left it.'

CHAPTER 31

Sylvia retreated into her art studio after Max left for his appointment. She took a fresh piece of paper. She always purchased the finest quality handmade paper for her painting. She prepared her brushes and paints. The sound of a pencil against the rough paper was as familiar as her breath to her. The only other sound was of a bee trapped at the window. She opened it and watched the bee fly high into the Chatham air.

She began to lightly sketch out her painting. Her hands were mottled with age but once she began to sketch it was as if they were young again. When she was painting her interior world took over. Her body only a vessel of what she would create. The image was already in her mind. It was as if her hands were in control as she began at first to lightly sketch out her painting.

Then she mixed some paints and water and in what seemed like hushed tones of lightest grey, she began painting the most delicate hues as a background. She adored watercolours. They were gentle. Yet there was no room for blunders. Her balance was affected but it did not affect her hands. At least two hours passed, and she did not stop. She was completely in the moment.

She had to allow the painting to dry before she could begin painting in the flowers. It was of course a painting of the wildflowers of Ireland.

Strange how a scent could evoke such memories. She had no idea where it had come from. Like a whisper from the past it had caught her. In that moment, she knew somehow the time had come. How her mother had loved that fragrance and how abundant the flowers were in Blythe Wood and at the rear garden of Eveline . . . She remembered even where they grew in the garden. Peeping out beneath the frosted ground. How she had dreamed of that garden!

She knew she needed to be strong now. She had tried not to allow her memory to go back. She had carved out a life that she felt at peace in. Chatham had offered her solace. The sea, the pretty quaint fishing town with its quirky shops and painted stores. She had everything that she needed here and most of all she had anonymity. She had even begun to sometimes go out for some food. Doris would take her to see her paintings in the gallery. They were framed in large white frames. Doris would do lots of talking so she could just observe. It wasn't that she did not like people – she just found it difficult at times and preferred to be at home in her studio or by the seashore. How blessed she was to have Max and Doris in her life! They were in ways her family now. Yes, she had found peace here amongst the pretty houses and the beaches.

But now it was as if something had shifted. The ghosts of the past were pulling her back. It frightened her. But she knew that there was always going to be a time that she would have to at least revisit Draheen, even if it was only in her mind.

Max arrived back and knocked on her door before peering in at her.

'Sorry to disturb but I thought you might like a little treat. I have brought your favourite chocolate chip from Buffy's.'

'Goodness, yes, I will be out in a moment,' Sylvia replied, smiling.

She was not the type of person who had gathered friends over the years. Her life was reclusive. She had of course entered the art world but only from a distance. Enough to get her paintings into some galleries. Other than those outings, she only met the world outside when she wanted to. But Max was different. He was part of her world and she cared deeply for him. In ways perhaps the son she would have loved to have. Doris was like a large flower, always full of bloom and happiness, with her colourful dresses and her easy ways. Neither ever intruding on her inner life.

She tidied her paints. She would come back to her painting tomorrow. She knew what she was trying to capture. She needed to capture the scent of those wildflowers. Because for that fleeting moment in the garden earlier she had felt close to her mother.

Max was sitting in the bright airy kitchen. He had bought some beautiful lilac and put it in a vase, the colour instantly lifting the room.

'They are so pretty. In Ireland they grow so wild on the hedgerows,' Sylvia said almost in a whisper. 'How strange you thought to buy them just now! Thank you.'

Max handed her the ice cream. Cool and sweet and reviving all at once.

'How did your meeting go?'

'Good, I suppose,' he said as he devoured his ice cream. 'We had a good chat about where I'm going. But I feel there is something out there that I really want to write about, but I can't find it. We were searching for ideas, but I will mill over them.'

'I am sure you will find the right project when you least expect it.'

'Yes, I hope so.'

'My mother was a playwright.,' she said cautiously.

'Your mother was a playwright!'

'Yes, quite famous in London in the late forties. She had two plays written and performed to critical acclaim. Unfortunately, the third was never published or put on stage.'

'What happened, why?' Max asked, his blue eyes trying to hide his astonishment at this news.

Sylvia put down her ice cream and looked at her friend.

'Because, my dear Max, in 1950 my beautiful mother vanished in Ireland and to my knowledge has never been found.'

'*What?*'

'Yes, my mother was a playwright. Oh, her plays were not put on in Ireland. Ireland was a land of a very strong Catholic faith and my mother's writing was frowned upon. In the winter of 1950, I became very ill. And while I was sick my mother vanished. She was last seen walking up the street in Draheen on January 12th, 1950. She was incredibly beautiful and the most wonderful mother.'

'What happened?'

'Well, there is a wood at the edge of the town, called Blythe Wood. Her silk scarf with a tinge of blood was found there and the key of our home. After that the trail went cold. Max, I need to find out what happened to my mother. I can't explain it, but it is as if the past has awoken and the truth must be told. Will you help me?'

'Of course.'

'I will tell you what I know.' Sylvia closed her eyes, and, in a moment, she was in Eveline.

CHAPTER 32

Draheen, Ireland 2019

Four months had passed, and Peggy was improving. She was now in a nursing home to recuperate. Emily and Jack got down to her as much as possible. But it was clear that she was going to need lots of care.

Her mother had not spoken of Eveline since and neither had Emily. She knew she would have to but for now it was a case of letting the dust settle until her mother was stronger.

There was a lot more work needed in Eveline than Emily had anticipated. But it was all moving along a lot quicker than she had anticipated. So many decisions on plumbing, electricity, general repair and decorating. She wanted to try to be in for Christmas. But considering the contracts went through so quickly, she reckoned she would at least have her workshop opened and her studio.

She had asked Jack to help with it. To her amazement, he was delighted and had moved up to stay with her in Stoneybatter. He was out in Draheen every morning and was taking care of everything like a proper project manager for the past few months. Enormous work had been done and without him there was no way she would have made such progress. The heating and plumbing were complete.

There had been huge issues with the wiring, and it had taken more money than estimated but at least it was now all taken care of. They had even managed to get the Aga cooker working.

She could not believe the difference in Jack. It was as if he had a purpose now and it had totally taken him out of himself. He was putting all his energy into the house, which allowed her to concentrate on her brides and of course her mother. To her delight, he was investigating going back to college as a mature student. He was highly intelligent and was considering his options.

Things were looking up in other respects too.

Preparing for the showcasing of her two bridal gowns at the charity ball had been chaotic with her mother ill, but she had managed to get them finished and they went down a storm. Her lace creation was inspired by Princess Grace's wedding gown and her pink fairy creation had almost brought her to tears, it looked so angelic on the model. She had acquired more commissions and was busy trying to balance work and marketing her business. Soon she would need some help.

Sebastian had gone back but would be in Ireland for Christmas. He was looking at an apartment in Barcelona and was loving it out there. Emily was happy that he was happy – that was all that mattered. She would not allow herself to be sad that he was not in Ireland. She had him close for so long and it was not as if Barcelona was so far away. But at times she just simply missed him. She was glad she was so busy it gave her less time to be thinking about him.

Her phone rang while she was up in Eveline trying to design the work studio with the carpenter. To her surprise it was Gerry Hynes.

'Good afternoon, Emily. I hope you are well settled into Eveline House. It's Gerry Hynes here from the *Draheen Post*.'

'Oh, hi, Gerry. Yes, lots has happened with the house and I hope to be settled in for Christmas. How can I help you?'

'Would you mind popping into the office, Emily? I need to talk to you about Eveline. It's a little sensitive.'

'Okay. I'm in Draheen. I'll come straight away if that suits?'

'Perfect.'

'What's all that about?' Jack asked when she hung up.

'I have no idea. But he was helpful when I asked him about the house. Oh God, I hope he hasn't been digging and realises who Mam is.'

'He possibly wants to talk to you about advertising the business,' Jack suggested.

'No, I don't think so. Why drag me up to the office?'

'Was he cute? Maybe he wants to ask you out?'

'No, that's definitely not it.' Emily gave him a dig.

Neither Jack nor herself were lucky in love so far in life. Both had had relationships, but they had never worked out. Jack had so many girlfriends when he was younger but then when he was in recovery he had stayed away from any relationships. Emily had got so used to being on her own that she wasn't even sure if she would want something permanent. Her mother despaired of either of them ever having a relationship. But in truth Emily was always wary of relationships when Sebastian was young and now she liked her life as it was. She did go out now and again, sometimes even on a blind date set up by her friends. They had normally ended in pure disaster.

Gerry Hynes was waiting for her in his office. He looked quite animated and excited.

'Thanks for coming up, Emily. I received a letter and I wanted you to have the chance to read it. It is in connection with Eveline and very intriguing. I will print some of this. I feel you have the right to know what is going on.'

Emily did not like the sound of this. He handed her a printout of an email.

Dear Mr Hynes,

I see you are the editor of the *Draheen Post*. My name is Max Bradford and I am a close friend of Sylvia Ward. Sylvia is the daughter of Henry and Violet Ward.

Her mother Violet went missing in January in 1950 and to her knowledge vanished without a trace. Sylvia now lives in Chatham in Cape Cod in America but would very much like to know any updates on this case. We tracked some information on the internet, and we see that you have followed it and indeed have done some investigative journalism on it.

We have also written to the local police station to see where the case is. We have been told that the case is still open pending new information. We also see that the house has been recently sold.

My friend Sylvia wants to do everything she can to try and discover what happened to her mother. There was a belief that her mother simply ran away, but Sylvia is quite confident that this is not what

happened. We would very much appreciate your help.

I am adding Sylvia Ward's phone number. If you wish to verify who she is, she is an artist here in Chatham and very well respected. Her work is in many galleries throughout the area.

Sylvia has told me everything that she knows but is at a stage in her life where she would really like to know what happened to her beloved mother and at the same time clear her father's name as she believes he was under suspicion for her murder.

I look forward to your response,
Max Bradford

Emily felt sick. Why now? Why after all these years would she decide to reappear?

'What does this mean? Why does she suddenly want to investigate it? You tell me this woman is missing since 1950 – why leave it until now to figure out what happened?'

'Well, I have no idea why now. But as a journalist I would like to print that Sylvia Ward is alive. As I told you, she was called "The Jeweller's Daughter". The story of the Jeweller's Daughter has passed down through the decades in the town of Draheen. Almost folklore. Except it is all true. Well, what we know of it. I will contact her and ask her permission to run a story, but I think it is in her interest as some new information might come up. People who did not want to talk then may just decide to talk now.'

Emily scanned his face. There was no way he would have connected that girl in the photo to her.

'There is no mention of the housekeeper that went missing. I thought she went missing with them.'

'No, there is no mention of her or Sylvia's father. I looked up this Max Bradford. He is a published author. Has had some success and has done a little journalism too so just to let you know I have checked him out. His reputation is very respectable as far as I can see.'

'But what age is this woman now?' Emily asked.

'I think she is in her late seventies. So, the housekeeper and her father may well be deceased.'

'You told me that this child Sylvia was unwell?'

'Yes, well, he doesn't mention that. Not just unwell but as I said some said she was possessed. Personally, I have no belief in any of that. I have yet to respond. I wanted to check it all out to make sure it was quite authentic. I have even checked out her paintings. I am no art connoisseur, but they are quite striking. Mostly of the sea and of the landscape around the Cape Cod area. She is quite respected but possibly not very well known. But as far as I can see there is no reason why she is claiming to be this woman if she is not. The house cannot be claimed back by her. The deeds were gone to the bank and now you are the rightful owner. From the letter all she wants to know is what happened to her mother. The question is, though, why now? Why decide only now to look? I felt it only right to tell you. I think if we put an article in the paper it will put pressure on anyone with any information and there will be a bit of interest in the house. He said that they have also contacted the gardaí here in Draheen. I am not sure if they will do anything about it though. As far as I know there is no more evidence.'

'What could they do?'

'Well, it is a cold case. I suppose if there was any new evidence, they would have to act on it. But as far as I am aware there is none.'

Emily felt nauseated.

'Alright, I appreciate you telling me. If there is any more news, I would appreciate the same.'

'I certainly will.'

'Just one thing. The young girl that was in that article. Do you know anything about what she may have known?'

'No, it was a dead end as far as the gardaí were concerned. Poor girl was traumatised, I am sure. Whether she ever really knew anything or not, no one ever found out. Maybe she did but maybe the beating silenced her. Hopefully they might even follow up that line of enquiry. But, sure, if she is alive, she must be in her eighties. She could be dead.' He paused and looked at Emily. 'Are you okay? You look a bit shaken?'

'I'm fine. Really, do you think they will try find this girl who was beaten?'

'I have no idea. But it never looks good to have crimes unsolved. The papers will love it all, of course. Sure, Violet Ward was like a film star. A ringer for Vivien Leigh.'

'Yes, I can see why they would. But if there is no new evidence? What good will come of it?'

'Well, someone must know. Maybe the woman did have an affair. There was talk of the parish priest and her being very friendly. It was a different Ireland. There were many secrets.'

'Right, well, I'd better let you get on with it. Thanks again for letting me know.'

When she got home, Jack said that a local garda had arrived to speak with her and had left a number.

Emily felt sick. This was not going away.

'Sis, you have to show them that letter.'

She had eventually shown him the letter she had found and since then he had been urging her to show it to the gardaí.

'But what about Mam? If they find out that Mam was the young girl? She might not be able to cope with that. Oh God, I feel so guilty!'

'How could you know? She could have warned you of what you were getting into, but she didn't!'

'She couldn't go there, Jack! The whole thing was traumatic for her!'

'Emily, stop. Beating yourself up is not going to help you or anyone. Ring that garda.'

She rang his mobile. His name was Garda Vincent Ryan. He asked if she could call to the Garda Station. It was in connection with a missing person.

'Sis, you have to at least show them the letter. Say nothing about Mam until we see what they know. This is unreal. I need a fag. I'll make you a cuppa first. But you must tell them.'

'Jack, there is something else.'

'What?'

'Jack, can you ever remember being here in Draheen before? When we were children? At the woods – Blythe Wood? Please try to remember.'

'Now that you say it, I did think something felt familiar since I came here. But I can't remember just when I felt that. Feck, it's just after coming back to me. Mam has an old biscuit box with all those memory cards. I saw a cutting from an old paper and what I think may have been a picture of this house! I am sure of it. Shit! There is also an envelope. I was looking for Mam's passport – that time she was going to Lourdes last year. Her passport went missing and we were tearing the house apart looking for it. I came across the box and the envelope and she nearly took my head off for looking in the box. I actually had the envelope in my hand. It looked an old envelope. There was something in it like a small box. There was a name on the envelope. A name but not hers. Oh Jesus!'

'What?'

'It just had a name on it. Oh, I can't remember. But Mam nearly went spare and grabbed it from me. There was something strange about it all. Seriously, she went spare. And she wasn't right for a day or two after. Oh, yes – she asked me if I had opened the letter. I had to show her that it was sealed. I just thought it was something to do with her religious pilgrimages. Some relic or something. In fairness, it probably is – you know what she's like. Sometimes I think she would have been happier as a nun. If she is not at Mass, she is talking about it. Praying at home. It's obsessive. Did I tell you? A few months ago, she took to saying the rosary every evening. Down on her bad knee. It is fanatical.'

'Oh, still it's worth checking out. This box.'

'Yeah, we should. Jesus, sis, this is all a bit bloody much. Poor Mam! But somehow it makes sense. I often wondered did something happen to her. Sis, you must show the letter to the gardaí. It is evidence and you are withholding it.'

'Okay, I will.'

Emily went down to the station. The gardaí had received a letter similar to the one sent to Gerry Hynes, who had just contacted them to say he was going to run a story. They were going to put out an appeal for any new information and felt they needed to alert Emily to the fact. Garda Ryan apologised to Emily, saying that he was sorry that a new resident of Draheen should be embroiled in an unpleasant matter which basically had nothing to do with her, apart from the fact she had bought the house in question.

Emily felt herself flush. If he only knew, she thought.

Embarrassed she said nothing about the letter.

'*Why did you not tell him?*' Jack asked, highly frustrated, when she got back.

'Let's try and find out what is in Dunmore East first and at least be prepared,' she said. 'I'll go down in a day or two and check it out.'

The following day she was at Eveline with Jack when she got another phone call from Gerry Hynes.

'Just to let you know that Sylvia Ward has hired a private investigator. He means business. He has contacted different people here in Draheen, trying to find out anything he can. But he won't find out much. Most are dead.'

Emily knew she had no choice. She would have to confront her mother. Sooner or later they would find her and drag it all back up.

But first she would drive to Dunmore East and find that letter that Jack saw.

'Look, I'll go with you,' said Jack. 'Why don't we just stay here tonight, go early in the morning and then I can get back to meet with the carpenter in the afternoon.'

'Stay here?'

'Yes, we can use the beds in what will be Seb's room and the one in the guest room. You've bought some bedclothes, haven't you? We can work on the studio tonight and get the design right. Let's get a takeaway, get some kip and then head for Dunmore East at about six. I have my key with me.'

'Okay, you're right. I will do up the beds and then we can get down to measuring the designs. Oh God, Jack, there is so much going on I can hardly cope.'

'It's okay, sis. We can cope together. First things first, let's see what is in that box.'

They ordered a curry and worked on the studio design, eventually coming up with something they were pleased with. It was after eleven before they finished up.

They got into their respective beds, exhausted.

It felt so strange to be finally sleeping in the house. Emily planned to sleep in the main bedroom when she moved in but there was so much work to be done on it first. She had splurged on a gorgeous embossed duck-egg wallpaper. It would look gorgeous with the wood floor.

She lay there, everything going through her mind. The house. The commissions she had. She was trying to come up with a design to suit Jenny Wright. It was proving very challenging. Eventually she fell into a fitful sleep, dreaming about wallpaper and Jenny Wright's dress.

But all too soon she was awoken.

'Emily! Emily! Jesus, Emily! Wake up!'

She shot up in the bed. The light was on and Jack was bending over her.

'Christ, Jack, what's wrong? Are you trying to give me a heart attack? You frightened the bloody daylights out of me!' she shrieked.

Jack looked completely shaken.

'What's wrong? Is it Mam?'

'No, no – I just thought I saw something!'

'What? You gave me the fright of my life because you *thought* you saw something. What is it that you think you saw? *A bloody mouse?*'

'I thought I heard something, and I got up. Jesus, I think I'm going mad. I need some air.' He walked out and she heard him open the window on the landing.

Emily got up, grabbed a jumper and tracksuit bottoms and pulled them on. She shoved her feet in her runners and went out to the landing.

'Jesus, sis, am I going mad?' Jack whispered.

'What's wrong, Jack? You look like you saw a ghost.'

'Sis, I bloody think I did.'

'What?'

'Oh, look, it must be the drugs still affecting my head after all these years.'

'What do you think you saw?'

'I saw a woman in a green dress. A long dress. She had dark hair tied up and she was walking down the stairs. The light from the hall was hitting off little jewels in the dress. Millions of them. But in an instant, it was as if she disappeared. I thought I was going mad. It frightened the bejesus out of me.'

A sense of dread came over Emily as she thought of the green silk dress of Violet Ward. It had lots of glass beading. There was no way that Jack had ever laid eyes on it. She had put it into the cleaner's, and she had only collected it and put it back in the closet that day, all covered up in a special sealed bag.

'What do you mean she disappeared?'

'Look, sis, I know it sounds mad, but she just bloody disappeared. Vanished. I need a fag.'

CHAPTER 33

They cautiously went downstairs and put the kettle on. Jack lit a cigarette and opened the window to let the smoke out.

'I'm so sorry, sis. I know I've freaked you out. It must be just tiredness or something.'

'Tell me again exactly what you thought you saw?' Emily asked cautiously.

'I was asleep and I suddenly woke up. For some reason I thought that there was someone in the room looking at me. Then I switched on my lamp and obviously there was no one there. Then I thought I heard footsteps on the stairs. I called your name. I thought you must be up and not able to sleep or something. But there was no answer. So, I got up and then I could hear nothing, so I thought I had imagined it. I decided to go down and check things out anyway in case you were in the kitchen. The light was off over the stairs but there was enough light from the downstairs light to shine up. I looked down the stairs and I saw a woman in a green dress that almost touched the floor. It was dim, but her hair was dark and pinned up. It was as if the dress had lots of jewels or something on it as they were all shining. I was about to shout out I was so stunned and then it was as if she turned and vanished into thin air. I never saw her face. I rushed down but there was nobody there. Christ! The drugs obviously fried my brain after all those years of abuse and now I am imagining things.'

'I am not sure you imagined it,' Emily replied.

'What? You think I saw a ghost? Stop, sis. Hopefully both of us are not going cracked.'

'There is a long jade-green dress with tiny crystals and pink appliqued roses. I got it cleaned. It was Violet Ward's. It's exquisite. It has little gems attached. Did you see it?'

'No! Where? When?'

'I didn't think you could have. I only collected it from the cleaner's yesterday. I left it in the master bedroom. Come on, follow me.'

'You are freaking me out even more, sis.' Jack took another puff on his cigarette and then discarded it.

They grabbed their tea and went upstairs to the main bedroom. Emily took the garment out of the closet. It was completely sealed up in a white cleaner's dress bag. She took it out of its packaging.

Jack looked like he would be sick.

'That's the bloody dress.'

'Oh my God, Jack, you must have seen the ghost of Violet Ward!'

'Stop, Emily, I don't believe in ghosts. It must have been my mind playing tricks on me. Maybe you told me about the bloody dress.'

But Emily could see that he was very shaken. She put the dress back in its cover.

They went back to the kitchen and Jack lit another cigarette.

'I could murder a straight whiskey,' he said.

'Don't even say that. More tea must suffice. But I do have some nice cake.' Emily grinned, trying to lighten the mood.

They never went back to bed but, as soon as daybreak came, they locked up the house and headed for Dunmore East.

They stopped at a garage and bought some coffee and croissants.

'You okay?' Emily asked.

'Yeah, in the light of day it all seems ridiculous. There is obviously some explanation – it must have been a trick of the light.'

'Possibly.' Emily thought it better to say no more for now.

They drove on down to the cottage. The sea looked inviting and she wished she was just there to relax for a couple of hours. She didn't feel right about snooping in her mother's stuff. But they had little choice.

It was dark inside the kitchen and for the first time Emily thought it a little eerie with all the statues. Normally she didn't mind them she was so used to them. But she had never realised just how many there were. Every saint imaginable was there.

'Can you remember where the box is?' she asked Jack.

'Yip, follow me.'

He went into his mother's room and got down to look under her bed.

'It's not there. Hopefully I didn't imagine that too,' he said with a grin.

They began to search. There were lots of memory cards and holy pictures and boxes with bills and bank transactions. But no sign of that box.

Then Emily noticed that there was a pillowcase at the back of the wardrobe in her mother's room – a pillowcase that looked rather bulky. In it was an old brown wooden box with scratches on it. It was locked.

'That's not the box I saw. It was more like an old biscuit tin from years ago.'

'Well, what could be in this?'

Jack easily broke the delicate lock. Inside was an envelope. Jack took it out.

'This is the envelope that I saw in that other box. I am sure of it. She must have moved it. I wonder where the other box is?'

'Look at what it says on the envelope,' Emily whispered.

In faded ink and big sprawling handwriting was written: *To Violet Ward.*

It was sealed. She picked it up. There was something like a small box in it. It looked like it had been opened and resealed.

'What will we do?' she said to Jack. 'Should it go to a solicitor – or the guards?'

'We have come all this way. Just open the bloody thing.'

Emily took it out. There was a small velvet box and a letter. In the box was a locket in rose gold.

With her hands shaking she opened the letter and read it aloud.

My dearest Violet,

I do not know where you are, and my heart and soul are broken. I have searched and searched.

Forgive us for leaving you. But, if I stay, they will surely throw me in jail and I will possibly hang as they think I am to blame for your disappearance. I cannot leave our little girl alone in the world. Betsy is loyal to the end and is leaving with us to help look after Sylvia. Where are you? In my darkest hour I imagine something dreadful has happened to you. Please God let that not be the case.

If you should return, go to London to the pub where I first told you that I loved you. There will be a message there as to where we are. Please come back to us, Violet.

Forgive me for not heeding you and not leaving this town before. I love you.

I am sending you this locket as token of that love. Inside is something to remind you of your beautiful child and your loving husband,

Henry

Jack carefully opened the locket.

Inside were two locks of hair. One golden, one a white-gold curl.

CHAPTER 34

Draheen, January 12th, 1950

Peggy McCormick loved the two hours before the shop opened. It was the only time that Miss Doheny was not watching her like a hawk. She had written to her aunt and asked if there was a different job she could go to. But she got no response. Miss Doheny's shop was worse than anywhere. Surely there was somewhere a little easier than this. At least somewhere that she might have someone to talk to. Here she had no one. Miss Doheny treated her like a simpleton.

Peggy had taken to rising early and getting out for a walk before she began her day. She loved Blythe Wood. She loved the way the cobwebs glistened in the early-morning frost. She loved to hear the birdsong and watch the birds build their nests high up in the trees. She loved the colours and how much they changed. In autumn they were a haze of reds and oranges and even purples and of course every green and brown imaginable. It was darker in the wood now, but she loved the frost and if she was early enough it was like a glass wood, full of new clear shiny ice. She looked forward to escaping there every morning when Miss Doheny was preparing herself for the day and thought she was still asleep. She knew that Miss Doheny awoke early, prayed and then read the bible and the *Far East* magazine in her room while keeping an eye on the goings-on on the street outside. But Peggy knew how to escape her beady eye and run to the woods. Her only way to cope with the day ahead. It meant she was exhausted by the end of the day, but she had to find some way to cope. It didn't matter if it was cold or wet, she still went. In fact, it was better with the cold because she would run then and for a time forget what her life was like. She had never thought that this could be her lot. She was determined to make a life away from here.

Away from Ireland. She had seen so many go but she had no one to go with and no one to go to. Her aunt said she was too young to go to America on her own and where would she get the money for the passage anyway? But, as miserable as Miss Doheny was, she was paying her, and she was saving up every penny that she could. Her Aunty Katy had written saying that she should send any money to her and she would look after it for her. Her aunt had even tried to persuade Miss Doheny to send her money to her. But Miss Doheny had insisted that she would only pay the girl herself. If she was responsible enough to be sent to work in her shop, she should be responsible enough to look after her own money. Peggy was very thankful for this small mercy as she was sure she would not see a penny of it if it went to her aunt.

She often wondered if her mother knew about the hard life she had. Why had she gone mad? When she was little, she did not remember her mammy being mad at all. She remembered her as being full of fun. She would take her for long walks and they would pick wildflowers and blackberries and make blackberry jam. They would decorate the tree for May Day with broken eggshells and then sit and have a tea party with her teddy and her doll. Her mother told her that her life would be wonderful and told her stories of Cúchulainn and Tír na n-Óg. She remembered baking bread on the fire and at Christmas she would get some raisins and currants and her mother would make a big currnie loaf and they would eat it hot with butter running on it. She would sing to her and tell her stories.

She had little recollection of when it changed. Her mother would stay in the bed and not get out. There would be no dinner and then her father took to staying in the pub and not coming home, sometimes for days on end. She often picked nettles and boiled them and made soup because she was so hungry, her mother still in the bed. She picked wild mushrooms and cooked them herself. Her mother stopped giving her a bottle of milk and some bread-and-butter and sending her to school. But she hated school anyway. It was an old school that had only one small window. The fire took ages to light and sometimes she would sit and feel her fingers go numb, praying that the teacher would not ask her for her composition. She had used all the excuses that she could think of. She had written a composition about a tree. Her teacher had laughed and made a mockery of it.

When the fire did light, they put their dusty lemonade bottles full of milk beside the fire to warm. Then the milk tasted sour or like buttermilk. Sometimes she had no milk and would run to the river for a drink as the other children laughed.

Then her father forgot to come home altogether. Peggy often wondered if he lost his way and forgot where he lived. She often set out on the road to find him but by dusk would return without him, her mother still in bed. Maggie Joyce said he had run off with a fancy woman to Dublin and left them. She had wanted to wallop Maggie Joyce across the face for saying such filth.

On Fair Days she would go into the town to see if she could spot him. It was always full of men. They seemed to have their own language. Then they went to the pubs and drank the money, while the wives waited outside grumbling and whining.

Then the priest arrived and told her mother that her husband was dead. Found dead in a ditch. His corpse gone off with the crows feeding on it. It all changed then. They took her mother away. Screaming and roaring. They said there were rats in the house and the child was half starved. It was years later that she realised they meant her, that she was half starved.

Peggy had hidden in the henhouse, but they had found her. She did not know where they had taken her mother. They sent Peggy to Katy's. They said she was Aunty Katy. That's what she was to call her anyway. But she never knew she had an aunt. Her mother never said.

She often wondered, if her mother knew how difficult her life was, would it make her less mad and maybe she could come out of that awful place that she was in. If there was any cure for her madness. Madness was the worst thing, she did know that.

She had gone to see her once. Aunty Katy had taken her in a pony and trap. They travelled thirty miles to where she was being kept. A big huge building with a long drive down to it. With a hundred dark windows. There was a long corridor that seemed to never end. She hardly recognised her mother. Her mother did not recognise her at all. Her mother's teeth were all gone. She was crying and roaring. She cried like an animal. All the people there frightened her. It was a terrible place and Peggy wished that her aunt had not brought her there. There were young people there too.

'Be careful you don't end up like them,' Aunty Katy had warned her. 'Or you could be in with her. It's in you. The madness is in you.'

Her Aunty Katy had no time for her from the minute she arrived. She had a bed and she worked for her cleaning and cooking. She never went for any more schooling. Her aunt had shipped her off to Miss Doheny's as soon as she was fourteen.

If only she had a friend to talk to. Betsy Kerrigan had smiled at her and looked kindly at her. So had the lovely lady that she worked for. The lady that Miss Doheny and the women were always gossiping about. She had such pretty clothes and such pretty hair. She wished she could go to work for her instead. In the gorgeous house. It was like a fairy castle. She had heard she had a little girl who was very sick and had some strange thing happen to her. She had heard she was all white with blonde curls. She wished she could visit her and maybe talk to her. Maybe even play with her. She longed to talk to someone other than Miss Doheny. Miss Doheny had warned her not to talk to the customers. Not to say any more than 'Good morning, ma'am' or 'Good afternoon, sir'.

The woods had a mist this morning that reminded her of home before her mother went mad. Although she hardly knew what home was now. At least here she was away from the watchful eye of Miss Doheny. She liked to lie down under the big tree and just think and dream about what it might be like when she would go to America. She would go as soon as she had the passage. She had heard of New York and all the bright lights. Her aunt would not stop her. Miss Doheny would go mad if she thought she was wasting her time training her. Using her as a skivvy more like and making her look a fool and her all superior.

Not allowing her to take any money in case she made a mistake. Standing over her when she was measuring flour or sugar, just waiting for her to give an ounce too much. She had seen her watching her, correcting her at every turn. She never allowed her out. She might as well be living in a prison. Her aunt could say what she liked. But she was saving the fare to America and that was that. She didn't want to end up like some old dried-up prune like Miss Doheny. She would run to Dublin and get a passage to New York. She was not afraid. She was alone here anyway. It could not be any lonelier than here. She would feel bad to leave her mother, but there was no way she could save her now. The madness had got hold of her.

She was tired of Miss Doheny making her look a fool. She watched the birds grabbing their breakfast. How free and easy their life was here in Blythe Wood.

Then she got a fright. There was someone there. She crept behind the tree.

She spotted Mrs Ward walking along. It was very early for anyone to be in the woods. She admired her beautiful coat all snug and warm-looking and a beautiful soft shade of green with a fur trim in a rusty-red colour. How beautiful she looked with her fashionable clothes and hair like a movie star! She had seen some magazines and she looked like she could be in them. The doctor's wife was glamorous too and wore pretty clothes, but Mrs Ward was like a movie star. She had gone to the pictures once and saw for herself how beautiful they looked. Yes, she looked like she could be in the movies. Peggy wondered how someone was so lucky to be born with such beauty. Miss Doheny did not approve of her. Yet she seemed to never stop talking about her. 'Did you see what she had on today?' one of the customers would say and her clothes were discussed at length.

Peggy wished she could see the letter-writing that they were all talking about. It was meant to be shocking. Some said she was cursed and that's why her little girl was sick. Miss Doheny had said that she wrote filth for the stages in London. Peggy thought she looked like something exotic with her dark hair and her pale complexion and her daring red lips.

She followed her on as quietly as she could.

She had heard the women talk about her. Now they were saying that she was having something to do with the priest and that she was being punished and that was the reason her child was so ill. God was angry with her. They were all angry with her. They said how scandalous she was. Nellie Cooke whispered that she might be having relations with him and that it would have to be stopped. Agnes the Cat called her a harlot.

Mrs Ward's husband was the most handsome man that Peggy had ever seen. Well, except for Father Quill but she thought it might be a mortal sin to think he was handsome. Or perhaps a venial sin? Although she was not sure what that was. But she had heard of it. Then they were saying that Mrs Ward was much more than friends with Father Quill. ''Tis more than sherry he is having in Eveline,' she

291

had overheard Agnes the Cat say. When Agnes came into the shop she would have to get the Jeyes Fluid out afterwards and wash the part of the shop that she stood in because of the stench of cat off her.

Peggy was thrilled to hear that Mr Ward gave Miss Doheny a good dressing-down. He put her in her place. The poor daughter though sounded dreadfully sick. They were saying terrible things about the girl – that she was cursed and that she could die. There was talk of the bishop coming to Draheen to pray over her.

She knew she should go back but curiosity got the better of her. She wanted to see where Mrs Ward was walking to so early in the morning and to look at her lovely clothes for a little longer. When she got to New York she would look for a coat just like hers. She would get her hair changed to a different colour and she would buy a scarlet lipstick just like Mrs Ward's.

That was when she heard them. The group of women that went to Mass every chance they got and cleaned the church every morning except Sunday. Mass was not for another two hours. Peggy watched as she saw them walk into the woods as if creeping after Mrs Ward. But not letting her know that they were there. It looked like they were following her. There were five of them. All with headscarves, except for Agnes who wore a knitted brown cap that looked like an old tea cosy. She knew all of them. Nellie Cooke had a dour look on her face and thick glasses that made her eyes look three times bigger than they were. Molly Walsh with her bottle-green coat that she wore no matter the weather and the two Grey sisters Kitty and Nora looking all pious with their pinched faces. The two sisters looked a little simple and younger than the others.

Then at the back was Agnes the Cat. Peggy was afraid of Agnes and she was afraid of her brother Mike Dillinger. She had heard from Miss Doheny that he could kill a hen and eat her raw.

She stayed a safe distance from them to see what they were up to. They kept creeping ever so gently. She thought she better go back, Miss Doheny would wonder where she was, but she knew something was up. It was the way they were creeping softly so as not to let Mrs Ward know they were following her.

They came to the clearing near the graveyard. Mrs Ward was calling out she knew someone was following her. But they were saying nothing. They were trying to frighten the living daylights out of her, Peggy reckoned. Peggy was unsure what to do. She wanted to warn her but in truth she was afraid of Agnes the Cat and she would tell Miss Doheny that she was in the woods and goodness knows what she would say.

Then they came out from behind the trees. They were circling her. Peggy gasped. They looked odd as if they had some evil in them.

Then Agnes spoke.

'*You did not listen to us, Violet Ward. We told you to get out and leave our town,*' she hissed.

The others nodded but the two Grey sisters looked away.

Mrs Ward turned on them, her eyes bright as shillings.

'You horrible women! How could you? It was you all along. Writing those letters. How could you be so cruel to a child?'

'You have only yourself to blame. You brought this darkness with you and we want you out of our town,' Agnes the Cat spat at her.

'Don't worry, I am leaving this place and I will never

293

look back here again. You have your wish. Get out of my way. Let God be your judge, you evil women!'

But Peggy could see she was terrified too. She was so afraid for her.

'You must look for absolution first,' Molly Walsh said.

'You are a sinner, Violet Ward. This is what happens to sinners. We have our own way to deal with them,' Agnes snarled.

'What are you doing following me?'

'What are you doing with Father Quill?' Agnes spat again.

'What are you talking about?'

'We know he visits Eveline. You are an evil dirty woman, Violet Ward, and Draheen has no place for the likes of you? God has sent this terrible thing to your daughter to punish you. Repent and leave here and don't come back.'

'*I told you I am leaving. Stay away from me!*' Violet screamed.

Peggy looked around to see if there was anyone she could run to for help, but they had timed it well. There was no one about.

Then Agnes took a bottle out of her bag.

'Witches burn unless they repent.' She was foaming at the mouth.

The Grey sisters held each other's hands in fear. Nellie and Molly Walsh gaped at the scene in front of them, their eyes almost coming out of their sockets.

'*That's right, Mrs Violet Ward!*' Agnes was roaring now. '*Witches are burned. Beg for forgiveness from the Almighty. Stay away from Father Quill or you will be burn!*'

'*Agnes! Enough!*' Molly Walsh shouted.

Peggy could hear her own breathing. She wanted to grab a piece of a stick and run at the women. They were terrifying her. She was caught between fear and anger at what they were doing.'

'*Leave me alone. Do you hear me?*' Violet Ward screamed at them.

Agnes the Cat ordered them to circle her. She held up the bottle.

Peggy didn't know what it contained but it looked a murky green colour.

Agnes threw the liquid into Violet's face. Violet screamed and tried to rub it from her face. Peggy could now smell it on the still air. The smell of lamp oil.

'*Repent! Repent! Repent! Repent! Repent! Repent! Repent! Repent! Repent! Repent!*' Agnes chanted.

Peggy could hear her own heart beating.

The two Grey sisters began to tremble and Molly Walsh and Nellie Cooke continued to gape at Agnes, their hands over their mouths.

'*Repent! Repent!*' Agnes hissed and she spat at Violet.

'*Stay away from me!*' Violet screamed.

'*Repent, you whore!*' Agnes spat again.

Peggy could take no more. She was about to scream at them when Mrs Ward took to run and break away from them. But Agnes caught her, pulling her by her hair and pushing her to the ground.

'*Repent, you evil woman! Beg for forgiveness or you will burn!*' Agnes hissed.

Peggy had never seen evil before but looking at Agnes she could feel it.

Agnes let go of her hair and kicked her, then threw more liquid.

295

'*Alright, whore! It's your choice! Now you must burn!*'

'*Noooo!*' screeched Molly Walsh.

Agnes had pulled a box of matches from her pocket.

The Grey sisters were frozen to the spot, their mouths gaping, as Agnes lit the match.

Nellie Cooke grabbed Agnes's arm and tried to blow out the match.

Violet Ward got back up, made a run for it, stumbled and fell.

Peggy heard the crack. Like when a brick hits a cold pavement. One clear crack. She knew it was her head. Bright blood oozed onto the stone where she lay. The women gasped and stared at Violet. Peggy could see that her eyes were open. Peggy had seen dead people before but only at wakes when they had been laid out, never like this but she knew in that instant that Violet Ward was dead.

CHAPTER 35

Peggy watched, barely able to believe her eyes. She was terrified to move in case anyone knew she was there. A twig broke under her foot and her heart leapt to her throat.

Molly Walsh screamed. The two Grey sisters began to wail. Nellie Cooke had her hand on her mouth.

Agnes the Cat looked around as if she was checking if anyone was watching them.

Violet Ward lay still, blood now coming out of her mouth and nose.

Molly Walsh began to scream louder.

'*Shut up!*' Agnes the Cat shouted.

'We have to get the doctor!' one of the Grey sisters cried.

'For what?' Agnes the Cat whispered. 'She is dead, you fool!'

'*Oh my God, look at her eyes! She is dead! We have killed her!*' Nellie screamed.

'Keep your voices down. We must act quickly,' Agnes ordered.

'Will I run for the doctor and Father Quill?' Kitty Grey asked, her voice quaking.

'*Are you mad?*' Agnes hissed.

'But she needs a doctor or a priest!' Nora Grey cried.

'It's too late!' Agnes spat at Nora.

'*No, no, no, no, no! We killed her!*' Nora cried and the two sisters began to howl.

Agnes slapped each of them across the face.

'*Never let me hear you utter those words again!* We need to act quickly. Come on, grab her legs and arms. We'll hide her, cover her up with leaves and branches until I get help.'

'Are you getting the doctor?' said Molly Walsh

'You stupid woman! Do you want to be thrown in jail or worse the madhouse? Or hang? Are you all mad? Well, I am not hanging for her. It was an accident. We only meant to frighten her. But there is nothing we can do now the woman is dead.'

Nora Grey was a slight woman so thin that you could almost see through her, her lined face almost identical to her sister's. She knelt and began to say the Act of Contrition into Violet Ward's ear.

'*Oh my God, I am heartily sorry for having offended Thee and I repent my sins –*'

'*Get up, Nora Grey!*' Agnes the Cat roared. 'It's too late for her to look for forgiveness. She made her own bed, the whore. Right, come on, grab her.'

Peggy was still in the same spot. Tears flowed down her face as she watched, trembling, while the women dragged poor Mrs Ward's body into the bushes and covered her with branches and leaves.

'We'll need help to get rid of her,' said Agnes.

Then she left, warning the others to hide if they heard anyone coming.

They barely moved and time passed.

Agnes arrived back with her brother Mike Dillinger. She pulled the branches back.

'*What the fuck have you done?*' Mike roared.

'I'm telling you it was an accident – but no one will believe us,' Agnes said.

'*You fuckin' mad bitches!*' he shouted at them and raised his fists threateningly.

The women cowered away, terrified. Only Agnes stood her ground.

Mike lowered his fists and spat. He looked at Violet Ward.

'We have to leave her here for now. I'd better cover our tracks.'

He got to work to cover the place where she was hidden even more thickly with leaves and branches. The sweat rolled off him. Big beads of sweat that even reached his nostrils. Then he began to sweep the area around with a big branch to cover any tracks.

'Gather around, ladies!' Agnes ordered in a tone not to be messed with.

They obeyed.

'I warn each of you – what happened here this morning will never be spoken of again,' she said.

'You can sing that,' Mike Dillinger growled. 'You have me implicated now, you stupid bloody women! *Speak of this and I will kill each one of you with my bare hands! Are you listening?*'

They all nodded, trembling and white-faced.

'What will you do with her?' Nellie asked.

'The Bullock will have to be told – he can help,' Mike said, referring to Molly Walsh's husband. 'We will come back tonight and deal with her. I warn you, if I hear a whimper out of any one of you, you will all end up where she is going!'

'We won't say a word,' said Nellie Cooke, her voice shaking.

Mike glared at Molly Walsh. 'You tell the Bullock. Tell him to meet me here at dusk. It won't take long with the two of us. I'll bring some tools.'

He stood and glared at each of the women in turn.

'*Remember, not a word or I'll come for you.*'

With that he walked away.

The Grey sisters were weeping.

'Stop it!' Agnes ordered. 'Stop right now and forget this ever happened. There will be a right fuss over her when the alarm is raised. Not a word, any of you. We must go now before anyone sees us. We must go to Mass like we always do. So stop that snivelling right now.'

They left, Agnes leading the way.

It was raining now, and the woods had become darker. Peggy listened to the sound of the raindrops on the leaves. Her clothes were soaking. She tried to move her legs, but it was as if the use had left them. She wondered was she mad like her mother? Could she have imagined what she had just witnessed? It had been too horrible and evil to be real. She began to sob and heave, terrified that Mike Dillinger would come back and find her and put her with that poor woman. That poor woman who only an hour earlier she thought was the most beautiful creature she had ever seen. Now lying with her head cracked and rivers of blood oozing out of it. Her eyes staring. Dead. Like the dead mice and rats in the woods. She had to get out of there.

She tried to move but her stomach heaved. She retched

up bile and began to weep. The rain was pouring down now, covering all tracks.

There was no sign of the horrific scene and blood of earlier.

She crept out of her hiding place. She wanted to go over and at least pray over poor Mrs Ward, but she was too afraid.

As quietly as she could she crept out of the woods and went back to Miss Doheny's. She changed her clothes, but she could not stop shaking. She was terrified to tell Miss Doheny. That man could kill her.

Miss Doheny was about to open the shop.

'Where were you?'

Peggy did not answer.

'Why are your hair and shoes wet?'

Peggy looked at the eggs she had collected earlier before going to the woods.

'What? You went out in that rain to collect eggs? Oh, for goodness sake! You look sick. Go on, get a cup of tea and get yourself together. I cannot have customers looking at you like that. Hurry now!'

She stayed awake all that night. Trying not to think about what those two men were doing with poor Mrs Ward.

The next day she heard about the searches and watched poor Betsy look for her. Her poor husband going out of his mind. Her heart was broken for the little girl too.

Two days later she was in the shop measuring flour into bags. Agnes the Cat arrived in for some bacon. She looked at Peggy and said hello. Peggy could not reply. She knew she was staring at her, but she could not help herself.

'Peggy is not herself,' Agnes remarked.

Peggy spilled some flour.

'You can sing that, Agnes,' Miss Doheny retorted. 'She's not been herself for the last few days and if she does not improve she will find herself back where she came from!'

Peggy dropped the whole bag of flour on the floor and Agnes stared at her.

And Peggy knew that Agnes realised that she knew something. She didn't sleep that night.

A week later, on Sunday, Miss Doheny went to see her sister in Dublin. Peggy visited the church. She went in and prayed and prayed for some strength. She knew she should tell somebody what had happened. She felt weak. She had barely eaten since it had happened. She slowly dragged herself from the church to go back to the house. But something compelled her to turn and walk towards the woods. She couldn't go in – the very thought of the woods terrified her. But she wanted to get closer to where poor Mrs Ward's soul had left her body. She wanted to pray for her there and maybe work up the courage to go to the Garda Station.

Then someone grabbed her from behind.

'So, what do you think you know?'

Agnes the Cat was in front of her. Someone had grabbed her arms behind her back and held them so tight it felt like they would break. Without seeing him she knew. She knew that Mike Dillinger was her captor

He dragged her into the woods. She would meet the same fate as Violet Ward. She tried to scream but her throat was frozen with terror and no sound came out. She looked to the sky. Then she could see only the tops of the trees over her head. She felt something hit her back and then her head. She fell. She was hit again, this time in the stomach and then again on the head. Blows from a heavy stick rained down on her. She felt the kick of a boot to her face.

'*You will die here, Peggy McCormick, and nobody will even care,*' Agnes the Cat snarled.

'*Whist, there is someone coming!*' Mike Dillinger hissed. He knelt down, putting his mouth close to her ear.

'*Say a single word about us and I will wring your neck like a chicken's. Do you hear?*'

Then he was gone.

She felt a final blow to the head. Then there was only darkness.

She did not know how long she was there. He eyes flickered opened. It was blurry but she could see the sky. She just looked at the sky and the clouds moving across leaving patches of blue.

She did not scream. She knew one thing. If she were to survive, she could never speak of what happened in Blythe Wood.

CHAPTER 36

Peggy 2019

She had known this day would come. She could feel it. It was as if that day in Blythe Wood began the end of her own life. Her youth, her innocent belief in what was good vanished, and she knew that pure evil existed within the world that she lived in. Her life had begun and ended for her that day. It was over but, unlike Violet Ward, she must still exist. Exist in this world of darkness and light where the light shifted and unleashed its anger into a terrible darkness.

She was only a child of fourteen but as she stumbled from Blythe Wood that morning, she knew that hour would haunt her for the rest of her time on this earth. The twigs had crackled under her feet, the twigs breaking. Every break reminding her of the dead woman that she could not speak of. Then, as she reached the church the day began to brighten. It was like a lie. Why would the clouds move now and the sun come out? The world was full of darkness. She had borne witness to it.

She had turned into the church, her only sanctuary, and collapsed in front of the little shrine to Saint Therese, the light of candles glimmering and blurring before her eyes.

'Peggy! Peggy! Do you hear me?' A man's voice. A gentle voice. 'Peggy! Who has done this to you?'

She opened her eyes and saw Father Quill before losing consciousness.

In the convent where she had gone after her beating, she had found some solace. She prayed to the cold statues – they never answered her, but she believed that they heard her. Without the confines of the church in the convent she would have lost her mind. Now she had someone to listen to her. The statues looked down on her as she prayed. She prayed to Saint Therese most of all. To protect her and to protect the little girl now motherless and on the run and, if she was to believe the whispers and the women, a child who might be possessed by the Devil.

Some said that the child could die. The evil would consume her. But one kindly nun told her this was codswallop and totally untrue.

The winter of 1950 robbed so many of so much. All because of the wickedness of these women and the two men involved. But as the years passed Peggy wondered if they suffered too?

The Grey sisters didn't survive for long. They hardly left their house again. They all but stopped eating and soon after Nora died. Her sister was not long after her.

Nellie Cooke carried on as did Molly Walsh and the Bullock.

Mike Dillinger fell down the stairs drunk and broke his neck. Soon after Agnes the Cat was not seen for weeks. No one ever dared to go to her house. Eventually Molly Walsh went up with Father Quill. They knocked but there was no answer. But the door was not bolted. Molly Walsh reckoned she'd been dead a few weeks. The stench made

Father Quill throw up. Agnes was dead in the bed. The cats had turned on her body in the end.

Peggy wondered if any of them ever thought of Mrs Ward. Her body's whereabouts were only known to the Bullock and Mike Dillinger. Did anyone secretly come and leave flowers for her at the place that she died? Did they pray for her? Did they feel remorse? Did they sleep in their warm beds, knowing that they had played a hand in this terrible deed?

She had played a hand in it by her silence.

She had been a coward and she had lived a lifetime with it. The child with the blonde curls, never knowing where her mother was. If she had died or simply left.

At least she knew where her mother went. She went mad and into a madhouse. There was no comfort in that but at least she never had to question if she had just left her. It was her poor mind that had left her. But that day in Blythe Woods had haunted her for her lifetime. How often she had wondered where the child was and the husband and Betsy? How she would have loved to have told them!

She remembered how kind Father Quill was and how kind the nuns were in the hospital. She had never returned to Miss Doheny's. The nuns in the convent in Draheen had taken her in.

Miss Doheny had arrived at the convent to see her. It was then she had told her. She was never quite sure if she believed her or not.

'Don't say such a terrible thing,' Miss Doheny had said.

But Peggy had seen a terrible fear cross her face. Maybe she did believe her but was fearful too of being implicated in any way.

But Miss Doheny had warned her not to say any more. No one would believe her, she said, and they would possibly lock her up. Sure, wasn't her mother mad and in a madhouse.

She stayed with the nuns in their convent. But talked little. She had literally lost the ability to talk. Slowly they had helped her, and she began to speak again.

She never ventured out of the convent. She thought she would become a nun and stay there. It was peaceful there. She loved the prayers – it was the one time her mind felt free. Or when the nuns sang and it reminded her of an ancient time, a time when she was not even born. She told them she wanted to stay. She would stay and pray and work with them. She forgot about America and New York. She was safe here. The nuns would keep her safe.

But Mother Superior told her that fear was not a reason to stay. She cried when they told her she was leaving. One of the nuns gave her a statue of Saint Therese. Another gave her one of Saint Martin.

One day shortly before she left the convent, she was in the nun's office dusting and she found a cutting from the paper. There was a picture of her. It said she was mad, and someone had beaten her up. It said that her poor mother was in a madhouse. It said she was possibly a simpleton. It said she had no family. It was just a small piece. Not worth a big mention.

Father Quill got her a job in Kerry to help a housekeeper in a parish near Kenmare. Mrs Canaan was a kindly lady and had looked after her. She was kinder to her than anyone. She loved the fresh smell of the water in Kerry, the mountains and the sea, but she knew that no matter how beautiful the day could be with lemons and oranges in the sky, there was a darkness that could come from the shadows.

Then she met her husband and he was a good man and he brought her to Dunmore East. She was almost thirty and the years had somehow passed. She left Kerry for a little fishing village that at times was too beautiful and pretty. Too hard to watch the perfect sunrise, knowing how imperfect her world was. But she finally felt she had some peace though she was still haunted by what had happened. It was years before she had her children. First came John to be called Jack and then came Emily. There was a nun in the convent, and she was called Sister Emily. She had the sweetest singing voice that Peggy had ever heard. They said she was from France. Sister Emily told her of a country that sounded like a piece of heaven, where the lavender grew and made the air smell so beautiful. Sister Emily sounded like an angel when she sang. Sometimes in the evenings she would bring Peggy in to clean the convent church and then she would sing beautiful French hymns that made Peggy think she was in heaven.

When her husband died, leaving her with two young children to rear, she felt she was being punished for not being brave and telling the truth, but the years passed and she never could tell. She tried to do her best. Jack was a bonny child with looks as good as a film star but then he went down that dark road. Again, she felt she was being punished. When Emily got pregnant, she wished she was closer to her. She wished she had been there for her. But there was no use in crying now. But Sebastian had been the light she had never seen coming. She feared terribly when he said he was going away. She wanted to keep him safe. She could not be punished any more.

She had lived a life of fear and guilt and now the time had come.

Now she knew she would have to tell the truth. Somehow the past had found her and dragged her back to Draheen and Blythe Wood. She had gone there over thirty years ago and left some flowers at the tomb in the graveyard. She begged Violet Ward for forgiveness and wept for all that was lost. She begged her to forgive her for leaving her there alone and for not telling anyone that she knew. She wept as Emily and Jack played in the woods, unaware of her secret.

The nurse came in to take her temperature.

'How are you today, Peggy? Is there anything that you need?'

'Actually, could you do something for me?' There were tears rolling down her face.

'I certainly will if I can. Peggy, are you alright?'

'I need you to call my daughter and my son and a garda. I have some information on a missing person, and I need to tell them now. It cannot wait any longer.'

CHAPTER 37

Peggy had told them all she knew. Emily had cried hard through most of the sad tale of her poor mother's life. If only she had known.

'Oh, Mam, why did you not confide in us? I cannot believe you've been carrying this all your life,' Emily cried.

'I couldn't, Emily.'

'But if I had never seen that advertisement all this would still remain untold,' Emily sobbed.

'It was meant to be that you would find the advertisement and buy the house,' Peggy said sadly.

Two gardaí had arrived. A young man and a young woman. They wrote everything down.

'What will happen now?' Emily asked them.

'Well, we will report back to Draheen Station with this statement that your mother made,' the woman garda replied kindly. 'She is quite sure and sound of mind, so we have no reason to believe any of it is untrue.'

'If only it had been so simple then,' Peggy said. 'But it was a different Ireland. One of many secrets that lay buried for decades. Now at least the secrets are not buried anymore.'

Jack had remained quiet throughout.

'Jack, are you alright?' Emily asked quietly.

'I think I need a fag,' he whispered. 'I'll head out. I'll be back in a few minutes.'

'Do you think they will do a search of the woods and possibly Eveline again?' Emily asked the gardaí.

'I am really not sure what the next step is. It will be up to our superiors,' the male garda replied.

Emily went in search of Jack.

'Jack, what's wrong?' she asked.

'That night I thought I saw someone? I keep thinking about it. Did I see a fucking ghost that night? Was that this woman? I feel bloody freaked out to be honest!'

Emily could see that his hand was shaking.

'I don't know. I don't know what I believe. But that woman meant no one any harm. She was a victim of a terrible incident that robbed a child of her mother. A child that was very ill. But Jack, the letter. Mam never mentioned the letter that we found. Why does she have that?'

'Oh God, please let it be a simple answer. I cannot take much more!'

'We will have to ask her.'

'Wait until the gardaí leave. They have literally taken down everything that she said. I have a feeling Eveline House will be in the news for all the wrong reasons,' Jack replied wearily.

'I know and I had hoped to open for Christmas. At this rate I might be opened and shut down all before Christmas!' Emily said with a sigh.

The next day the woman garda contacted Emily to inform her that a search of Blythe Wood was going to take place and they had also spoken to Sylvia Ward who was going to send someone over here to represent her.

'Oh, what do you mean?'

'I am not sure. But I suppose in case we do find remains she would like someone to represent her.'

'How will you know if it's her? I suppose you'll have to do a DNA test but that will take time, won't it?'

'There may be some identification. Look, I'll keep you posted.'

'Will my mother be in trouble for not reporting this?' Emily asked.

'It's not for me to say now, to be honest.'

That was not reassuring. She was a woman in her eighties. But she had hidden the evidence. Oh God. She wondered if this nightmare would ever end.

CHAPTER 38

The search only took two days to complete, and human remains were found. The search party had noticed that one of the tombs in Suaimhneas Graveyard was tampered with. It was in the walled part of the cemetery and the last person had been interred in 1870. But one of the searchers noticed that the heavy stone tomb cover looked like it was not completely aligned. Had it been removed and then replaced? Any relatives of the interred were now dead. The lid was lifted. Human remains of an obviously later date than the 19th century were discovered. The scene was closed off. There would not be any more information until a forensic examination was carried out.

Three weeks later it was confirmed that the remains found in Blythe Wood were those of Violet Ward. Missing since January 1950. The gardaí made a statement to say that a full investigation was under way.

It was on the national news and in the national newspapers. Reporters arrived into the town and took photographs of Blythe Wood and Eveline House.

There was an interview on the news with the priest who presided over the parish at present. Father Nolan was a sincere man who was known to love to sing and indeed had formed a very respected choir within the parish.

He said that the whole town was extremely saddened and that their thoughts and prayers were with her daughter Sylvia. He announced that they were planning a special service to pray for Violet Ward, and all were welcome. Emily had invited him down to the house. She was not religious but the whole incident with Jack and what he thought he saw had freaked her out. The priest had blessed the house and said some prayers. Even Jack had lowered his head and prayed.

Emily had a number of visits from the gardaí. They did a search of the house and a careful search of the basement. Nothing was found. Emily showed them the letter that she had found in the drawer and now they were in possession of all the evidence.

Well, almost all. Peggy had asked her to get a letter and a locket she had hidden in her wardrobe in Dunmore East. So Emily had to confess that she and Jack had already searched and found them. Peggy understood and had told her why she had it. She said she wanted to post it to Sylvia herself. Emily and Jack got a postal address from Gerry Hynes and, although worried that they were withholding evidence again, retrieved the letter and locket and gave them to Peggy to send it to Sylvia.

The last couple of months had been a blur for Emily. It was getting near to Christmas and she had transformed some of the downstairs of Eveline. She had ordered her sign and *Emily O'Connor, Eveline House of Bridal Couture* was opened.

The drawing room was now a showroom, the parlour

was her workshop and the study was transformed into a boudoir-style changing room. The downstairs bathroom was retiled and grouted, and all the plumbing, painting and papering was completed downstairs.

She still had to convert the kitchen and the bedrooms upstairs had not been touched but she had moved in and so had Jack for now anyway. They remained in Seb's room and the guest room for now. There had been no more sightings of ghosts or anything else and Emily had fallen even more in love with the house. Jack was going to continue working on the house and in January would apply to go back to college to study. He was still not sure what course to do. But there was a great change in him. He looked fitter and healthier and was trying to give up the cigarettes. He had joined a running club and had met a girl called Rachel who he had dated a few times. Emily could not wait for Sebastian to see the change in him. She was so looking forward to Seb coming to Eveline for Christmas.

Peggy was better but still needed a lot of care. She was quite comfortable in the nursing home and Emily thought that she was more at peace than she had ever been. There was a lightness to her now and she seemed to have lost some of the melancholy that had ruled her life.

Emily was reading an article in the local *Draheen Post* about the upcoming service for Violet Ward that evening when her doorbell rang. It was very early. She had the sign up and she had to keep reminding herself that it was a business now as well as a home. She needed to get an intercom and new gates. There was endless stuff she needed to do. But it was so early it was bound to be Jack who she had begged to go out and get her some croissants. There was a new shop and deli that had opened, and it sold the most divine croissants she had ever tasted. Jack had obviously forgotten his keys, not for the first time.

When she answered the door a man with tanned skin, chestnut hair and blue-green eyes was on the doorstep.

'Sorry to bother you. But I am Max Bradford. I am a friend of Sylvia Ward. I'm sorry – I should have called first. But I just arrived into the town for the service tonight.' He had a soft American accent.

Emily could barely speak. She knew she must look a fright, and she could feel him staring at her. For the first time in years she felt what she could only describe as something strange. He was handsome in a rugged sort of way. He was a bit taller than her and possibly about her age. But it was his eyes that she could not take her own eyes off.

'You'd better come on in,' she replied.

She wished she had at least tied up her hair or had a decent-looking robe on. She had a big fluffy flowery thing on that made her look at least a stone heavier. With big slippers that were ancient and fluffy ankle socks. Her hair was wet from her shower and she had not a scrap of make-up on.

'Sorry,' she said. 'I thought you were Jack.'

'Oh, your husband?'

'No, my brother. I'm not married.' She could have kicked herself. Why did she say that to a perfect stranger? She might as well have asked him if he was available. 'Would you like some coffee? Or tea?' she asked, trying to keep her voice normal.

'Love some. Coffee, please. The house is so like Sylvia described it from the outside. I see you have a business here? It looks cool. I think Sylvia would approve. I gather you are Emily O'Connor. The designer on the sign outside?'

Emily loved the way his eyes crinkled up. He had a very open face if there was such a thing.

'Yes, just starting up. How is Sylvia?'

'Miss Sylvia is okay, I suppose. Perhaps more at peace.'

'Miss Sylvia? She never married?' Emily asked.

'I have always called her that. It's not that she would ever want to be addressed like that, but she was so secretive when she first arrived at Cape Cod that we could never find out her surname and my dad began calling her Miss Sylvia. It stuck. Everyone in Chatham calls her that now. She is the closest person I have to family. I think I am to her too, to be honest. I have known Sylvia over thirty years but never knew about her past. I hated leaving her, but she was insistent that I came. I am glad now. I think it is easier for her knowing that she has sent me. She is so strong really. I am so glad they have found her mother. At least she can find some sort of closure now.'

Jack arrived in with a bag of croissants. She introduced them and ran to change.

She found herself really fussing over what she wore. Discarding clothes like a teenager, eventually settling on a long flowy skirt and a sweater in a soft pink that really flattered her. She blow-dried her hair and tied it to the side, put on some make-up and went a bit overboard spraying some Chanel Allure. Even Jack did a bit of a double take when she arrived down.

They had more coffee and Emily tried to stop looking right into Max's eyes, but there was something so attractive about him.

Jack asked her to go over something before the carpenter arrived and Max went outside to see the garden Sylvia had told him about.

'You okay, sis? You're a bit distracted,' Jack said with a smirk.

'Sorry, yes, I have a lot on my mind.'

'Yeah, and it's nothing to do with a handsome American who can't seem to take his eyes off you or you him by the way?' Jack grinned.

'What? No way!'

'I might as well not be here.'

'Oh gosh, I can't really concentrate on anything for a few minutes,' Emily admitted.

'Go on – I'll talk to you later. Your head is not really in the right place for designing cabinets right now!' Jack said, smiling.

'Is this outfit okay on me? I'm just not sure,' Emily said worriedly.

'You look great. Beautiful actually. Nice perfume by the way. Are you sure you sprayed enough on? Hope he is not asthmatic.'

Emily threw a cushion at him and got up to go into the garden but not before checking her make-up and hair in the hall mirror. She grabbed a jacket from the coat-stand and went out.

She had done nothing in the garden yet except bring up her mother's big marmalade cat, Lucky, who had had taken to the garden as if she had always lived there. Striker seemed to be happy with the new addition to the garden.

'The garden is gorgeous,' Max said, admiring it.

It was warm for December. There was a chill, but a winter sun shone down.

'Yes, I hope to tackle it in the spring. It's wild but so beautiful I agree. Look, there are some gorgeous Christmas roses in bloom. There are some really pungent wildflowers there too. Can you get the aroma?'

'Yes, I can. I know that this house meant so much to Sylvia. She told me about the garden and the wildflowers, would you believe?'

'Can you tell me about Sylvia?'

'Oh, she is a really special lady. Unique and incredibly artistic. I am just a bit heartbroken that all this happened to her in the past and I never knew all these years.'

'I guess you know that my mother was Peggy. The girl who witnessed what happened?' Emily said warily.

'Yes, Sylvia told me about her. She told me that the housekeeper Betsy had often mentioned her over the years and wondered if she was alright. For what it's worth Sylvia is not the type of person to hold any ill feeling towards your mother. I know that Ireland of 1950 was a very different place to now.'

He told her what he knew, and Emily could see how deeply he cared about the woman. He told her about his writing, and they ended up talking for over an hour. Back in the house, she showed him the personal belongings the family had left behind. She told him that there was a heritage house in Draheen which might be glad to display the memorabilia of a famous playwright. However, the wonderful painting of Violet and the photographs would stay in place in the house – unless Sylvia wanted them of course. And she would not evict the dolls from their home but now felt that perhaps they should go back to Sylvia.

Max smiled at this and nodded. 'Or at least the one called Petite Suzanne. She has talked to me about her.'

Then Emily realised she had better get dressed, as Jenny Wright was coming for a fitting.

'I am sorry, but I have a client coming and she is due soon.'

'Look, can I take you to lunch later? I am going to go now to Blythe Wood and the church. Pay my respects to the last places where she was.'

'I would love that,' Emily replied. 'Can I ask if you know what happened to her father and the housekeeper?'

'I am not sure. They are both dead, that is all I know. I think Sylvia has been living in Chatham for about thirty years. So, I think they are dead a long time.'

They arranged to meet at one o'clock.

* * *

Jenny Wright arrived with her three bridesmaids again and her mother and this time her wedding planner.

Emily had a design created. She had the fabric samples and a mock-up of what the dress would look like. It was just the way she worked. But she was very unsure of what Jenny's reaction would be. She had tried to incorporate what Jenny wanted but tried to stay true to herself too. So, she turned to Hollywood yet again and the golden era. The pearl-white Carrickmacross lace dress-design was fitted but flared into a chapel-length train. It had quite a revealing halter neck and plunged back. Emily thought it was a complete showstopper but a throwback to the glamour of the golden era of cinema. It was different to what Jenny had shown her in her pictures but it did incorporate some of her requests.

She had a sample of luxurious Swarovski Crystals that would adorn the dress. It was bling, showstopping, sexy, luxurious and was going to cost a fortune. She liked to imagine who would have worn such a dress if it did exist in the golden era of Hollywood and looking out the window watching Jenny get out of her BMW it came to her. She could picture Joan Crawford in her heyday in such a dress.

She opened the door to let Jenny and company in.

'Cool house,' Jenny remarked.

'Thank you, come on in. I have the mock-up ready for you to try.'

Jenny tried on the mock-up dress. She stopped and looked, and Emily held her breath. It was only a mock-up but, on her body, she could see how beautiful it looked. It was certainly a showstopper and the train was quite incredible. It gave her the most fabulous curves and tiny waist. She showed her the lace and the crystals.

'*We have a winner! I love it!*' Jenny shrieked.

Her bridesmaids heaved a collective sigh of relief and immediately took out a bottle of champagne and some plastic flutes.

'Sorry but we have to celebrate,' one of the bridesmaids said as she popped the cork.

Father Nolan had put a lot of effort into the service for Violet Ward. The chapel was packed with only standing room and the portrait of Violet that hung in Eveline House was at the altar. It was not a funeral service, he said. It was Draheen's token to remember a very talented woman who lost her life in Blythe Wood. He said any judgements were for the courts to make and reminded everyone that there was a full investigation of the tragic loss of Violet Ward going on.

An extract from one of her plays was read and in it she spoke of Ireland and the beauty of it. A man and a woman sang 'Ave Maria'. It was very beautiful and moving and

Emily thought very fitting. Afterwards the parish had organised some refreshments in a local hotel for anyone who would like to come.

How different Draheen was now to the Draheen her mother had described, Emily thought.

'How long are you staying?' Emily asked Max

'Just a few days. I want to visit where Violet was born. Sylvia said that she often spoke of it and I promised to go there. It's near a Lough Deeravaragh.'

'I can take you.'

'I would love that.' He grinned.

It was a beautiful Irish December day as they looked out over Lough Deeravaragh.

'Miss Sylvia said that her mother used to tell her a legend and it had something to do with the lough.'

'There is a legend called 'The Children of Lir'. There was a king called Lir and his three children were turned into swans by their jealous stepmother. They swam here for three hundred years before moving to the Straits of Moyle for another three hundred years and then on to another place whose name I forget for yet another three hundred years. They did regain their human form in the end but of course they were ancient people over nine hundred years old when they did. But they were baptised as Christians before they died.'

'You Irish are a melancholy lot, aren't you?' Max said with a grin.

'I think it's the history and the ghosts of the past. I think it has changed so much but when my mother was a child and Sylvia was a child there was nowhere in the world that seemed to live as Ireland did. A land that carried a history of coffin ships, famine and oppression. A Church that ruled with an iron fist and fear was the bread and butter given to all.'

'My goodness, I thought the Irish were a merry lot and liked to drink Guinness and sing.'

'Oh, we do but sometimes I think the Irish sang and drank to forget. But, as I said, that is the Ireland that Sylvia left. How can you tell her how much it has changed?'

'Perhaps you might come over and visit and tell her yourself,' Max whispered.

'Is that an invitation?'

'You bet.' With that he leaned over and kissed her.

CHAPTER 39

Peggy knew she had one more thing to do. For the first time in all these years her dreams were not full of sadness. There was a change. Now her sleep was more peaceful, and she didn't awaken and clutch at her heart.

She was happy in the nursing home. She missed her house, but she could not imagine going back. She was content here and that was something she was not sure she ever was before. It was not like a lot of nursing homes that she visited. There was plenty of activity and she liked her room. It was painted in a vibrant yellow with a window that looked out into a garden. Emily had brought in all her statues to her. They were dotted all over the room. Saint Therese was on her locker. She had even brought in her picture of Daniel O'Donnel. She had her little cassette player and she often listened to her music and read the prayer books and holy magazines for hours. She had company if she wanted it. She needed help in dressing and her left leg had decided not to move after the stroke. But she had improved. She liked to sit in the little day room when Emily or Jack arrived. There was a little room converted into a place for prayer too. She liked to visit it every day.

She could not believe the difference in Jack. He looked more like the old Jack and was constantly talking about his new plans.

So Violet Ward's remains had been there in Blythe Woods all these years. She prayed that finally she would be at peace.

Emily had told her that there was to be a full investigation into what had happened.

All the women that Peggy had recalled and the two men, the Bullock and Mike Dillinger, were now dead. Her regret was that it took her so long to tell what had happened. But age was a strange thing. She knew when she awoke from her stroke that she had to tell the truth. This was her last chance for that woman to be laid in a peaceful resting place and her daughter to know the truth and to have her father's name cleared.

She could not forgive herself for not being brave enough to tell what happened at the time. But she tried to remember that she was only a child then and somehow to at least make peace with it.

She had asked Emily to buy her some good-quality paper. Emily said she could write a letter on her laptop and print it. But Peggy felt that the very least she could do was to write a real letter to Sylvia. Her hands were not good, but if she took her time she would manage it. Not to explain or look for forgiveness. But just to write to Sylvia Ward.

With her hands shaking she wondered how to begin. How could she tell this woman that she had haunted her life? That not a night had gone by but she prayed for her. How she often spent hours wondering what happened to the little girl with the blond curls and the white skin. With tears in her eyes she began.

325

December 14th, 2019

Dear Sylvia,

I cannot ask you to forgive me for not telling you about your mother. I don't expect your forgiveness or even your understanding. But please know that I have thought and prayed for you all my life. I was just fourteen when your mother died, and I am afraid fear has ruled most of my life.

I remember her as so very beautiful. I also remember your father and how handsome he was. I also can vividly recall the incredible pain he suffered when your mother disappeared. I only wish I had been braver and tried to let you know the truth before. I believe there will be an investigation, but I have told the story as it happened, and you have my word that is what occurred that dreadful morning.

There is always one ringleader and the evil that emanated from her still has the power to frighten me, even knowing that she is long dead.

In 1985 I received a letter and a locket from the solicitor of the Miss Doheny that I worked for. Inside the envelope was a note and another letter. It was a letter written by your father to your mother. He wrote it the day he left with you and Betsy and posted it to Miss Doheny.

In her will Miss Doheny requested that it be sent to me. It was to be given to Violet Ward if she ever returned. I will make sure it is sent to you together with the locket.

I am so sorry that we never met, but I feel our lives were intertwined all my life.

I pray you are at peace.

Peggy

CHAPTER 40

Sylvia drifted into the dream again.

She was in the garden and the aroma of wildflowers was permeating the air. She could see her mother dressed in a pale-pink taffeta dress and white fur stole. Her hair pinned up. She was smiling and looking at the flowers. Betsy was there and was feeding Milky the cat.

The dream shifted to the kitchen and there was her father. Grinning and laughing and telling Father Quill a joke he had heard in London. Father Quill was sipping sherry with his long legs resting on a footstool.

Then the dream shifted to her bedroom and she opened the gift her mother had brought from London. It was wrapped in the prettiest pink paper. A beautiful silk coat with pearl buttons for Suzanne her beautiful doll. She knew she would adore it. Suzanne knew all her secrets. She put it on her doll, and she looked almost as beautiful as her mother. Her mother's hair was pinned up with a comb of sparkling crystals. She found a tiny brooch similar to her mother's ornate hair comb and placed it on Suzanne. She put her with the rest of her dolls.

Then Sylvia awoke. The dawn was just setting in. She had

left the curtain open last night. Petite Suzanne was gazing at her from where she sat at the end of the bed. Emily had sent her with Max from Ireland.

Max had rung her while he was in Ireland and told her all about Eveline and all that had happened. The beautiful service that the priest had held for her. She was glad he had gone there.

Part of her had wanted to go but part of her just could not go back. All these years later it was all still too painful. She had lost too much. Her life was irrevocably changed that winter. She had told him she was worried that the flight was too long. But truthfully, she knew it might be too much for her emotionally. She could never forget what happened to her at Eveline. The fact that it could return frightened her in her darkest hours.

What did really happen to her in Eveline House she never really knew. She felt safe in the house but it was as if something evil was outside of the walls. She remembered going into the garden with her doll but that was all. She had no recollection of what happened after that. She had no recollection of how she came into possession of the letters. Had someone given them to her? Had she somehow been exposed to something evil without her knowledge? She knew some believed she was possessed by a demon. It's strange how the mind can shut down any memories of something that has the power to terrify them. There was one other similar episode.

Shortly after arriving in London they went into hiding in a flat near Putney. One of those nights she became unwell. She could recall very little about it but she remembered screaming at Betsy that there was something terrible happening to her. Then it was as if her mind went blank. She did recall a priest there. But mostly she remembered Betsy holding her. She could recall a dreadful darkness almost trying to take over her body. Betsy had told her later that she thought they would both die that night but somehow it passed and they had lived through it. She often thought that if it was something evil then it was Betsy who had stopped it from killing both of them. A fight between good and evil. Betsy was her protector. An angel sent to protect her. Or maybe it was her mind that had some terrible breakdown. Betsy had never really told her what had happened that night in London. Had the priest performed some kind of exorcism? Perhaps Betsy knew that she could hardly handle knowing if it had happened. The world was a strange place and there was a lot she still did not understand. But at least now after all these years she finally knew what happened to her beloved mother. She did not leave her, and she knew that Peggy was telling the truth. Her father's name was clear. Their persecutors were all dead it seemed.

How strange that it was the frightened young girl who held the key to knowing what happened. Strange how Betsy had talked about her over the years. Wondering if she was alright. Did Betsy have some inner sense? Sylvia had often dreamt of Blythe Wood. Now she knew why. She dreamt about it when it was blue with a haze of bluebells and she dreamt about it when the frost left jewels on the trees. She could smell the aroma of rotting twigs mixed with the wildflowers that grew between the cracks. Her mother was buried inside a tomb. Left there. It was too unbearable to think about. The people who had done this were dead. But perhaps in another life they would have to answer for their crimes?

329

Betsy and she had talked about it so much over the years. Betsy believed that the letters were written by those women, but she could never believe that it was they who had been responsible for her disappearance.

Max had visited the village of Whitewater where her mother grew up. There was nothing left of the house except a ruin of an old farmhouse. He visited the graveyard and found their grave. Her mother had never fully recovered from her own mother closing the door to her. He visited the lough and it looked as beautiful as her mother had described. How she had adored the stories of the lough. The Children of Lir who were turned into swans by some evil curse. The world was full of good and evil. Light and dark. That she was certain of.

Max would wake her early this morning. They had one more thing to complete.

Her father was buried in Boston but somehow she felt that her mother would not wish to be buried. Max had arranged for a cremation and then brought her ashes back to Sylvia.

They were ashes. But they represented so much. So much loss, such lost years. Her beautiful mother gone for so long . . . but, in her mind, she was forever young. She felt she would like Chatham.

Max woke her early. He brought her usual coffee. She dressed and then they took the ashes down to a small boat. He very carefully helped her in.

It was a beautiful crystal-clear morning. An azure-blue sky and the sun just coming up. It could not be more perfect.

He rowed out from the shore until she asked him to stop.

She looked at the sky and opened the urn. She shook the ashes into the soft breeze.

'Fly free now, my beloved mother! Be free at last!'

She watched as the ashes almost took flight like butterflies on the ocean and it felt as if the soul of her mother was finally free.

Back at the house, Max made some lemon pancakes for breakfast and they ate outside. Mostly in silence.

'I have a gift for you, my dear,' Sylvia said. 'Go into my studio. There is a package behind the door. Would you be a dear and get it for me?'

Max brought it out. It looked like a painting gift-wrapped.

'Open it, dear, it is for you,' Sylvia said.

He opened it. She had finished the painting. It was of a vase of Christmas roses and wildflowers in an earthenware jar, the same jar and flowers that Betsy filled the house with that winter of 1950.

She looked back on her own life. She knew she felt pain deeply. Not pain of the physical but of the soul. Poor beloved Betsy, how she missed her! She was so full of goodness. In a strange way, with Henry, they had formed their own little family.

They had moved first to London, then into hiding and then moved on to Boston. Nobody knew who they were. They lived a very quiet life and were lucky that Henry had managed to grab what money and jewellery he had before they went on the run. It gave them a start.

But her father took ill shortly after arriving in Boston. He could never forgive himself for not leaving Ireland when Violet had begged him to. He drank and got into bad health. At times his anger would spill over and at other times he cried like a child and if it weren't for Betsy being there to calm him, he would not have seen the morning. His heart would have killed him. Sylvia loved her father. But his despair at what had happened did little to help her. He could not help it. It was his own malady of the heart. He never worked again as a jeweller – instead he took odd jobs as a night watchman in places that no one ever cared to know his name. He could not cope with what had happened.

He died in his sleep. The doctor thought it was a massive heart attack. He was forty-eight. Betsy believed it was simply a broken heart. A broken heart for the woman that he had loved and the country that had taken her that he would have given his life for.

Sylvia would have been alone in the world but for Betsy. But somehow they had made a life. A simple one but one of a love as pure as the snow of Mount Leinster. Betsy loved her as much as any parent could.

After Henry died Betsy took some part-time jobs at times to keep the roof over their heads. It was Betsy who encouraged Sylvia to show her art and to their delight her paintings began to sell.

When Betsy took ill it was Sylvia's turn to take care of her and when she died Sylvia did feel alone in the world. She felt she had lost a second mother.

They were both buried in Boston. Nobody really knowing who they were. Small indiscreet graves with just a name and date of burial. It was after Betsy's death that she decided to move to Chatham. It amazed her, the strength of the will to live. But the memory that she had of love had kept her going. That and her painting. Betsy had always encouraged her to paint and, thanks to that, she had lived a good life and was independent financially. Her painting was her saviour.

The family was gone now except for her. She held the locket her father had made for her mother, opened it and stroked the precious locks of hair within with the tip of a finger. How beautiful it was. A last gift. She was so glad Peggy had sent it to her. Poor Peggy! Sylvia had a feeling that Peggy had suffered very much too.

She would add the locket to her will. She would send it to Emily O'Connor. How strange that fate played a hand and somehow Emily the daughter of Peggy was drawn to Eveline House. But life was full of the unexplainable. That was something she was certain of. She would keep it for now. She had a feeling from Max that he had fallen for this Irishwoman. Some good had come from all the pain.

She wrote a little note to be added to her will.

To Emily O'Connor, my red-gold locket and its contents. And my Petite Suzanne. Thank you for buying Eveline House and helping to find the truth. From Sylvia.

Now that you're hooked why not try

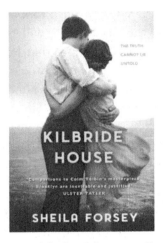

also published by Poolbeg

A STORY OF ENDURING LOVE, SIBLING LOYALTY AND A SECRET PACT THAT LASTS A LIFETIME

Here's a sneak preview of the
PROLOGUE AND CHAPTER 1

PROLOGUE

Kilbride Graveyard
1954

An old graveyard. Surrounded by a stone wall, crumbling, in need of repair. Jagged steps lead up to a stile and there is also a rusted iron gate. It creaks on opening. Adjacent is a small Protestant church. In daylight you can see wisteria wrapped around it and in summer a wild rambling rose covers the mottled wall with silken petals and an evocative scent of the past.

Edward Goulding and the local vicar walk silently side by side, dressed in heavy overcoats against the cold. Edward is carrying a small coffin. The vicar lights the way with a torch. They find the spot, big enough to fit, yet small enough to hardly notice. It's close to the stone wall, sheltered by a willow tree. Slightly away from the rest of the cold grey slabs.

This very church is where Edward attended Sunday service every week of his childhood. As children they had run up and down the stile steps, clip-clopping and chasing each other. If he closes his eyes he can almost hear their laughter – Victoria and Edith, dressed in velvet coats and hats, all pink cheeks and rosy lips. Edith holding Victoria's hand, just in case she slipped on the withered frosted leaves. Edith, always looking out for Victoria. Victoria who seemed to have no fear, just a wild curiosity. In winter the stone steps would glisten like crystal, cracking under their warm boots as they jumped and hopped, and Edith held Victoria's hand, just in case.

'This is the spot,' the vicar says, dragging Edward back to the present.

Edward is glad his friend is with him – a brother could not have been more loyal. The charcoal night is lit by a thousand ancient stars, like street lamps in the velvet darkness. The call of a nightingale breaks the silence. Something scurries near them. A flash of the torch reveals a mouse. They can see their breath as they breathe. Edward takes out a cigarette and a matchbox. He strikes the match and the little flame flares. He takes a long puff and the tip of the cigarette glows as he inhales.

He walks back and gets two shovels from the car.

The ground is hard, it takes longer and is a more difficult task than they anticipated. The earth smells of rot. They discard their coats and hats. The dawn is almost upon them. Eventually the task is complete, and they lower the coffin in. They throw the earth back, filling in the grave.

There is so much to say, yet they say so little.

'You did the only thing that you could,' the vicar whispers.

'I am broken inside.'

'Time, Edward, time will help.' The vicar fixes a simple cross to mark the spot.

They bow their heads and pray for a new day.

They put their coats and hats on and gather up their spades, then walk back towards the stile.

Edward takes one last look. The small cross is barely visible. The smell of the night air fills his nostrils and he knows it will always make him remember. Even when his hair is silver, and the years have passed, the scent of this place will haunt him, remembering all that was lost.

CHAPTER 1

Kilbride, Dingle Peninsula, County Kerry
1954

Canice Meagher loved and hated Ireland in equal measure. Born on the mystical Great Blasket Island, the cliffs, the gulls and the hardship of the ancient landscape was in his very being. He had left before, but it was as if the Dingle Peninsula could claw him back, denying him any chance of a different life.

To escape, he had left the peninsula on different occasions, losing himself in the dark pubs of Cricklewood and Kilburn where the Irish sang and drank and talked of Éire with sentiment – a land of love, song and poetry – not like his rugged island. A piece of land in the wild sea that tore at his soul and dragged him back to it. Over the years, everyone who could leave had left, with their battered suitcases and few quid. They would find a squalid place to live and dream of coming back as The Big Man. Some did. But most got married over there, the long nights eating at them. They married their own or met a Londoner and began a new life, away from the Island, the sea and the shifting fog. But some might never make it either way, caught in some no man's land off Kilburn Road, eaten up by memories.

And now, of course, there could be no more returns to the Great Blasket. In 1953 the government had removed its people from their harsh lives and increasingly extreme weather, and housed them on the mainland in Dunquin, leaving only their sheep to reign over the island.

It was almost dusk, and the haunting sound of a curlew broke the stillness. Then came the muffled thuds of a galloping horse. It was then that he saw her move across the bog field on a majestic grey mare whose hooves were digging up the wet earth. The gallop softened to a canter and they headed straight for the ditch.

He thought she was a vision summoned up by the Celtic stories that had filled his head since he had first heard them from the island people. This strange beauty of a woman was confidently negotiating the jump. It looked far too risky. She was oblivious to anyone watching. His mind was racing – it was madness to think of jumping it.

He had seldom seen such a display of fearlessness and to make it even more incredible it was a woman, a woman so striking that he wondered had the longing for porter brought him to imagining her. But she was as real as the dirt on his shovel. He thought of trying to stop her, but he knew it was too late – he would only startle the mare and that might lead to something worse. He blessed himself and watched as they made the jump, her body in harmony with the mare's as if they were one. It had to be six feet wide. The graceful horse jumped like she had been taken up by the wind, landing heavily on the other side as her mistress screamed in pure delight. Canice was caught between fear at what could have happened and admiration for such a daring jump. The horse was now cantering towards him. The woman drew on the reins and slowed the horse down.

They reached him and halted. The girl – she was just a girl – stared down at him.

'Are you trying to kill yourself?' he said.

'Of course not,' she said haughtily.

'It was dangerous,' he pointed out.

'I am more than capable and who are you to question my jumping skills?'

'I never questioned your ability, I just questioned your common sense, to jump such a ditch here in the bog. You could have fallen and broken your neck and the horse's too.'

'I would never put my horse at risk. You must know very little about horses.'

'Granted, I know more about work horses than fine thoroughbreds. And she is a fine one – what is she called?'

'Silver.'

'Suits her. And what, may I ask, is your name?'

'You can tell me who you are first and what you are doing on this land.'

'Canice Meagher.'

'Where are you from? There are no Meaghers around here that I know of.'

'An Blascaod Mór – the Great Blasket Island – up to a few years ago.'

'Ah, I see.'

He wondered what exactly she 'saw'. He grinned at her and wiped the sweat from his brow.

'I'm putting up a bit of fencing for the Gouldings.'

He knew who she was, by her clothes, the quality of

the leather saddle and bridle, the way she spoke and the horse that she rode. She had to be a daughter of the Gouldings. But he wasn't going to say that. He had met another daughter briefly, up at the Big House when he was working on a roof. Edith Goulding, striking too but very prim, maybe slightly older. Looking at this girl, he figured she couldn't be more than seventeen or eighteen.

'So, are you working on the farm too or are you just trespassing to use their ditches to jump?' he teased.

'I most certainly am not trespassing! I am Victoria Goulding – we own the land,' she replied with an air of authority.

Canice grinned. 'So, you are one of the Gouldings. I had no idea any of them were like you.'

'What is that supposed to mean?'

'I would expect you to be at piano lessons or doing needlework, not out here trying to kill yourself on a wild horse.'

'I have no interest in needlework or piano.'

He knew straight away she was out of his league and not only his league but his religion. He was a Catholic born and bred and Victoria Goulding was a wealthy Protestant. But in that bog field, for now, religion could be forgotten.

His mother would warn him not to have anything to do with a Goulding. They were gentry, he was an islander. But what harm could there be in a little flirtation?

'Where do you live now?' she asked then.

'Ventry.'

'Ah, I see,' she said again.

'We built a cottage there after we left the island.'

'You have a family?'

340

'Just my mother.'

Neither of them noticed the hare jump from the ditch. The mare startled and reared, but the girl kept her seat.

The mare whinnied loudly as Canice caught the reins. He whispered to her until the fear had left her while the girl also soothed and patted her.

He put his hand on the girl's in reassurance.

'Are you okay?' he asked softly.

'Fine.'

His hand remained on hers, his eyes didn't leave hers. Then something happened that almost knocked the use from his legs: she leaned down from her horse and kissed him, full on the lips. It only lasted a second, but he knew he would remember it for a lifetime.

With that, she laughed and rode off, galloping away from him, leaving him wondering if the fairies had taken his brain and tricked him into imagining the whole incident.

It was in Kilbride village that he saw her again, her dark curly hair pinned back under a hat. She stopped to chat to another girl and he pretended to tie his boots, then he walked on and followed her.

'Hello there, Miss Goulding. How is that fine mare of yours?' he said as he drew level with her.

'Silver is fine,' she replied, not breaking her step.

'I am heading out to do a bit of fishing later this evening. You are welcome to join me,' he heard himself saying. It was out before he thought about it. She might tell her brother Edward or that mother of hers who would scare the life out of you that he had propositioned her. He would never get work again on the estate. He was about to say that he was only joking when she spoke.

'What time? I'd better see if I can get out of my needlework class.'

He could hardly believe it.

'About four. Down past the lake, at the bog entrance.'

'Look forward to it,' she replied.

'Bring something warm, it gets cold on the boat.'

'See you then.'

She walked off and again he wondered if he had dreamt the whole conversation.

If anyone knew, they would surely stop it. He knew himself it was not right, but he also knew that the wilds of the sea in all their power could not stop him from seeing her again.

Buy *Kilbride House* from
POOLBEG.COM